Book of PRAYERS

By Author and Minister
Lynda Hackford

Publishers:
Inspiring Publishers
PO box 159 Calwell ACT 2905, Australia.
Email: inspiringpublishers@gmail.com

National Library of Australia Cataloguing-in-Publication entry

Author: Hackford, Lynda

Title: **Book of Prayers, and Short Stories**/*Lynda Hackford*.

ISBN: 9781925477849 (pbk)

Subjects: Short stories
            Prayers|
            Devotional exercises.
            Worship—Biblical teaching.

Table of Contents

About the Author

Hi welcome to my peace I give unto you, my first prayer book, it's going to be hard trying to explain where these prayers come from, for I have never had the gift of writing prayers before, I turned to my Lord a few years ago, I needed to turn to someone to give me back my life, to change me into a better person.

I needed God in my life, I needed faith; I needed someone that I could trust; someone that I could turn to, someone who wouldn't cause me pain and heartache; someone who wasn't willing to push me into a corner with no escape and trample me even lower than I was already feeling.

I crumbled to my knees and lost all my built up emotions, I was an emotional wreak, with rivers of tears rolling down my cheeks my hands held up to my Lord I begged like I have never begged before, I knew always in my heart that God existed; I have always believed, I was just lost in this world.

I won't go into all my ups and downs because there are so many suffering people all over the world, many people with way more problems than mine, you know the old saying, there is always someone worse off than you, and that saying is so true.

I was at a point of no return, and I prayed to god every day, I use to curse, and my tongue was really bad and the more problems I faced the worse it got, I was wanting to hurt because I was hurting, but you know deep down in my heart I found myself disliking what I was doing, I knew it wasn't me I had this voice saying to me, you don't really want to be this person, you are hurting because you are trying to hurt someone who is causing you harm your pain is intensifying because it's not who you really are.

Then after a while I realized my tongue had stopped cursing (this was truly one of Gods miracles) I wasn't crying day in and day out, I was completely feeling transformed all that I had asked for from God was becoming a reality, I knew without a shadow of a doubt that God almighty had answered my prayers.

I knew I had to take this further I can't explain this feeling, it's a feeling so deep within, a inner knowing from God, even to this day I feel different; a transformation that our Lord God after prayer brings to you; I started reading the Holy Bible which I had always with me, I didn't have the wisdom that our Lord Jesus can give to you to understand it, to comprehend the parables in how its worded, how Jesus speaks.

I have had many encounters over the years, which the Lord had given for me to walk in the way of God, but I was still wrapped up in the world to see his calling to the right path of righteousness, the sins and the repentance which is needed to turn your life around and for God to take you by the hand and say to you, come to me and welcome child for its better late than never.

God was working in me all along but you cannot see this because your eyes are spiritually blinded, I never thought I could love like God has given, I started to write things, it started with songs when I had lost my mother, I was grieving for her so terribly I was depressed knowing I couldn't hold or call her ever again, for 5 years I grieved.

God had healed me at the same time as the rest, I cried for mum every day, then mum came to me in visions and fulfilled me; that she was alive and ok, and gave me many truths that it was real, her coming to me that which could only be validated by family members, the most amazing one was mum thanking me for the gift I gave her, when mum was in her coffin I took of my cross of the Lord from around my neck and put it on my mum, that was validation enough for me to know that she came to tell me to stop grieving and that she was with the Lord, and he was with me.

God had sent me in the comforter and my life has been completely changed, my songs started to turn to these amazing prayers which must be given to all his amazing children to read, all you who are my brothers and sisters; The prayers were given to me at all different times I would wake up hearing them and I would try and write them down in the dark, trying not to disturb my husband and our son, I would be working and I would receive another prayer, I would be in prayer and receive another, it started with me having 10 prayers written, and I was awe struck with how amazing and beautiful they are but they kept coming, and coming.

I have written many of these in less than half an hour; it took me a few weeks to realize that I could not even remember the prayers and what I had already written, I would read back on many of these God inspired prayers and I thought really I wrote that, it's then when I realized that they were not from me but from our Lord God, these I knew were meant to be shared to all.

These prayers were from Heaven to give to all who need and want something special in their life, all who really need the word from our Lord God, and I cannot take any credit for these wonderful prayers, when I read these prayer to other members of God tears roll down our faces, you can hear God in these words he speaks to you directly and directing you on the right path, he is leading you in the right direction, you are touched by Gods grace.

The walk with our Holy and righteous heavenly Lord is an amazing journey a journey I wish to never leave its a joyous ride of love, joy, peace and happiness, because God is pure devoted love, and that's all he wants for all his children, he doesn't want anyone to suffer, he suffered to give us a new life; a walk in Christian faith as believers in God, to pick up yourself and turn to him as your Lord and your saviour.

These prayers are for all to read every day at anytime, for God he is always with you, if you believe in him with all your heart and all your soul, his promise to you is that he will never leave you; all you problems you can give to him and he will heal you, put your faith, love and trust into his hands.

If you have a bible pick it up and read it ask God to lead you to understanding and you will find that it will become easier, he will work in you a little every single day, if you have a church near you then attend, but listen to me, do not feel that God will not love or forgive you if you do not attend church, your church is your home, remember god dwells within you, draw on the God within to show you the way, remember he will never leave you nor forsake you.

I have become a devout follower of our Lord and saviour, to spread the word of God, to help and save as many as I possibly can, these prayers are a story from God which can and will reach you the reader, prayers that will change and transform your heart, filling you with love and faith, that God he will teach and reach you within.

I love the walk with God I never feel alone anymore, he is someone I can talk to anywhere and at anytime, he is someone I can fear enough to keep me on the right path, a path that I do not want to stray from, the fear is of losing God, and do you know all the sins which you have committed against yourself and God, he forgives you, he loves you, he died for (yes you), he remembers them no more, the walk will your Lord it stops you from sinning, you do not want to sin no more, and that is an amazing gift from God, AMEN

Repenting when you turn to him for all your sins is the gift of salvation he gives you to have everlasting eternal life in the greatest kingdom in heaven; the love you have is the love he gives to all his children who believe in him, trust in him, love and have faith in him.

The walk with the Lord God and our Heavenly Father is a family of truth and everlasting love, many of Gods believers are ridiculed, but don't let that stop your love and your walk in faith with Jesus, because this has been on ongoing problem since the beginning of time, I work in a business 7 days a week and I can see and have many conversations with many people and people's faith and believes are very far and few, which is very sad, but it's taken away from schools and now Easter and Christmas, many people take and enjoy these festive holidays without the knowledge of the seasons holidays background.

I can't even give away for free on a counter religious books of our Lord, I do not push anyone to take them, they are there in plain view, but no one with take them, they grab a free truck book though, how disappointing is that; my point is do not let anyone mock your love and faith in your Lord and saviour, he is your Lord, even if it's a family member who does not walk in your path, do not give up, do not force them for its they're free will, and this is very important, do not judge them for there is only one judge and that is God; you may need God to help you in that, as I still do, I still have human limitations and frailties, just as you have and I still have much to learn as well, but with our Lord by our side, we will continue to love all, for God loved us first, forgive all because God also has forgiven us.

I pray and hope that these prayers given to you from our Lord God give you as much joy, faith and love, as it has given me in writing them for you, this journey that you are on is a calling from God, it's a calling for me and that is why I am writing to you the reader today, I would never thought I would have been called to do the work of God, to help feed underprivileged children and families, writing for God, saving people to return to their maker giving people hope and faith in the word of God. **AMEN**

It is my Deep devoted love that obligates me to write and teach the word of God;

The word of our beloved Lord Jesus, I say unto you and my Peace I give unto you, to all who have ears let them hear.

I hope you enjoy my first book of prayers as I have enjoyed writing every single one, may God bless you with love and peace.

Unity, Devout Christians of Jesus Christ;

I am forever grateful to our Heavenly Father for his guidance, trust and faith in me to bring you and his beloved children his guidance and word, love and prayers.

Introduction

Welcome readers to the Book of Prayers, and short stories; The Prayers and the love will bring joy into your learning and will bring blessings upon your life, the Prayers have been written by me as a gift from the Lord, to share with you.

This is a gift given to you so that you can read these Prayers, giving love to the Lord after you have read the word of God. These can be read to the Lord as worship to him from you, with love, joy, praise and thanksgiving.

The Prayers that I wrote were ones that I have done on inspiration to the Lord; for all that he has done for my life, and the change he has brought upon me; and my feelings that were poured out into the prayers.

I found myself in a different light while doing them and trying to explain the inner feelings that I had while writing the prayers to the Lord was difficult, inspiring, joyous, and enlightening.

You can sum it up in many different areas of feelings that the Lord can bring into your life. Your Holy Spirit for instance, this is where God resides and I believe this is where God gives you all your blessings and how he transmits his love to you, and the messages he wants you to receive.

Grace abounding in you from the word of God is transformation in you, the blessings to actually transform your life in such a way, that you are changing everyday without you even realizing.

It's the feeling of the greatest love, love that you can never experience with anyone except our lord Jesus our Messiah and your Father in Heaven.

Bringing the word of God and changing your life and your ways and bringing new into your daily living is being reborn in Christ; The Lord Jesus he died for us, giving us a second chance to be saved for our sins and to have peace, joy, happiness and faith as Christians and children of God.

Prayers and the Love are the most wonderful faith bringing comfort that you can give yourself and the Lord, the Lord rejoices in the love you feel for him, and knowing that God and Jesus hears you and loves you as well, this will bring joyous comfort to you on a very deep level, these prayers are a story of faith and trust all on their own.

Your prayers can be done anywhere in your most personal place, whether that's in your office, your lounge room, your car, anywhere were you want to have your private time with the Lord.

I pray that all my Prayers, stories; bring you much joy and happiness, hope and faith believing.

Now I welcome you to Unity, as devout Christians of Jesus Christ.

Prayers

1

Jesus Son of God

1 My Lord Jesus; son of our God most high, Jesus show me the way, teaching me to pray for,

2 My heart has been troubled and so deep in pain; and I'm calling on you Jesus to show me the way.

3 I will put my faith in you with all my heart, for my Lord and my Saviour; I know you paid the ultimate price, for all of our sin's "yes" which we have done.

4 Had a crown of thorns placed upon your precious head, and was that just to show us that you are truly our King of Kings.

5 But little did they know that when they placed that crown, that you'd be our King to the very end of days,

6 That your love for us was ever so strong, and it is a true love, that many have not really known.

7 Showed me such strong faith, it's a faith that I know I must embrace; Thankyou my Lord Jesus, for I will forever keep this faith, But please know my Lord Jesus that you are my true grace.

8 I glorify you my Lord Jesus that it's you that I've been longing to find; for that love that I now have with you, it will be forever divine.

AMEN MY LORD AMEN

Praise = prayer = power

2

Forgive me Father

1 Holy gracious father in heaven, forgive me for losing sight of my visions, for becoming discouraged, because I do not think things are coming for me quick enough.

2 I repent my Lord, for I feel selfish; I have opened the doors of darkness and depression and defeat, I believe that I should repent, for not keeping my faith.

3 My heart focused on you, within your word and your promises, my trust and love within,

4 For tomorrow my Lord it's a new day, and I will covenant in you, to hear your voice; setting my mind on the things that you have ordained in my life.

5 To trust and wait on the provisions promised, and to do all that I can to reach my goals, in my Lords name.

6 As a child of the King, I have the mind of Christ, I do not count myself to have apprehended.

7 But one thing I do, is forgetting those which are behind, and reaching forward to those which are ahead.

8 I will press towards my Lord, a prize for the upward call, a divine goal of God in Jesus Christ.

9 My Lord I praise you that you have entrusted me, with the blessings of my heart; my true trusted faith, my love for you.

10 To achieve what I accomplish with the words of my Father, my love for Jesus Christ, my love for you both.

11 I know that you know my true heart, for you know all about me; and I know that my love, faith, and trust are in your hands.

12 To teach me, to trust and rely on you, to forgive me Father for all that I have sinned; and I repent my Father, to you deep within.

3
Steps of Faith-
"The World"

1 Your steps of faith are they not directly from God, the Holy Spirit, and the deep within.

2 Walking upright for God's grace, is this your true call, Time to trust in the Lord, so you will not fall.

3 My Lord how hard is it, why don't we all see, are our eyes truly blind, that we just cannot perceive.

4 Is the world to us just so perfect, that we are so willing to miss your call, are the risks of going to the pit of hell, worth the risks to us all?

5 That you're deep love for us; is worth risking "shall" we all fall; for your loving god, your kind, so why can't you see, that world.

6 The steps of faith my Lord God, you know that it's all that we need, its directions from you Lord, world just open your eyes and see.

7 Call on the Lord people and change your lives, is the pit of hell worth it "world" the world over God.

8 And if it's not what you want world, then open those eyes; steps of faith in the Lord, is all that you will require,

9 Leaving the darkness behind, opening the Lords light to come in, for the Lord is waiting with open arms, and with his divine love, he will let you in.

10 But you must repent world, so that you can be saved, now the world is crying, for the steps of faith; Lord, please don't let your beloved, children stray.

11 I hear you my dear Lord, I repent and I have changed my ways, and I thank you my Father, for now I know that I am truly Saved.

4
I'm singled eyed: Filling my call

1 My Lord Jesus, I am you and made in the image of the Father, my promise as a child to train myself, through scripture and knowledge.

2 My Lord you are graciously guiding me, into the word, in righteousness I will walk, in what's the truth, I will learn.

3 With my finetuned ears I will hear, what my Holy Spirit will reveal, and my sight will show me the way and the truth.

4 For my eyes they will show me what is the truth, what's real from the grace, that's abounding in me; for greater is he that is in me than this "world".

5 The evil one he cannot touch me, for my lords name is engraved on my forehead; and I am singled eyed filling my call.

6 My Lord Jesus you are coming, in the clouds for all to see, I will not fear my lord, for you will defend me, I love you my King of Kings, I am yours and I am free, I will dwell in your house; all of my days.

7 I am born of you my Father, I'm your beloved child; I have eternal life, for Jesus you have set me free, free from past, present and future sins, free from guilt and grief from this sinful world.

8 The stronghold of my life is my Lord, Holy Spirit I love you, My Lord Jesus, the power of your spirit, it surrounds me, and your power is directed towards me.

9 I know you are near, my heart will not fear, I feel it in my heart, but one thing that I ask, one thing that I see, that I'm now raised up in Christ, my body a temple of the Holy Spirit, Christ.

10 I see your Glory, I see your face, sending me to my knees, love brushing over me, I felt your touch Lord, I believe in you, I trust in you, and I have faith in you, for I am singled eyed, filling my call.

11 I will fill my destiny, that my father gave me to call, it's a power you gave me, that you have given me to walk, your grace abounding in me; that is filling my call.

12 Now I feel myself getting more of you, for I'm living a life more pleasing to you, but it's you Father, your loves controlling me, and I know now that you're taking care of me, grounded in truth, for life is hard, but you're reaching out your hand saying; come follow me my Child.

13 My Father I'm singled eyed, filling my call; I am living for you, praying to you, letting you know that my old ways have passed away, and it's all thanks to you.

5
For I'm in your Holy Hands

1 My Father God I thank you for accepting my love, the change and the faith that you have given to my heart, the life that you have now given me, making me reach deep inside, to give me your comfort, I'm in your Holy Hands.

2 Waiting on your love to rescue me, to hear my voice to hear my cry, with my prayers, I reach deep inside, Father are you working it out for me.

3 Father is faith made from these moments, are you seizing my heart, have you healing for the broken, giving with love, a giver of love, I'm in your Holy Hands.

4 Your mercy deep within, for I chose to believe, to have blessings upon my life, to bless, to love, with the help of your Holy Hands, helping the needy, being a giver of life, hope, and faith believing, that someone else deeply, loves.

5 I will reap by your words, your teachings and promises, God my Father, your love coming after me, I find myself running to you my daddy, letting your love rescue me, My daddy , I'm in your Holy Hands.

6 I will focus on my Daddy's grace everywhere I go, sometimes thinking I've lost my way, but I have to focus on his gaze, keeping my eyes on my daddy's hand.

7 No more excuses anymore, chose in the trusted ways, break the pain, a new day dawning, trusting in myself, preaching the cross every day, trusting in conversations in the Lord, my Saviour, I'm in your Holy Hands.

8 Living for Heaven everyday whatever it takes, living like Jesus, laying down my life my Lord; your ultimate grace, I love the Lord for he listens to me, and he takes care of me, and all it matters is Jesus, and I want this world to know, how you are watching me grow.

9 How my Lords eyes they see me, with tears rolling down my face, feeling his amazing grace, how I have prayed to you, and cried oceans of tears, and you have heard my prayers father with the washing of those tears; and my Holy Spirit its thanking you, How I believe in you, But how can I not my Lord, for I trust and rely on you.

10 Through you Father, I'm being nourished by your words, washed, cleansed and renewed, for the King and I are now entered in rest, because I am now living in the word, My Father I am loved and you let me feel this love, for I'm in your Holy Hands.

6

Fathers Mercies upon me

1 choosing me Lord from the beginning, and learning from my saved life, that I have found you again, was it your mercies that came upon my life,

2 How my heart feels, to have found these blessings from heaven above, it's an inheritance from heaven a partaker; you my Father have established the truth in me, and my life.

3 Hearing me Father, when I have needed you the most, my troubled heart was way too much for most, It took me to my knees, nearly took me to my grave, but you knew my Father, that I needed to be saved.

4 Saving me my Lord, I just couldn't stand the pain, I needed mercy from someone, just to carry the pain away, you sent your Holy Angels, to save my heart to pick me up, to put me on their wings, to save me from my sins.

5 Father God your mercies are upon me, my Lord forgive me from my sins, I know you love me Father, for you have forgiven and blessed me.

6 And when wrath is upon the world, I know I can be relaxed and calm; for I will have Jesus' love protection and comfort, directly by my side.

7 You are coming back my Lord Jesus, for you are the one who has the power over all, I reign in you my Lord in this age and the next one to come, to watch the beauty and love, completely surrounded by grace, Fathers mercies upon me, I'm totally embraced.

7
My Father in Heaven

1 My Father in Heaven, thank you for hearing my prayers, what you have done for my life lord, I am so glad you are there.

2 There by my side whenever I call, loving, trusting me, my Lord, how I have it all; when I hear you calling, Oh, how you have made me feel, my spirits it's alive in me; the divine within.

3 I know my Lord that you are watching, but what do I do, but I can promise you this Father that I will live and breathe your word.

4 I know that you are teaching me, my dear lord, and what is my call; but you have told me Father it's not yet for me to know, the love and change in me daddy it's becoming so surreal,

5 But its grace that you have told me and that it is real, My Lord what I am now writing it's not really from me, Its grace abounding from your love, that you are teaching me.

6 And to share with others, to teach and to heal; the passion for the lost, to tell them that yes, Father, Jesus and heaven are real.

7 Not just real in my heart, but it's from Heaven above, its love, grace, peace, joy and more; and it's amazing how I have always really known, this place of grace; that its real you know.

8 And yes these visions that I have are just not my own, there from Father above and he is my daddy you know, I'm a child of the Lord, and I will never be alone.

9 Faith is made from love, when God knows what you want, to make a difference to the world, just let the Lord know, by just trusting him, loving him, and Making him your own, and living like a child of Christ, living for Heaven; for my Father in Heaven.

AMEN

8

Explosion of Love

1 How grand is Heaven, to be there at last, to find the explosion of love that I've never really had, never in the world that's now left behind.

2 Much beauty has one ever seen, the colours, the lights, it's Just so real, such a wonderful sight; the angels are rejoicing just to welcome me, and to see Jesus standing there reaching out his hand, rejoicing for me.

3 What does one say when you meet such love, do I bow down on my knees to this wonderful grace, the explosion of love that I feel for this man, my Lord, I' am home; at home at last.

4 To see the king of heaven, and hearing the harps play, never has such music played, this is really grand; nothing can compare now, to my wonderful true name.

5 People glad to see what was once called my face, but did I once know you, that's yet to be said, many people standing around, feel the happiness the joy, all you can hear now; is a trumpets call, a new arrival is hear, now that's real love you know.

6 This is truly God, and it's an amazing place, now look at those Gates so tall so gold yet so grand, the pathways to take, and flowers to see, now look at that ocean and smell and feel that breeze.

7 Nobody to harm you, just peace and calm all around, they say that heaven is love, real love spread around,

8 The explosion of love that I am feeling right now, it's because I am home with my daddy, I'm really home with him at last, that explosion of love, for my daddy who is now holding my hand.

9 He's glad to see me, I'm his child you know, I love you my daddy and yes I am glad to be home, It took me a long time in the world that I left, but please tell me daddy, that I did my best.

10 It's not that easy in the world you know, but I called on you just to let you know, I struggled I cried and you felt my pain, You opened the door my Father and you took me by my hand, and you taught me in my Holy Spirit what to say.

11 To teach the world who would listen, to feed the poor to lend a hand, Lessons to learn in this world; but it's been really hard; my Lord, but finding you again, my father, has stopped my heart from being cold.

12 My hearts, not so troubled because I feel you near, telling me what to say and do, it's becoming really clear; the explosion of love, it's the Holy Spirit I feel, it's my daddy's love , That's because I know you're now near.

13 I will reach home again one day; this is my story to tell; that my daddy's he is with me, to share the truth with you as well, listen to me people, for I know what I tell, pick up the word of God, and you too; will be saved.

9
I've surrendered, my Heart to You

1 I feel the need to totally let go, for my soul loves you, my Lord, my Father; you are real; my Lord I promise I will never let you go.

2 I am veiled at home, not in public you know, veiled in private only for you; but you will let me go, to be serving only you, to teach to the world, so they can love you, Like I do, for I've surrendered my heart to you.

3 I will never, not reach out to you my Lord, for your love and mercies I send praises to you, King Jesus and father daddy, draw me close to you, I depend and I need, for I love thee, and I will run in all directions, all directions after thee,

4 I will always write and teach the word for you, for the spirit of truth is Jesus you know, Moved by the spoken spirit of God, is this what my writing's is all about, and you will expose to me Lord, what is yet to come so I know.

5 The foundations of walking and writing for the Lord, is transformation for me, baptized by the word of God, by the desire to serve you; for my Lord I've surrendered my heart to you.

6 Surrendering all my wrongs, which have been made right through you, my Lord I'm totally focused on you; Yes I'm singled eyed for you my Lord.

7 I've been shown the fruit of the vine, the fruit of the vine, sent from the divine, given me a sign of your face, was this Lord to fill my Life, with your grace, oh Father I've surrendered my heart to you.

8 You showed me a Letter from the Bible; Chapter Jude, to tell me to keep focused totally focused on you, I cried to you and this is what you said, I read it my Lord, and I love you, that was the best, I realized then what you are telling me, I will get through all the pain, If I stay focused on you Lord.

9 I thank you my Lord for the words spoken from you, yes I have love and faith and I have trust in you, I believe in the name; of the son of God, and I believe my Daddy I have eternal life, I believe what you tell me, and I believe what I write, I've surrendered my Heart to you, my Lord Jesus Christ.

AMEN

10

Life is in your Blood

1 What is life, what do you really see, does your life, your blood, flow really free?

2 Is it really yours, to do with as you please, for life is in your blood? But it belongs to God, why can't you see,

3 Do you believe in Christ, I guess that's for you to really believe? Its Life, that is in your blood.

4 Didn't Christ die on the cross, and wasn't it his blood that was spilt on his hands,

5 And he died for us you know, and he suffered at the hands, Off people who didn't believe, that Jesus Christ was the son of man.

6 Life is in your blood, how much, do you really understand, and how important it is to take Jesus as the son of man.

7 That he died for us; to save us from our sins, and that he suffered at the hands of man, to make you understand.

8 Now life is in your blood, and Jesus died for us that day, to save us from our sins, and to turn your life around.

9 Now our blood may not mean too much to us, if we cannot change our ways, so take up the cross of Jesus, for our blood is in his hands.

10 Many of us just don't realize how important it is, to follow Jesus and the word of God, and really take it in, Hold it in your hands and feel that love, for the Lord's love is in your blood.

11
Oh what a Wonderful Lord (With the Amazing Heart)

1 My Lord, you're my life,
How you can read our hearts well,
For your knowledge, and how you can fix it at last,
How you can set us all apart,
For the one's that needs you now,
And for the ones that you say, can just wait, Oh what a wonderful
Lord, (with the amazing heart).

2 How you can touch our lives, and touch deeply our hearts,
To reach out to those, who can call on you at last?
How you have waited so long, for us to reach out to you.
Oh what a wonderful Lord, (with the amazing heart).

3 You've opened your loving arms,
So that you can hold us at last;
For we are father's beloved children and you look lovingly upon us,
With those beautiful eye's, and with that gracious smile;
Oh what a wonderful Lord, (with the amazing heart).

4 Your loving warm embrace, your holy gentle touch,
How can anyone want to let you go, of this wonderful love that got you at last?

5 The Holy glory of Gods embrace that's finally got hold of you,
Don't ever let go, for he has never set you apart,
For it's not God, that wanted you to wait for his touch.
Oh what a wonderful Lord, (with the amazing heart).

6 My gracious Lord, my love, my life,
With your wonderful embrace, how you can change one's life,
When crying out to you, in the middle of the night,
While reaching out to you, one glorious night,
With stars so bright, I know that you are there,
Oh what a wonderful Lord, (with the amazing heart).

7 You sent your Angels in, for me to hold on to,
To wipe away my tear's, and to gentle kiss me too,
To the one who doesn't want to wait no more?
I've now found God, who I can really turn to, and so can you,
Oh what a wonderful Lord, (with the amazing heart).

8 Your compassion oh so loving, for the one who puts hope in you,
But without this hope and trust, then who has one to turn too,
I'd have nowhere to go Lord, that's why I'd never let you go,
For you are the one, to call upon;
To pick me up, to hold me tight, and to put me in touch with Heaven at last,
Oh what a wonderful Lord, (with the amazing heart).

9 I can look at the oceans; I can even look up at the stars,
But what does beauty really hold,
When one can finally look at God at last,
That's beauty, that's love, that one can be around,
And no one can give that to you, but only God's given touch,
Oh what a wonderful Lord, (with the amazing heart).

AMEN

12
Spiritual Eye's

1 Spirituality is it deep within, can you feel, can you see, have we always let it.

2 Let God tell you please, do you really know, and do you believe, Have we to spiritually grow within, do you have Gods spiritual eye's to see.

3 Look around you, with your spiritual eyes,
It's everywhere; it's everything that you look at, that your father in Heaven made grow.

4 It's how you perceive it, it's also how you feel,
But when you look at the beautiful sunset, how can you not melt within, your spiritual eye's they know what they see.

5 The beauty of the flowers, of all different kinds,
There magical-gracious, when God had them in mind, 'He knew how we'd feel, when you'd hold one in our hands;

6 But don't let it stop there truly just look around,
Your spiritual eyes have so much to show you all around,
Let God touch your soul, let God touch your eyes.

7 The colours of a rainbow are so much more than you see,
Look at the rain falling down, do you think of it; as life, and what
it'll bring, for we can't live without it, neither can much on our world,
neither the air that we breathe.

8 But we do take it for granted, even its beauty that it holds,
The waterfalls, the rivers, the oceans and so much more,
For they hold so much life, and it's not just marine life you know.

9 For it is what's all around them, the mountains and the trees,
all the wildlife too, open your spiritual eyes and you will know what
I mean.

10 God knew what he was doing, when he made our world,
His spiritual eyes, what a blessing, and the beauty they hold.
We'll never see, what God sees at all,

11 When you go for a long drive, take your eyes with you to,
Stop and look around at the beauty it really holds,
Not just at people, but the wildlife, the flowers and the trees,

12 Don't forget the nature, that surrounds all of these,
Our spiritual eyes, that God gave us, I hope you use them, and look
and see.

13 Now look above you, during the day, and especially at night,
There is so much that God gave us, apart from our sight,

14 How much are we really missing, with this special gift that
God gave us, yes our sight?
Loving our spiritual eyes and this amazing life, with our God given
beauty our amazing sight,

15 Now take a good look at what you really have when you get
home tonight,
For they are truly a blessing from God, that he gave us from love,

16 Your spiritual eyes need to open, and focus on what you
really have,
For family are important, and they are a God given grace,
Open your spiritual eyes, and look at what you already; truly have.

17 We are all from Heaven, spiritual beings from the Lord,
Spiritual eyes are a blessing, from God, didn't you know,
You can use them or lose them,
It's really all up to you,

18 The beauty that surrounds us, that we don't always see,
But God gave us something special, are you not glad now God has
made you see,

19 Do people really know what to do with them, these beautiful eyes
that we have so we can see;
Look into your children's eyes, are they Gods eyes or really ours,

20 But I tell you they are spiritual eyes from Heaven above,
There a treasure and we need to look after them, for they are Gods
children as well,

21 To let them see with their own spiritual eyes, that God gave them
to believe, for it's what they need to see and perceive.

22 I will look from within the caves, oh and what did I see, for Gods
marvellous works that he created with ease,
For all people and nations, to open their eyes and see,

23 And I declare his glory, for Jesus keeps me on the cross with him,
and he rules over the surging seas, when its waves mount up,
You still them Jesus, with your power, and with such ease,

24 How precious are your thoughts to me, and how vast is the sum of
them,
I know I couldn't count them oh Lord, for they would outnumber all of
the sands,

25 Thankyou my Father in Heaven, I will use my spiritual eyes, and look at what's around me more, with my God created eyes.

26 You have made me see; what a blessing in my eyes that I truly have, and how important sight really is, the beauty that is in it, truly; just everything, which you have blessed us with; to see.

13
A Holy call

1 I've been delivered from this world, redeemed from the curse,
walking by the spirit of God, it's a Holy call.

2 Do not carry out the desires of the flesh, Keep them under control,
do not lose your head,
Not losing your heart and soul, walk in the good faith, if you want
God's grace and this Holy call,

3 Father I need your strengthening, Jesus surrounds me by his love,
a Holy call is upon my life, renewed and entered into rest, for I know
you will help me in my times of deep stress,

4 Oh hear me Father, hear me in my prayers, grant me my requests
oh Lord, pick me up when I fall, my Lord give me, my Holy call.

5 I know deep down that you have called me, Father I know the riches
and the inheritance for me,
But the power that raised Jesus from the dead, Gods hands, Father's
blessings for a truly blessed and well beloved son,

6 I will train myself in righteousness, I will hear Gods words, I will
believe Gods words, I will speak Gods words, and I am complete in
Christ, A Holy Call.

7 Oh my Lord Jesus, I long for your glory, to feed me more in the word, Continue to open the door, to the spiritual blessings, which I need in my life, I will train always, during the day and at night.

8 The Angels you tell me are here all the time, watching Gods children, sending the Angels when I cry all day and night.

9 For they are Gods messengers' and they have much work to do, feel them over your shoulder, they are listening to you, They are loving and kind and are hear for you, don't stop praying Gods children, it's a Holy call within you.

14
I'm Flooded by Gods Love

1 I'm looking from within the caves my Lord; oh what do I see,
The beauty that my Lord has made, just for me to see,
Look at his marvellous works that he has created with such ease,

2 For all the nations and people around the world to see,
Oh I'm declaring God's glory, for Jesus he keeps me on the cross,
close to him; I'm flooded by God's love.

3 You rule over the surging seas, when the waves have mounted up,
you can still them with your mighty power, they ceased, they stopped,

4 How precious are your thoughts to me, Oh Lord how vast is the sum
of them. And if I could count them my Lord, they would outnumber
the sands. I declare to you Oh Lord, can these bones of mine live,
again I hear you say to me, I'm flooded by Gods love.

5 And prophesise to these bones of mine, my Lord said, saying to
them, Oh you dry bones, hear the word of the Lord, for these words
are just grand.

6 For your past sins are gone, by speaking the word of the Lord,
can God speak to these bones of mine, breathing his spirit to enter

them, so I can live in you my Lord, Oh all of my days, I'm flooded by Gods love.

7 So I can know and understand Lord, and realize as well, that you are the Lord and the ruler, over all of mankind, For you are loyal and obedient, Much more than this world, and know this my Lord, that my bones rattle and shake with excitement, every time I hear your words.

8 Now I know my bones they live, and I know that I'm whole, Whole in you, by the spirit of your breath, that has come upon me Oh Lord,

9 Given by you, how I delight so much in you, and your loveliness my gracious Lord, how I delight in your sweet gaze, seeking your kingdom all of my days, as I am flooded by Gods love.

10 Needing to go deeper, beyond what you want and feel, for I need to seek God first, for this is the power of my call, Gods given me the power as a Christian, a child that he so loves.

11 I'm the apple of Gods eye, Oh yes this is love, and I'm not ashamed of the intimacy, with neither God nor his grace, for his Holy Spirit it dwells in me, every day and every night **for I am**

Flooded by Gods love,
For God he dwelleth in me,
It's great to have Gods love,
Thank you for showing me,
And, what's deep love is truly
Meant to be

AMEN

15
God heals the broken Hearted

1 I am the Lord your God, the earth trembles at my gaze, I am the Lord your God and I can heal all your pain.

2 The Lord your God, of the most high, our Lord he is the great king, He reigns over all the Earth and all the lands; Our God he is close to the broken Hearted every day,
He rescues those whose spirits are crushed by pain, God heals the broken Hearted.

3 I tumble down with a broken heart; my entire broken pieces lord please cast them away,
The sacrifices of God, a broken spirit, a broken soul, turn to me Lord, have mercy on my troubled soul.

4 A broken and a contrite Heart, Oh my Lord, I know you will never despise, for I am fixed on you, for the rest of my days, you see I'm broken father heal my pain.

5 My heart a blazed too; I need to be renewed, renewed in you Oh Rejoicing in you my Lord, for all righteousness too, God heals the broken hearted, and he will do it for you to; Lord just to be in your presence, I surrender to you.

6 Every piece of me, you seem to praise, for someone has pushed me father, for Heaven's sake.
Take these pieces Lord and do with them what you can,

7 For my flesh is weak, and it may fail again today, but my god you are my strength, and you're in my heart every day, My portion forever, and through your strength I will grow, God heals the broken Heart, everywhere he goes, God I will give to you, from me everything.

8 Take the pieces my Lord, for there all I really have, as for me I believe in you, Oh my Lord; I say that you are my God, in this life that is something that I really do know for Sure,

9 I know Earth comes up as a great big world, I can tell you this, you can get very much hurt as well, It can break you, and you will truly fall, but God he heals the broken hearted, I will surrender always; to you my Lord.

10 My Lord all the kings horses and all of the kings men, couldn't put me back together again, But my Lord, my God, you will always save me, again and again; and you will put me back together again. God heals the broken hearted.

11 I can hear the broken hearted, I need fixing too, My Lord I've been broken, and trapped in this harsh world; And you've heard my pain, Oh so many times, But you have come and saved me each and every time.

12 You've made yourself known to me, the path of life, with eternal pleasure, seated at your right hand side, when I've suffered though, and I have cried, You have never denied me father, you just held me close by, and comforted me more, I know your by my side.

13 For I am your child, a gift from heaven you see, and even though I have been saved, I've just been broken you see; God heals the broken hearted.

I give you my heart my Lord,
I give you my soul,
I give you my all,
My Father, My Lord.

"Father he says"

My child give me your heart, search for me, with all your soul,

You will find me always,

Let your eyes, observe my ways, and then you will be in my presence day after day.

I love those who love me, and those who seek me diligently, Look and you will, find me always.

16

My God, My Father

1 My God, you are the one who control's history.

My God, he is the great I am, your memorial name to all generations.

2 My God, my father, he is the holy one, My God he is the one who remembers all, and my God he acts in salvation.

3 My God he is the one, who acts in Judgement, My God my Father he is the one, whose anger may be averted.

4 My God he asks for repentance, My God he is the one who speaks, and My God he is the one who cares, My God he is the one who is transcendent.

5 My God, My Father in heaven, he is the one who lives among his children, his people, My God he is the kindest Father, and he is the merciful one.

6 My God he is so faithful, to the ones who love him, love him with all their heart and soul, they are the children of God, and they are his chosen ones.

7 My God, My Father he is the one who comforts, My God he is the one, who will listens to your prayers.

8 My God, My Father, My lord, you are all that is written, in my heart and so much more. My God you are the knowing all, the understanding all, and my remembering all.

9 My God, you are the essential all, my God, you are the permanent existing, and you are my God, My Father, for you are my true strength.

10 My God you are the mightiest of power; you have done the greatest creations of all, My God, my Father and my lord, you are the gift to open my heart, to the beauty and mystery of life.

11 My God you are sending Angels to surround our lives, with love and protection for all, knowing in our hearts, that you are among us, to ease our burdens in our lives.

12 My God, my Father you are enlightening to our hearts, guiding us along our personal journey with you, our glorious and wonderful Father, God, I want to personally thank you.

13 My God, My Father we pray every day, for heavenly protection, knowing that we are in God's hands, as we continue on this glorious journey with you.

14 My God, My Father, we are committed to you, every day pouring out our hearts to you, with love and trust and so much more, with trust and spiritually, longing to hear from you.

15 My God, My Father I lovingly put my thoughts into my prayers, and over my head, I hear music everywhere, singing in the air, knowing that my father God is somewhere.

16 My God, My Father are you over my shoulder or are you behind me, I know your there, I sense your being, for I am content in my heart, knowing I am in your watchful care.

17
Angel, messengers' of divine love

1 Angels are messengers coming back and forth from Heaven to Earth, and God he uses his angels to tell us of his divine love.

2 Gods mercies enduring always upon us, to show us the way, he wants us to follow, to care, to trust, and to love one another.

3 Angels are a presence of wings and harps that glow, with robes of white that slide through the day and ever so gently at night, they are spirit beings bathed in light; invisible among us, for we walk by faith and not by sight.

4 Don't be afraid of Gods celestial beings, they are messengers of light, so just be open to receive, for they come with God's blessings, from heaven above.

5 With Gods heavenly business to teach us to learn, to also properly trust, to properly love, and sometimes my Lord you have come with a message so strong, especially when our lives are in a storm, and our spirits needing a gentle loving nudge.

6 Our hearts enlightened by the gentle whisper of your spirit voice, however when you approach us, with your message of help and tender love, and your compassion to help, was a certainty for us,

7 The surprise of your Holy voice, and your Holy touch, to help with Holy love, so immediately recognizing the message that was from you my Lord, but it warmed my heart to know, that you're watching over us, to help protect my family from harm and from being detached from God.

8 With your Angels and yourself my Lord watching over us, whispering encouraging words to help us and to heal, that's love in abundance, and that a divine presence is near.

9 Angels moving in mysterious and wonderful ways, speaking in Holy voices, in warm and gentle tones; there loving presence and there king words, covering us with peace and comfort, to show us their love.

10 To make your face just glow, the guardian Angel of our life, sometimes flying ever so high, moving way beyond our sight, and I know their always looking, down upon us.

11 But to sense the presence of your Angel Guardian is like feeling the wind around your hair, you can't actually see the wind, but you notice the movement that's ever so near.

12 Did you know that it's your Angel that is near; they're there with God's grace, your Angel so near, your life truly with never be ordinary again.

13 Angels reflect the magnificence of Heaven, the gracious home of God; that he has prepared for all to see, and for all of those who love him, you just wait and you'll see.

14 With perfect submission, and perfect delight, with visions of rapture now bursting in my sight, and seeing last night the cross of my Lord Jesus Christ,

15 The glowing, glistering around my lords head, that just took away my breath, now I want to be one of Gods angels, and with the Angels

I want to stand, a crown upon my forehead and a Heavenly harp within my hand.

16 Heaven abounds with Angels, of light, when our life on Earth is over, Angels that will whisk us up to experience perfection of eternal life.

17 To be shown around the Holy City, to hear in Heaven the Angels singing, oh what a glorious new beginning, I know that I am now in the presence of Heaven.

AMEN

18

I finally understand

1 My Lord and my saviour, thank you for always being near, fixing areas in my life, when you hear me, and calling in your ear.

2 I don't always my Lord have to much to say, because I know in my heart that you are so near, I finally understand.

3 You know what I need, for you know my heart so well, life is always a struggle, because I am here in this world, and life is much more pleasant, in Heaven than on Earth, I finally understand.

4 But isn't it how you want it my Lord, so that we can finally understand, to keep love and happiness, tightly gripped in our hearts and in our hands, our spirits, our minds, and the sands, Lord I finally understand.

5 Life isn't so different from thousands of years ago, its how our minds want to perceive it that makes us fail you know; and it's where you want to finally go, for there is only two choices, and its Heaven or Hell? And my Lord God, you certainly need us to finally understand.

6 God wants to show more love to you, for what you have been through, however it's not always about us, Gods children, but truly what you can do, Pray to God, and repent for your sins, he is always listening to you, for he has compassion within, I finally understand.

7 If we want to see you Lord, hear you, we need to look more deeply inside, have more faith, trust and love and compassion like Christ; and it's never really been about us, look for God, and you will see, then in your heart, you will finally understand,

8 Isn't that how we should have always perceived it, and what God should do, not thinking about the real deep genuine love, for it's always about you? Do you finally understand?

9 What people have become; started many of thousands of years ago, not much trust and love around, you can't hide it, for God already knows, do you finally understand.

10 God he wants us to understand, to feel and look more deeply inside, what's real, what's not, God he will show us the way, for a true genuine human being, is the key to the Holy gates, deep faith, a pure heart, pure love, a pure soul, to love and trust in God, is the key to your soul, I finally understand.

11 My Father, we want so much more from you though, much more than we truly want to give, and that must hurt you so much, how my Holy spirit it grieves; and I feel deeply for you, so much more than ever before, for you have touched my heart, touched my soul, am I starting to finally understand.

12 I hear and I feel for you so deeply my Lord, my Holy Spirit it feels you grieve, that is truly you, now living in my heart, my God, just talk to me more my Lord, showing me more to understand, I want more of your loving heart, because you are my dad; I now finally understand.

MY TEACHER, HE IS MY FATHER IN HEAVEN; HE IS MY TRUE DAD.

13 Now how lucky are his children to want to understand, to find their true father, their heavenly dad, to learn his true words of peace, love, joy and much more, I am glad I have found you, my heavenly dad, to finally understand, so much more.

19
Am I, favoured in your eyes, oh Lord

1 Am I, favoured in your eyes, oh Lord, as you watch over me, And have I pleased you my lord, in all of my years; did you plan for all of my wrongs, so that I can make them, all right. And have you watched over me every day, and every night; bless me oh Lord, for I hunger for your deepest love.

2 Am I, favoured in your eyes, oh Lord, when I try to make things right, even if I know it's not my fault, I know that it's right in your sight; and I know, that's what you want me to do, If I'm to be a child of the light; For I do always think of you, my Lord; every day and every night.

3 Am I, favoured in your eyes, oh Lord, when you have made it this way for me, since I have taken you in my heart, and I feel alive, finally; Your words alive in me, with so much, to still learn, it's Holy, It's scripture, it's the truth, and so much more, It's God its creation, for he has, created us all.

4 Am I, favoured in your eyes, oh Lord, do you know how wonderful, you are to me, the miracles that you have done my Lord, all over this world, for many thousands of years, and all done with your breath; and with your hands my Lord, what a wonderful sight, to watch you, that would have been for me, I want to personally praise you my Father, for all that you have done, for your children, and me.

5 Am I, favoured in your eyes, oh Lord, when tears are streaming down my face, when you have touched my heart, so deeply; an aching like I have never had before, its grace abounding in me, like a beautiful waterfall, of rushing love, rolling down my cheeks, because I've now found, my true love.

6 Am I, favoured in your eyes, oh Lord, when I need you by my side, when things don't work out for me, and I am losing sight; can you make it right for me, my dad, and heal all my pain, and take it away from me, my gracious dad, but I already know that answer, my father, for you always do, and yes my Lord, I really do love you.

AMEN

20
My shining light upon my life

1 My gracious Heavenly Father, your my shining light upon my life, standing in the mists of my everyday life; and knowing that you are their gives me the greatest delight, do you know how you make me feel, so deeply inside.

2 Your divine presence surrounding me, my heart fulfilled with the greatest of ease, that is because my Lord, that I know in my heart, your love for me; your my shining light upon my life.

3 Knowing that you're with me giving me all your support, wish I had found you so many years ago, but it doesn't matter, does it my Lord, because I have found you now, our bond ever so strong, to ever lose you now, you are my shining light upon my life.

4 Now I can go about my everyday life, I may still even struggle, but it's so much less, now in my life, for I have you with me now lord, all of the time; you're in charge to show me the way, to even tone me down, when I am getting out of hand, your my shining light upon my life.

5 How easy life can be, if you really make that stand, to have Jesus seated at Fathers, right hand; watching, and teaching me, and don't make a mistake, for you will get, daddy's hand, what a wonderful way to live every day, to have daddy's love, for he is holding your hand, your my shining light upon my life.

6 You have watched me grow my Father from a very tiny seed, and you have kept me safe, throughout my years, I have been waiting for you my Lord, in this swallowed up world, but to find you at last has made it all worthwhile, to hold you so close, within my soul; don't let me slip again my Lord, grip me tightly in your hands, keeping me totally in your control, for your my world, your my shining light, upon my life.

7 The power that you have over me, it's what everybody needs, if they could only find you and see what I see; Its love and its strength, that you have within, and that power of love, is the divine strengthening; the light within you, its God shining through, the faith, the trust, its God relying on you, to turn to him, to have all those qualities' your my shining light, upon my life.

8 Come and follow the Lord, and you will have his glory shining onto you, for he is your Father of love, and he is watching over you, hold the Fathers book, and hear his words, for daddy is teaching you, his glory will be upon you to, his shining light will forever be upon your life.

21

Show Daddy that you really care

1 You know how much I love you daddy; I thought I showed you every day, how I feel inside of me, you just take my breath away; I express my love in prayers, that I say to you each day, I do show you my Daddy, that I really do care, for loving you is easy, every single day.

2 To someone who loves you so dearly my Lord, you gave me life and showed me the way, the way to eternal life; and taken my sorrow away and replaced it with joy, only a daddy can do that, for the love of his child, I do show daddy that I really care.

3 Show daddy, that you really care, Is being a child at heart, to have the innocence, the purity, to hold Fathers hand, to never let go, of his gentle touch; I need fathers teaching, so I do not fall, I truly love you my Father, this is deeply my call.

4 Show daddy, how much you really care, is to tithe and to love, to never judge someone again, if you truly want daddy's love, it's not too much to ask, if you're ready to make a stand, standing next to him, on judgement day; I repent my Father, I hope my sins have been cast away.

5 Show Daddy, that you really care is to learn to forgive, to have no harshness in your heart, and to only love within, compassion, trust and faith, is what God is trying to teach; read the Bible my child, and feel the holiness within.

6 Show daddy, that you really care, is to worship you Lord for all that you are, for all that you gave us, the hope and the trust; to be able to reach out to you, father, you're the greatest gift of all.

7 Show daddy, that you really care, Father everyone thinks they are important, you know, But they really don't understand; that without you, we are nothing at all, for you created the world, the world in which we now stand; The beauty that we see, with our created eye's; the form that we have, created with your hands, I tell you daddy, I very much care, and understand.

8 Show daddy, that you really care, when you tell the world about his love, to feed the Lords sheep, giving his children, so much love, and hope, all of this, I tell is from heaven above, that daddy is always here for you, and that he just wants the world, to change, to learn the word of the lord, to grow and to understand..

9 Show, daddy that you really care, to save as many of his children as you can, to spread the word of the Gospel, teaching us to listen and to understand, for God really cares for us, he doesn't give up on us at all; only to give all of his children, hope; to save us from this world.

10 This world has been made corrupt, we need saving from all sin, we needed saving from this world, from Gods only begotten son, that's why, Jesus was sent, from Heaven above, to save us from all sins, it's because of his love, this love from Father, and his, beloved son.

11 I want to tell my daddy now, how I really feel; Daddy I really do care, for I have learned so much from thee, and I haven't even got halfway through, the bible, how it's such a great gift from you, a heavenly gift, from the greatest Father of all.

12 Show, daddy that you really care, is to say I am so glad I was born, for I have learned so much love, which was freely given from the Lord; when you pray to him each day, you will feel this joy from within, which is your Holy Spirit telling you that you have finally reached him.

13 Show, daddy that you really care, is loving-kindness, compassion, and grace, God hearing our calls and our cries when we hurt. Sending your angels, to comfort and heal, to laugh and to help us to smile again, you know it's from Father above, and he is trying to heal us within, keeping our spirits alive, it's our God, deeply within.

AMEM, TO OUR FATHER IN HEAVEN

22

Glory to God

1 The glory of gods face, you shall not look upon, but on judgement day, you will see; but until then, no one can see Gods face, which would live to tell.

2 For Gods face it is holy, he is pure, he is power and he is grace, Gods face it is sacred to you, to even look upon, Glory to god, and Gods for his magnificence, his wondrous works; the greatest creator of all, power of his creations, he even created us all.

3 Glory to God, for what he has done, for there will never be anyone, that can ever match what he has done; now don't even think or say that it can be done, for it was no big bang only the clap of daddy's hands, our father he is a Jealous God, he is the I am, he is the greatest one.

4 But we love our Father, for he has given us so much, the beauty surrounding us, day in and day out; and there isn't anything, that you can't see and touch, that God hasn't made, for our God he created it all, with his wonderful and blessed hands.

5 Many look up at the heavens, and love what they see, and why, wouldn't they, for it is an amazing sight to see; many have even tried to count the stars, and have failed, but our father in heaven, he knows them all very well, did you know in the bible it says that he has even named them all; as well.

6 Do you truly want to know your father better than you do "now", then read the Bible, it is the greatest book, and the greatest story to tell, and when you do, then you will know our Father very well; he will also know then, how much you love him, and he will also know, you have learnt something as well.

7 Glory to God, for what I now know, to read the book of God, that I wish I had acknowledged long ago, now I know what has been missing most of my life, it's my true father in heaven, the love of my life, the creator of everything, including myself.

8 I pray to my father every day, and give thanks, to the greatest creator of all – my dad,

For all that I have, it's because of you, saving my life so many times before;

10 I look up to the heavens, and smile before you, praying glory to God for my life was given to my mother, because of you; my beloved mother is now in heaven with you, Glory to God, thank you for my mother, my Lord, for I love my mum, I miss my mum; my Lord.

11 It was a blessing to have known her, to cry and to hold, to comfort and to love, to kiss each other as well, a special gift between a mother and child.

12 I've failed you my father, for all that I have done wrong, But, I feel blessed, to try so much harder, for my love for you, my-dad, you've changed me, and have turned my life around, and your teachings, so strong, for the love of your child.

13 Your ways and truths, mean so much to me and my life, I meditate on you my father everyday and every night; To get closer to you, brings so much joy to my heart, but you reside in me father, glory to God.

14 Oh teach me right now father, in every way; for it frightens me father, that I might misbehave, not intentionally though, for I want to please you, but I don't know all that's wrong, that's been written by you.

15 So I ask for repentance every day, and I am writing personally to you, so I can be saved; and I'm being honest my Father, to you; This is from my heart, for I deeply love you, and your only beloved, son, written from the heart of a devoted, loved child of Gods.

AMEN AND AMEN

23
By the Grace of God

1 For the mountains shall depart and the hills be removed,
but my kindness, it shall not depart from you, by the grace of God.

2 Neither shall my covenant of peace be removed, says I your Lord,
who will always have mercy on you, believe and love in all I do;
for you are all my children, I will show loving-kindness for you,
by the grace of God.

3 God, he will demonstrate his own love for us, for we are all sinners,
but our Lord Jesus, he died for us; saving us all of all of our sins;
for our Father he so loved the world; that he gave up his own beloved
son, glory to God.

4 So that whoever believes in him should not perish and have
everlasting life, for God he didn't send his son to condemn the world,
but the world through our Lord Jesus, to be saved of all sins, Glory is,
by the grace of God.

5 So again the glory of God has appeared bringing salvation to all
men, instructing us to the intent; to deny ungodliness and lusts, and to
live soberly, righteously, and Godly in this present world, all of this can
be achieved with love and trust in God,

6 However God he has said to me, my Grace is sufficient for all, for my power made perfect in weakness;

7 Pray and I will listen to all, for repenting has great value, in keeping you from falling; love me like I love you, for you weakness will weaken, saving you, by the grace of God.

24
A worthy God

1 The Lord in his Holy Temple is keeping his eyes on you, for everything our God has made is good; and nothing refused, but accepted with love, accepted with thanks, a worthy god, a worthy God to have on your side.

2 I confess with my mouth, my Lord, all wickedness from my forefathers, in their unfaithfulness, and all of the other sins, which they have committed against me, and any of their hostility towards me, but I have also acted with hostility towards them and others as well, so I confess and repent, with the blood of the lamb; to my worthy God with an *AMEN and AMEN*

3 My Lord in spite of this, I will not reject them, for I have forgiven them, as you have forgiven me; of all of our sins, for you are the Lord my God,

4 I pray to you oh Lord, to be worthy in your eyes, to re-establish a relationship, with you, my Lord; with what I have lost so many years ago, to be of value in your eyes, to not be set apart, banned or cursed, for I truly love you my Lord, to me you are truly a worthy God.

5 Lord speak to me through revelations, to help me to open my eyes, seeking all truth from Heaven, to re-establish my life, to change my old ways, to live my life more worthy to you my Lord, to speak and learn the word of my God; to the ones seeking me, to speak about you, in learning more about, my worthy God.

6 The heart of Israel, the blessed country of God, I pray for peace, and of love, for your beloved people my Lord, so deeply I feel my Lord, for your Holy land, I feel at peace, I feel at home, you're a worthy God, you and your Holy land.

7 Blessed oh Israel, for you're blessed by God, Blessed oh Israel, for you're the chosen ones of God,
Blessed oh Israel, for Jesus walked and lived on the Holy land,
Blessed oh Israel, for you're loved by so many, blessed oh Israel,
and you're Holy land,
Blessed oh Israel, for I love you as well, blessed oh Israel, for Jesus
is coming back soon, blessed oh Israel, for he will keep you safe
and well, blessed oh Israel, for God will provide, blessed oh Israel,
for God will give you peace at last,

All these blessings are from a worthy God above.

AMEN and AMEN, GLORY to GOD.

25

Jesus is coming

1To watch the Heavens open, and see a beautiful white horse, spreading its wings in the clouds; **a** wonderful sight will be seen, and the one, who is riding this glorious horse, is our Messiah our Lord Jesus Christ; He is faithful and loving and he is the truth, righteous and majestic, and he will Judge, a click of his fingers and Gods chosen ones gone, vanished in plain sight, going to Heaven above.

2 For our rebellious nation, its more than I can stand, come my Lord Jesus save our world from the Evil around, A false messiah that's going to deceive our world, and people will believe the evil of this man, come my Lord Jesus with your flaming eyes of fire, seeing you coming out of the clouds would be a wonderful sight.

3 Carrying on your head, oh so many crowns, you are royalty my Lord, you deserve that crown, placed upon your head, by father God, to lead the way, and the army of Angels right by your side, victory will be yours, all evil will be gone, to the pit of hell, once and for all, glory to you my Messiah Jesus Christ, I love you and father with all of my Heart, a thousand years of peace, thankyou my Lord.

4 The beautiful robe you are wearing is called the word of God, I understand this for it's the truth my Lord, the army of Angels following you, such loyalty by your side, what an amazing sight will your flaming sword from your mouth, which is the word, to strike many nations, to rule, with your rod of iron, non believers of the Lord, not trusting in God, with a click of the fingers, you should have believed in God.

5 For your our King of Kings, our Lord of Lords, all Christian believers understand its written on your robes, your robe flowing in the clouds, upon your white horse, you're a beautiful sight, my Lord Jesus Christ, the day of your coming all Believes can't wait, Lord Jesus is coming, to save our world, Israel saved, amen and amen.

6 Lightening flashing, from all sides of the clouds, my Lord Jesus he is coming, with the mightiest of power, save our world Jesus, bringing peace to save our sad world, taking away all evil, bringing back to us joy.

7 These words they are faithful, and they are truth, for my Lord Jesus he is coming soon, to save believers from this cruel world, I Feel blessed, I'm now happy, and I have my Lord to thank for that, For I have found my father and Lord Jesus, I am a devout Christian at last, For the one to take to heart, and believes in the word of God, take up your cross now and be a follower of our Lord and Saviour Jesus Christ.

8 My Lord Jesus who will send his Angels to testify against all, and to give assurance of these things, for the house of God (the bride); my Lord you are the root, the source and the life, the off spring of King David, the royal bloodline, to me my Lord Jesus, you are also the radiant morning star, my morning star my Lord, you are my life.

9 My Holy Spirit it says, come and hear all that I will tell, for the one who is thirsty, is the one who will drink, it's the water of life, without any cost; I do believe and trust in Christ, I am thirsty for the word, the word and truth of God, Hallelujah to God.

10 Yes my Lord Jesus, I believe in the word and all that is written, in the Holy Scriptures, the Holy Scriptures I read, the word of God, and I affirm these things, come quickly my Lord,

11 Come on your white horse, and sort out this world I'm in, for the grace of my Lord Jesus, my Messiah, my Lord, and my King, for all of your believers, for those that you set apart, set apart for God, Jesus is coming, Jesus is coming, Amen my Lord, Amen.

26

The Love of God

1 The love of God has been poured out within, within our hearts through the Holy Spirit given; given to us from the greatest creator of all, our beloved God from Heaven above.

2 There is no greater love to lay down one's life, for one's friends, for God says love thy neighbour, love oneself; from Heaven the Lord looks down, and he sees all mankind, he looks on you with love, and he looks at what you have done; for the love of God he will forgive, if you just repent for all of your sins.

3 The love of God, has set all the borders of the Earth, and made all of our seasons, for many reasons, to enjoy, to also walk in love, love as Jesus has loved; for Jesus has also given himself for us, an offering a sacrifice, to God as a sweet smelling aroma, a gift for the God we love.

4 For we are his workmanship, created in Jesus Christ, for good works; to follow him, to receive the word, to sin no more, to live a new life, created by God, a new child in Christ, the work of God, the spirit of God; now living in us, this is the love of God.

5 God prepared before hand, that we should walk in love, from Mount Zion, the perfection of beauty; God shines in glorious radiance, to bring eternal life to all who will listen, the son of man who came from Heaven, all of this to shine in us all; that God prepared before hand, the greatest creator of all, From the God of love.

6 God showed me the river, the water of life, clear as crystal, like a clear night sky; bathed in baptism, oh thankyou my Lord, proceeding out of the throne of God, our the words from our Lord.

7 The lamb of Jesus how sweet are our Saviours words, unto my taste, your words are sweeter than Honey to my mouth, divine and a pleasure to learn and express, the love of our God, to follow forever, my grace.

8 Send me your light again, your truth; let it lead me to your Holy Hill, your words of wisdom, for your wise words are like the deepest waters, flowing through me like an endless bubbling brook, holding many tears, from the eyes, of your beloved children needing your love; loving you Father so deep within, reaching out to you for the rivers of love, rivers of love that flow ever so deep within.

9 The love of our God who grips our hearts; changing forever within us, don't ever leave us my Lord, stay with us as we pray, for we are now forever in love, we live each day in a sinful world,

10 A world we can no longer embrace; we are now waiting for Jesus to come back soon, to rescue us from this world, we are true believers, believers of the son of God, this is from your child, a deep love of our God.

11 A sweet victory, when you realize that you have found your true love, a love you can have with no one except with God, he teaches, he trains, showing you what's wrong and what is right,

12 Is that not a loving caring father to save his child from real harm, harm from much evil that is corrupting our world, father is embracing his beloved children, holding out his hands, reach out and grab, your daddy's hands.

27
I Believe

1 Jesus he came, for he was sent by God, to find out what his children were all about, for God has been disappointed time after time, from the beginning of creation, when he made man, the first son he named Adam, we remember his name;

2 For Adam he sinned, this is tree of knowledge, don't eat from it said the Lord, for you will die, you will live no more; but the devil he tempted Adams wife Eve, saying take and eat its good, you surely will not die; so they took it and ate, for they were deceived, making the Lord angry, for they didn't listen to him, I know this story my Lord, I believe.

3 Now God he sent his beloved son, Jesus was his name, on a mission from God to save us from all of our sins, Jesus he first appeared to a fisherman, pulling no fish from the sea; when Jesus realized he couldn't get any, Jesus he helped him to believe.

4 The first of his miracles, impressing all who had seen; follow me said Jesus, leave all this behind, the first of his twelve
Disciples to follow him to the end, spread the word of God, make everyone believe, that I am the son of man, sent from God, teaching love and prayers, to believe in God; I know this story God, yes I believe.

5 Into the desert to be tested by the lord God, tested by Satan, to see if he would give up on his true father God, Jesus he walked the desert hungry and thirsty for forty days and forty nights,

6 Then Satan he tempted Jesus will many offerings, but Jesus he refused, saying no to all, God said you cannot live on bread alone; Jesus he didn't fail, he refused all Satan's lies; then Satan left, he was angry, not getting his own way, Jesus was loyal to his father, right to the very end; Jesus he is truly blessed, I believe in you too my Father and Jesus; your both the best.

7 Now with his twelve disciples by his side; he went out and he healed, many came to see him, to get his touch, he raised the dead, the blind could now see; the lame could walk, many sicknesses healed, by the touch of this amazing man, the son of God, was his real name.

8 Witnessed by many, for this was foretold, miracles of Jesus, the word was getting spread around, city to city, all came to see, the miracle man, many did believe; feeding thousands of hungry people with a few fish and loaves of bread, how can this be, with only a touch of his hands.

9 He walks on water; he does miracles to all, he casts out demons, even getting the dead to walk; surely this man, truly is the son of God, it's a miracle from Heaven, I believe my Lord, you have healed me also, I truly do believe, I believe also that Jesus is the son of God.

10 Jesus, deceived by one of your beloved disciples, deceived by many who didn't believe, no faith no trust, with all that you have done, you my beloved Lord are the true son of God, I believe in you Jesus, I am a devoted follower of you and Father God.

11 Arrested my Lord, for being the son of God, betrayed by someone you truly loved; accused and beaten, because of your love of God, none of your Judges would take your side; But I do my Lord, I believe in God, they Judged you unfairly, and sentenced you to Death, unfairly treated is the son of God.

12 Crucify him, is what they said, let the murderer go free instead, the choice was made by all who were present, crucify him, for he isn't our king; Then Pilot said, you sentence this man to be crucified, he has done nothing wrong in my eyes, you let a man go free, who has killed so many, then I wipe my hands of this man Jesus' blood, you will be sorry, for it is our law, crucify Jesus , the crowd they roared; If this is what you want, then it will be done, I will wash my hands though; of this man's innocent blood.

13 Walking the stony road holding his own cross, the body of the son of God, beaten and scourged to a pulp; carrying a crown which was made out of thorns, spat on him our King of Kings, making a mockery of the son of God;

14 Nailed to a cross in front of all to see, with two other men next to thee; forgive them father for they know not what they do, you still had mercy my Lord for the ones who crucifying you; I believe in you my Lord Jesus, I Truly do love you.

15 Long day on the cross, suffering all you could, given sour wine to quench your thirst, its finished was what you said to all, woman this is your son, saying to his mother before all; and Father I give my spirit to you, Jesus you gave up the ghost, dying for all, I believe you Jesus, that you saved us all, taken all of our sins, your love for us all.

16 Three days all alone, until an Angel came, removing the stone, which enclosed your grave, now risen from the dead, as foretold, then your saw a woman in which you knew, weeping heavily because she loved you, you said to Mary, woman, why do you cry" my teacher is missing "Mary replied" tell my disciples that I will come for them, don't touch me Mary I haven't ascended yet; I believe my Lord, *AMEN*.

17 You went to your disciples, to show them the truth; you've risen from the dead, as foretold, preach the word of God, as I have showed you, preach and heal; To all who will listen, believe and trust in all that I have said, live in me as I live in you; and you will have eternal life; if you lose your life for me, in my name, you will have eternal life.

18 Receive me says Jesus, and you will be saved, to the end of this world, I will be with you; thankyou my Lord Jesus, for all that you have done, I receive you my Lord Jesus, the son of God; I believe all that is written from the beginning of the Holy Bible to the end, the word of God is the truth, I'll pray.

19 You created all Father, and it is good; we have all sinned, and saved by your beloved son, I thank you my father with all of my heart, this is a story to be told to all, for the Holy Bible it's the word of God.

I believe and Amen

28
Fruits of Heaven

1 Jesus he says; I am the way, the truth and the life, and no one can come to the Father, except through me, Oh my beloved Lord, through the fruits of Heaven you have delivered me and my soul from death, and I say to you, have you not kept my feet from falling, so that I might walk before God in the light of everlasting life, living in Heaven above.

2 I will forever worship the Lord, my God, in the splendour of his holiness, lead my oh Lord to the fruits of Heaven, as I tremble before you, all the Earth, trusting in you oh God my Father, doing all that's good, before you, that you require from me, that I know and understand, as I dwell in the land with the fruits that I have been given, the fruits of Heaven,

3 Fruits to enjoy, a safe pasture, provided by my father in Heaven; now the one who provides the seed, to the sower (could that be me?) bread supplied for food supply and multiply the seed, you have sown says the Lord and you've increased, the fruits of your righteousness, for me.

4 Oh thankyou my gracious Lord, for supplying every need for me, done in accordance to the riches in glory in Jesus Christ our Lord, Oh praise the Lord, for he does provide for us all.

5 For as high as the Heavens are above the Earth, so great is Gods loving-kindness' towards those who fear him, the Lord he will guide you continually: giving you the fruits of the water of life, when you are dry, restoring to you all your strength, the fruits of Heaven, Gods loving -kindness to you.

6 God has provided the fruit of food; for all his people "who fear" ever mindful of his covenant to you, our God he has done good, for I am wanting for nothing at all my Lord, for I have your love and that is the best fruit of all, the best fruit of all, your fruits from Heaven, oh thankyou my Lord.

7 And God he does good, giving us the rains from Heaven. Fruitful seasons filling our hearts with food and gratefulness' so let us come before pour Gods presence, with thanksgiving for these fruits; let us shout joyfully to him, with prayers and rejoicing, for all that God has provided us, the fruits of Heaven.

8 I will walk with you my God, and Jesus he will walk among us, saying" behold my child I am with you, and I will give you rest, oh thankyou my Father, oh my Lord, for all the fruits of Heaven provided for all your children my Lord, for all that you have created, the fruits for us all.

9 I shout to you with praises and thanksgivings and Joy, fruits you gave to so many in all different ways, it's given by God; to you from Heaven above, my lips still pour with praises to you, because you have made me the new person that I am today; I will bow down to you, for all the Earth will bow down to you to, in worship my Lord, for the wonderful things that you do, singing praises like I do for you, praising your name, for all of the fruit from Heaven given from you.

10 My God my rock, I can come to you for safety, you are my shield and my strength; for God he is my defender, sending me the comforter when I am in pain, you are my God my complete place of safety. Amen

11 I can look up at the hills but where does all my strength come from, my strength and my help comes from my Lord, and he made all of Heaven and Earth, you know, he is all of my fruit, he is all of my joy, my Holy spirit so alive, with all the fruits from Heaven above.

12 No one is Holier than my Lord, there is no one else for me besides you; there is no rock, like my God; when I ascend into Heaven, lift me up my Lord, hold my hand for you have been my rock and my salvation, here on Earth where I now stand, your my fruits of Heaven, blessing me my Lord, lifting me up when I have been down, I thank you everyday my Lord for all that you have done for me, I wouldn't be the person that I am today if you had not come and saved me.

29
God Almighty is his name

1 He who has formed the mountains, who also has created the mighty winds, and who reveals his thoughts to mankind, who turns dawn into darkness; and treads on the heights of the Earth, the Lord God Almighty is his name.

2 Oh how great is our God, he is beyond our understanding, and the number of his years, is beyond uncomprehending; he evaporates the drops of water from the Earth and turns them into rain, oh what a wonderful God, we have; the rain pours down from beyond the clouds, and everyone benefits' from this rain which is Gods; the Lord God almighty is his name.

3 The poor and the needy seek water from the ground, but there is none to be found, their tongues failing from thirst, their skin is dryer than the sands; and I says the Lord will hear their cries, I the Lord God of Israel, will not forsake them, the Lord God Almighty is his name.

4 I will open the rivers in desolated heights, and fountains in the midst of the valleys waters will flow; I will make the wilderness a pool of water, and all the dry lands springs of water,

Mission provisions, from other countries I will send, for the Lord God Almighty is his name.

5 How great is our God, when he heals the ones who suffer and hurt, the miracles that he does day in and day out, for not many comprehend at all about what our God really does, but God he does care and oh how he loves us, compassionate is God, giving credit for what he had done, for God Almighty is his wonderful name.

6 Lord God, majestic is your name, for all that you have created, just for us to walk on, you gave us life, you have blessed us with all the beauty of the world, everything you gave life through your breath and that includes me, oh my Lord.

7 Lord God how wonderful you are to me, nothing else matters, but you to me, the creator of all, before all the mountains were born, before you even gave birth to the Earth, and the world; from the beginning to the end, you are my God Almighty, my Lord.

8 God he is the one he is the mighty I am, he made the mountains and created the winds; he makes his thoughts known to you and to me, so come and hear all that fear God; for you should, and I will declare to all, what God he has done for my soul today, For I now know the God I love for he has got so much of my heart.

30
From God on Love

1 I love you my Lord Oh my strength, I was put into your arms at birth and from that moment, you have been my God, my father, my joy, my salvation.

2 God he is love, and he says he who remains in love, remains in God, because he first loved us; take good heed, therefore unto yourself, that you love the Lord your God.

3 There is no fear in Love, but perfect love that cast out fear, for fear involves torment, but he who fears has not been made perfect in love, God says unto you, that you shall love the Lord your God with all of your heart and soul, with all your mind, casting out all sinful thoughts, this is the great and first commandment of God.

4 And the second like unto it is this, you shall also love thy neighbour as yourself, seeking the kingdom of God above all else and live righteously and I will give you everything you need.

5 Now it is high time to awake out of sleep, for now is our salvation, nearer than when we believe, I am the first and the last, apart from me, there is no God; I will continue to seek you my Lord God, there is no other God to me but you, I am Glad that we have found each other, *AMEN*

6 Oh my soul how it thirsts for you, oh how my life and Holy Spirit it longs for you;
Those who love me says the Lord, I will deliver them up, I will protect those who truly know me, and my name; when you call for me, I will answer them, I will be with them in troubled times, I will receive them and I will honour them, with long life, I will satisfy them and show them my salvation.
For Grace and peace I give to you, to all my children, your God the Father; and your Lord, Jesus Christ.

7 Now I pray to you, that I have found favour in your sight, for you have favour in my eyes oh Lord, let me know your ways, so that I will always know you, for you my gracious Lord, God; you are our sun that shines high above the earth, you are my shining stars that glitter before me at night, all which you created for our sight, you are my shield, my protection.

8 You have transformed my life in so many ways, for this I give you grace and all the glory, for you my Lord hold no good thing from those, who do what is right, for all the sins that we have done, no longer will be our master, because we are no longer under the law but now under the true grace of you my God, from your fullness, receiving grace after grace.

Amen and Amen

31

I Your God

1 I have swept away your offenses like cloud, your sins like the morning mist; so that it will return to me, For I your Lord God have redeemed you.

2 Oh my Lord, I ask of you to please wash away all of my guilt, clean me again, whiter than the snow, for I know that my Lord and Saviour Jesus Christ gave up his life to free me, from every kind of sin, all sins; to cleanse us and to make us his very own people; totally committed to doing good deeds.

3 The Lord on high is mightier than the noises of all the running waters; he causes his wind to blow and the waters to flow, for as the deer pants for the water brooks so does my soul pant for you, oh my gracious one, oh my Lord God.

4 The Heavens declare the Glory of my God and the skies announce what his hands have made, Oh Lord, Oh Lord, how excellent is your name, in all the Earth in which your children stand, who have set your Glory above the skies, the Heavens, its I your God.

5 Your Love Lord reaches to the Heavens, your faithfulness to the skies; you alone are my true and only God, of all the kingdoms of the Earth, you alone, created the Heaven and the Earth.

6 I the Lord made everything, stretching out the skies, by myself spreading out the Earth all alone, Heaven and Earth will pass away, but my words they will not pass away, says I your God.

7 Rain and snow fall from the sky and do not return without watering the ground, they cause the plants to sprout and grow, making seeds for the farmers, and bread for all people, making food for all, says I your God.

8 So shall my word be that goes forth, from my mouth it shall not return to me void; but it shall accomplish what I please, and it shall prosper in the things for which I have sent it, I your God.

9 The humble will be filled with fresh joy from the Lord your God, and the poor will rejoice in the Holy Land of Israel; for the love of God has been poured out into the hearts, by the Holy Spirit who I have given to you, says I your God.

10 All things were made through Jesus Christ, for he has never sinned, he has never lied, for in Christ Jesus lies many treasures of wisdom and knowledge; and being found in appearance as a man he humbled himself and became obedient to the point of death, even the death of the cross, I your God.

11 For there are only one God and one mediator between God and Man and his name is Jesus Christ, said I your God.

Amen

32
Oh My Mighty God

1 For the Heavens declare the glory of God, the skies proclaim the
works of my Lords mighty hands;
My Father "what God" is there in Heaven or on Earth who can do
anything as great as your works; and your almighty deeds, what
wonder they are, Oh my mighty God,

2 Your righteousness oh my mighty God, our the riches in Heaven; Oh
mighty God, you who has done such great things, for me my Lord in
my troubled times of need, you have came through for me thoroughly,
I believe in your touch and the wondrous works of your hands, you
have touched many believes lives in many different ways, there is no
one that can compare to you, Oh my mighty God.

3 I have asked for you to create a pure heart for me, a clean mind, a
pure body and a pure soul, Oh my mighty God, renew a right spirit
within me, for this I am so longing for, right standing, in your eyes, Oh
my mighty God.

4 I am longing for the fruits that the spirit brings, which are the love,
the joy, the peace, longsuffering, for without that we cannot, find
strength, kindness, goodness, faithfulness, and gentleness, to have

within us all this self control; help me Oh Lord to learn and have this understanding, its importance's, Oh my mighty God.

5 Oh my mighty God, the kingdom of God, it's not a matter of eating and drinking, but of righteousness, peace and joy in the Holy Spirit, being perfected, being in comfort, being of a sound mind, living in peace, living in the love of God, "the God of Love" then peace shall always be with you, Amen Oh my mighty God, completely in fellowship with you.

6 Today I make a covenant of my peace with you, That with everything just said, for it to be an everlasting covenant with them, for all that I have had, for they are now spiritually dead, because of the wrong things done, against my wonderful Father God; Oh my mighty God, how that has made me spiritually sad.

7 But my God he gave me a new life, with Christ, for he has saved me, by Gods grace, he has lifted me up, our God he gives more grace to the ones who ask and turn to him, for the scriptures say, God he is against the proud, but he does give grace to the humble; for the law was given through Moses, but grace and truth came through, my Lord and my saviour Jesus Christ; Oh my mighty Lord.

8 Therefore let me draw near with confidence to the throne of grace, so that I may receive your mercy and find grace to help me in my time of need, for the one thing I have desired of you my Lord, is that I will seek so that I may dwell in the house of the Lord, all the days of my life, where everlasting life and peace is, to behold the beauty of the Lord, to inquire in your temple Oh my mighty Lord.

9 Oh open my eyes, so that I can see, the wondrous things from your laws, for I delight in your laws, my God; to learn more in my inner most self; for my Lord my goal is that I may be encouraged in my heart and united in love, so that I may have richness in full understanding-completely in law.

10 So I do pray that my eyes of your heart may be enlightened so that you will know, I ask of you what is the hope of my calling for the Gospel it came unto me, not just in the word only, but of power in my Holy Spirit, and in as much assurance, Oh my mighty God.

11 My fear for you my Lord, makes me want to stay in your Laws, your word, that calling in us my Lord; is your plan all along for your children who love you, to not want to make any mistakes because they love and fear you oh my Father; to repent and say grace, the Holy Spirit in us, for it's a law all on its own, It does tell us real quickly when we have done wrong, I thank-you for giving me the wonderful Holy Spirit I have, that will keep me on track, Oh my mighty God, forever in fellowship with you. Amen and Amen

33
All of Your Heart and Soul

1 Is it not with you alone, that I am making this covenant with you, an oath; that you have returned to the Lord your God, and you have listened too and obeyed, obeyed his voice, with all of your heart and all of your soul; with everything I am commanding you, today, you and your children.

2 The Lord your God will lead your heart, and the hearts of your descendants, removing the desire to sin from your heart, cleansing and purifying your soul, so that you will love the Lord your god, with all your heart and soul, so that you may live with blessings granted to you by God.

3 The Lord your God will inflict all curses on your enemies and on those who hate and persecute you, and also with unfairness, judged on you when you are innocent, again, listen to and obey the voice of the Lord and obey; doing all of his commandments, which I will command you, today; the laws written in the Holy scriptures.

4 And if you turn to your Lord God, loving me with all of your Heart, your soul; your entire being, leaving all your fleshly desires' and thoughts behind, capturing them before they get out of control, for this is the first commandment given to you, it hasn't been given to you to be difficult and hard to reach and understand, for the words are very near to your mouth, and in your heart, it's so you will obey and command.

5 How is it that you do not listen and capture thoughts that result in out bursts of anger and resentment towards me your God; I have set before you life and prosperity, death and adversity, in that I command you today to love the Lord your God and walk and live every single day in his ways not yours. His commandments and not yours; his statutes not yours, his judgements not yours, and unto others; for I am right and you are not, I am the one and only judge, do all this so that your God, your Lord, will bless you.

6 But I say to you that If your heart turns away and you will not hear me nor obey me, for you are drawn away from me, I will call Heaven and Earth as a witness against you, today; for I have set before you life and death, the blessings and the curses; therefore love your God with all your heart and your soul, you shall choose life in that you may live.

7 Love the Lord your God by obeying his voice, by holding ever so closely to him, for God he is your life fulfilment for all of your days, so being strong, having courage and do not be afraid and tremble before your enemies for it is the Lord your God, who will not fail you nor abandon you, so do not be dismayed or fear.

8 Oh my Lord loving you is one of the easiest things for me to do now, and now that I have found you my Lord, do not fail me, nor abandon me, when I make mistakes, for you are my life, you are my heart and you are my soul.

9 I want to be ever so strong, and dependant on you, and not weak in my flesh no more, for I know it is detestable to you, you are right, removing the desired sins away from us , which cause havoc in our lives, it's like living in hell, causing so much grief and heartache, hell here on Earth where there is so much weakness in sin, replacing the desires of sin from my heart and replacing it with my God within, I love you my Lord.

AMEN

34
Oh Praise the Lord, what's Gods Love

1 My Lord will bless the righteous with Favour, will you surround him with a shield, do not be ashamed of the testimony of our God for great is his love towards us and the faithfulness of the Lord endures forever, Oh praise the Lord, what's Gods love.

2 Oh praise the name of God, forever and ever, for he has all wisdom and power, you are brought with a price, therefore glorify your God, in your body and in your spirit, which belongs to God, Oh praise the Lord, what's Gods Love.

3 My beloved, let us love one another, for love is of God, and everyone who loves is born of God, and knows God, if anyone is in Christ, he is a new creature, and old things have passed away, I say behold the will, become new, Oh praise the Lord.

4 A good name my Lord is more desirable than any of the greatest riches, to be a new creature is better than any silver, gold or rubies, all the riches in the world, I'm glad to be anew in you my Lord, learning so much of the world, what's right and what is not; finding you cannot put a price tag on love, that I feel for you and Lord Jesus, Oh praise the Lord, what's Gods Love.

5 Gratefulness' gratitude, for all things that you have done, praises for the loving caring God that you are, and for all the good things that you have brought back to my heart, you do not take advantage like the world in which we live, you love unconditionally not wanting or expecting, for its all about us, not understanding or caring, for that's not about love, for sharing and love is only what God can really give us, and that does come from God, with no price tag, attached for us, its unconditional, Oh praise the Lord, what's Gods love.

6 What do you really know about real deep love is it, sin, anger, jealousy, lust and thoughts that are not just; did I not tell you that these are detestable to God; I gave my son and so much more, more than you can do, I have given you tests, tests that you still cannot learn; you break them and fail and talk among yourselves, but you still take chances, and you wonder why you fail, I love you my children, I wish you would understand, try harder learn and then repent, Oh praise the Lord, what's Gods love.

7 Live in my law is it so hard to do, you read each day, so you are living in my word, is your flesh so important, taking total control of your life, look at the word, let love from me flow through your mouth, from Spirit and Heaven above, casting away darkness and lusts, and sins of this world; then you might find the true meaning of what's Gods love, if you reach deep inside, Oh praise the Lord, what's Gods love.

8 What do you want from me, if you do not listen and learn, do you want to be saved or do you want this world, I will listen when you pray, I have all the time to spare, I will wait a little longer to see if there is a change; remember the tests that I give to you all, It will still come down to this me or your world, Oh praise the Lord, what's Gods love.

9 I am compassionate and loving, I have saved millions, and then I won't, I give chances to the ones who I know that really do love me, the most; search your hearts and your souls, love and do not hate, be kind and not selfish; look within and not out, you have answers, but ignorance gets in your way, old ways sneak in, stamp them under your feet, for I have given you the power within, Oh praise the Lord, so what's Gods love, the Holy Spirit within.

10 I've given so much, with such little results, I've tried so hard, but I haven't given up on you all, I died on the cross to save you all from your sins, but many who want to be saved, will not give up the flesh of the world; If you want everlasting life, try then much harder than you do, for me and your Father that truly do love you.

11 Forget the sins of the world, to reach Heaven much faster, than you are today; but for the love of me and the Father says you shouldn't give up at all, we will be there for you so search deep within the answer is there its really all up to you, Oh praise the Lord, what's Gods love.

12 Is it such a gamble to really focus and understand the Love of Heaven or the Love of the worldly desires, the sin nature of the world, that has trapped so many, more than you can comprehend; give up the sin of the world and follow me through real love, not the love of the world, but the real love in Heaven above, compassion and trust, faith and not false hope, reliance of the Heavens; Oh praise the Lord, what's Gods love.

35
Real Everlasting Love

1 Above the voices of the many waters, the mighty breakers of the sea, Lord Jesus on high is much mightier than thee, so when I pass through the waters, I will be with you my Lord, for tears can be like the ocean, emotions running ever so free; I shall not overflow you my beloved Lord, for you have established in me peace and real everlasting Love, that God has given me within.

2 May the God of power and hope fill me with so much Joy, peace in believing that there is always hope, I'll abound in hope by the power of my Holy Spirit that God has given me, for you my Lord will give to whoever has a steadfast mind, in perfect loving peace; just because of the real everlasting love, that you have now given to me, true everlasting love that you have for me.

3 My Lord in peace I will lie down and sleep, for you alone this is my meditation on your love, that you have transformed in my life, I'm glad I have found you at last, you keep me now safe, for I waited patiently for you my Lord, you heard me sobbing so deeply, you knew I needed help, you brought me out of the horrible pit of hell of murky clay, setting me on a perfect rock, you established my step, my God that is real everlasting love.

4 Your putting new prayers in my mouth nearly every day, all these prayers from you, Oh what a joy to feel and learn, there from your heart transformed to mine and mouth, all grace abounding because of love, we are never far apart, always now ever so near,

5 longing always now for your words to grow inside of me, Oh love me my Father that's how a child of yours learns, a child that's needed, tender nurturing and loved, hold my hand, for you hold my heart, I don't ever again want to be lost, for a child to its Father, its real everlasting Love.

6 I now live in you my Lord; it's the new creation in me it's come forth a transformation, grace abounding from you to me, Oh my gracious Lord how wonderful you have been to me, you who resides the new me is now here; Oh how much different I've become how much you open one's eyes, when they feel your love deeply growing inside, real everlasting love, from my God and his beloved son My Lord Jesus Christ.

7 My Lord as is your name, God so is your praise, to the ends of the Earth I will follow and love you, for you fill my Holy Spirit with so much love and joy, your hands full of righteousness, your name will endure in me forever, your name shall continue longer than the sun; and all your beloved children my Father will be blessed in your name, and all nations will be happy, because of you, and everlasting love spread around the world, the Holy Scriptures are your word.

8 You're a wise and understanding God you are, your ways have proven to be, compassion and Love that's you my Lord, and honourable life you've given me; saved and blessed are Gods works, with the humility this comes, and wisdom, "God's love" given within, always be humble, gentle and patient, excepting each other with love; this is Gods way of teaching, to God's chosen one's, from God to us, this is everlasting love.

9 When God speaks, loved clothed in his compassion, kindness, humility and grace, gentleness and patience, his divine power, he has given us everything we have received from him, everything we need everlasting love.

36
Creation

1 The Heavens will praise your wonders my Lord, your faithfulness is also the assembly of the Holiest ones, the creation from your hands for all to enjoy.

2 The Heavens proclaim the Glory of Gods skies, displaying his craftsmanship, all over the universe, for it wasn't a big bang that many do think; it's the wonderful power of God himself, he is the creator, his breath and his hands; through our Lords mercies we are not consumed, because his compassions fail us not; they are new every morning, for great is your faithfulness, for I tell you it's I your God, your God that does never change.

3 For our God he is faithful he is our true Father you know, who will not allow you to be tempted above, above all that you are able to withstand, for he will drive out your enemies before you, teach you to trample them under your feet.

4 for the eternal God is your refuge and underneath are the everlasting arms, God he will pick you up, and strengthen you with pure love, creation of your Holy Spirit within, you're his created child.

5 Now thanks be unto God who always causes us to triumph in Christ, and makes manifest the fragrance of his knowledge, by us in every place in our hearts, a creation only given by you.

6 Your unfailing love Oh my Lord it's as vast as the Heavens, your faithfulness reaches beyond our clouds, you are my Lord, I'm truly devoted to you, I will exalt you, I will give thanks to your name, you have worked wonders in me, plans I believe formed long ago, with perfect faithfulness finding you, an empty journey for me finally fulfilled, creation from you my Father, your grace to praise, hallelujah and amen.

7 In the beginning my God you created the Heavens and the Earth, and the creation of the highest Heavens belong to you, Oh my God; also the Earth and all that is within and that's including me my Lord, your reaching out to your children in need, we are reaching out seeing this beauty that you have created, creation for all to see, how you are worthy, to receive the honour from your beloved children, who deeply love you within; your power is to be praised for the creation from your wonderful hands, your pleasure from your love within.

8 Loving you my Lord, I shall go out with joy and led out with everlasting peace; the mountains and the hills shall break forth into singing before you, and all the trees of the fields shall clap their hands in joy, holding your hands splendorous, exalting in love, creation from God for his wondrous works for all of us to enjoy, for everlasting peace I will now finally hold.

9 My voice you shall hear in the morning, my Lord in the morning I will direct it to you; as I look up in the Heavens seeking you, I will hear what my Lord will speak, he will speak of love and peace, to all his children who will have ears to hear, my gracious Lord I seek you, I will listen to what you say, I open my heart to your words, for they are of wisdom beyond our years, knowledge and understanding, that you are teaching me; not all I will comprehend, but one day I will be with you and then I will totally understand.

10 Though my God is not a God of total confusion but only that of total peace, as in all the churches of the saints, the Heavens are yours, as is the Earth; in all its fullness you created you founded it all on your own, no other creator could have done this, only the true creator God.

11 Come unto me all you who are heavily laden with burdens, beyond your control, for our God and our Lord they will tell us, they will give you rest, sending you in the comforter, helping you to recognise and to learn from God for he says I am meek and lowly at heart, you shall find rest unto your souls, I will give you the peace that you need, to have happiness and love.

37
Message from God

1 I am writing to you my beloved dear ones, that you should love one another as I have loved you, this isn't a new commandment I give, but one from the beginning of time; and about your love for one another, we should not need to send a message to you, for you yourself have been taught by God, to love each other, for the word of God is truth, it is love, it is God himself.

2 Now this is a message that's been heard from the beginning, to live your life in the law of God's word, it's absolutely clear that I gave you a free life, but I didn't give it to be abused, to destroy your freedom, but rather you use your freedom to serve, for freedom grows with love, Gods love that grows within his children who hear and live in the word.

3 Faith, love and hope will remain these three, but the greatest of these ones is love; the Heavens declare the glory of God, but the universe shows us Gods hands, what was made from love for all to see, God said I did this all on my own; my love reaches to the Heavens and my faithfulness to the skies, but my true love I give you inside.

4 The Holy Spirit it has so much power to the one who holds it true in their hearts, you might make mistakes, but give it straight back to me, and I will truly forgive you, because you now understand how I will feel, when the Holy Spirit, it weeps, from the pressures of this world and the people that you met, that turn your life upside down, but I do understand and I do forgive.

5 Listen to me and understand, keep turning to me all the time, and I will give you back your peace of mind, it's not hard to do when you learn my ways, think like me and how I would feel, and you will win each time, keeping love in your heart; and forgiveness for all, for I know you have compassion already, in your heart, that is why you struggle at times, but remember do not fail or fall short for what others do, remember you are a child of Gods.

6 My Lord, my God, your my wise teacher from Heaven, with all my soul I desire your love every day and every night, by my Spirit within me, I will seek you as early as the dawn, for when my eyes are awake I do think of you all the time, I only want to live in happiness, love and peace, to me this would be a great start to my day, then I will truly know in my heart, that you my loving God are not too far away.

7 Your love is breathtaking filling my life with joy, facing a day without you would be like facing a day in jail, your life brings to me peace, joy and happiness, and you can only have this if you have the love of God's word.

8 My word God said is forever, you cannot live without it in this world, for it's the truth without sin, lust, hatred and lies, that people have made the world in which you live in, and only my children will comprehend all this; now preach my word and my love, to all that you meet, for the ones that will listen are the ones who can be saved; for they took the time to listen about me, they care and believe and are willing to hear, a seed planted by me that day, when you meet.

9 Thank the Lord your God for seeking you and showing you the way, I've watched you grow from a seed in the womb, and I knew you even before I placed you there, I have known your heart all along, and I knew all the mistakes that you would make, I also knew that you would come back to me, and you knew I would forgive you as well, I had planted that seed long; long ago, you just can't comprehend it at all, but deep down you do know the truth, it just hasn't surfaced fully yet, don't push yourself to far or struggle in what I say, live your life as best that you can, for you will be with me again one day, live peaceful my child, you understand.

10 I am a true believer in God, and I have a Father in Heaven who has saved me from my sins, he has opened my eyes to so many things, I will never turn away from him ever again, for I have found the truth at last, I love what my Father has done for me, I love my Father and his son, The word of God, I'm a true Christian at heart, the God of Israel, he is the I am, a love for his child, a gift from God, a blessed message received, amen.

38
Holy Spirit

1 My heart has heard you say come and talk with me awhile, and my Lord my heart responds to you, I am coming my Holy one, for I delight in you my Lord, giving the desires of my heart to you; I long everyday for my embracing on my thoughts, thoughts and dreams as we talk.

2 My heart totally fixed on you my Lord, singing praises, letting my heart be perfect in your eyes my Lord; to work in your word, your law to keep your commands, my Holy Spirit as alive as we embrace.

3 Oh Lord your name is called wonderful councillor for almighty you are to me, an everlasting Father a Father of peace, my soul it cries out to you when I don't feel you around, my Holy Spirit just doesn't feel the same,

4 You will show me the way of life, you have granted me the joy and the pleasures of living with you forever, I feel my Spirit alive with this thought, your mercy for me is in the Heavens above, and faithfulness reaches its hands out for love.

5 I praise you for the acts that are mightier than all, praising according to your excellence and greatness, for the things which I have learned and received from you, which have given me so much strength and power to my life, a Holy Spirit so strong a Holy Spirit that's alive and it's all because of your my Great God.

6 So let the Heavens be Glad, and the Earth know rejoice, and let us say among the nations that the Lord he reigns, and that God he has made everything beautiful including me, my Holy Spirit alive, it's because of God; he has set eternity in my heart, from the beginning and even to the end.

7 I do not set aside the true grace of God, for righteousness comes through the law, then Jesus Christ he died all in vain, you shall give up all that you can, and more in the name of the Lords sake,

8 For if you do you shall have eternal life, in Heaven above if you believe what I have done, believe in the word, believe in God, you Holy Spirit it will thank you for then you truly do know me, more than the world in which you now live.

9 Search now your Holy Spirit, that I have given to you, what do you feel right now, for your heart should be humbled, your mind more focused and stable, your body more healed, more focused on the Good and not evil; more focused on the word, the truth of God, which is the law, more focused on love and not lusts of the world;

10 Do you truly understand the importance of what I have given you, your true elements of nature of what's in Heaven above, not of the nature of unbelievers of the world, in which you now reside; A true believers loving Holy Spirit resides in everlasting life in heaven, not the riches of the world but a living intimacy within the source, an expression and manifestation of Gods words, and actions of your Holy Spirit, your soul destiny is in Heaven.

39

Washed and Cleansed

1 Although we were spiritually dead, because of the things we done wrong, against God our Father, he still gave us a new life in Christ, being saved only by Gods grace, God he gave us more grace as it's been said in the scriptures, God he is against the proud, but gives grace to the humble, now washed and cleansed, spiritually clean.

2 Our lord God is a sun, and he is our shield, watching and protecting, what is truly his, for the Lord he will give grace, and Glory to the ones, and no good thing will he withhold from those who walk upright, washed and cleansed like polished glass.

3 So let us walk and draw nearer with confidence to the throne, the throne of grace, so that we can receive all Gods mercies, to find Gods grace to help us in our time of need; for the one thing that I desire of my Lord, that I seek, is to dwell in the house of my Lord, to be ever so close to him, open my eyes so I can truly see, the truth and your law, washed and cleansed just like pure gold.

4 For my true goal is that my Father can encourage me in my heart, uniting me in true love, to have full rich and complete understanding, Gods plans for us all we never will know until we are in heaven to be judged, But I pray my Father that the eyes of your heart may enlighten me so that I can know what your hope is for my true calling, please wash and cleanse me so I am ready my Lord, to do my good works for you.

5 Tell me Oh Father that you have washed and cleansed away all my offences, like a cloud, my sins like the morning mist, to evaporate, by the sun, so I can return to you washed and guilt never more to be remembered by me and my God, washed as white as snow, for I do love you so, with all my heart and soul.

6 For the Lord he gave his life to free us, from every kind of sin, to cleanse us to make us his very own; totally committed to doing only good deeds, now I know why you're the son of God, your totally washed and totally clean, He causes the wind to blow, and the waters to flow, washed and cleansed, crystal clear like glass.

7 Your love lord reaches to the Heavens your faithfulness to the skies, I the Lord made everything stretching out the skies, by myself and spreading out the Earth, all alone; I seek to keep my children, perfect in every way, washed and cleansed in water; to keep you safe and warm, I've done my part to bring you where you are today, I trust my love inside you, will guide you the rest of the way, keep faith and trust in what you have learnt from me, the word in the truth so follow me, Live in me and I will live in you.

8 Search your heart for the rest of your days, finding me always, listen and you will hear me, for I am guiding you every day, you will know when I am not happy, you will feel it in your heart, I don't want to tell you when you have done wrong, I want you to learn all on your own; your Holy Spirit its now renewed, you know you are my child, trust and believe until you are back home, back in my arms my child, you're feeling me aren't you, My child of mine, don't doubt my love, I do know your heart, very well.

9 You won't go back to your old ways, you can't and you do know why, and why you are different now, it's your spirit being trained, in a totally different law, to what you are use to in the world, you will struggle sometimes and you will be tested for sure, for strength and its nothing you can't handle, I promise my child, just keep me close in your heart.

10 Don't doubt like you do, you already know the truth, of who you are, where you belong, what to do, and how to be strong; what is right, what is wrong, your different now, know and trust in your Lord, where you now belong in the love of God, your washed and cleansed, baptized in love.

11 I am your God, I know your heart, I know you love me, just you now be strong, keep up with what you are doing, for I am watching you, I know your reading, and I know your believing, I'll be with you every step of the way, focus on me, I will lead you all of the way.

12 Your thoughts are sometimes troubled, and yes I do know; but I am still with you every time, don't resist what you know is wrong, change direction and turn it to around, back around to me, listen and learn what your Holy Spirit is telling you, it will not lie, for it is full of the light.

13 So don't lead it astray or it'll change overnight; you will not notice it straight away, until you change your thoughts, back to true grace, the love and the light; Holy and true, not ungodly for its not my world, if you want answers then ask me your God; don't tell me that I am not listening or answering you, you are now washed and cleansed and totally clean.

40

I'm rejoicing for the light my Lord

1 For the life of every living thing that is in my hands, and the breath of every human being, be on your guard and stand firm in your faith, be courage's and be strong, oh my Lord you have made me strong for you have given me life, I worship you and sing many praises to you, and in your name I always pray amen, my life is in your hands, and I'm rejoicing in your light my Lord.

2 The love of you my Lord has been poured out in our hearts, By our Holy Spirit which was given to us by your love and your grace, in our Lord Jesus Christ; My Lord in you lies hidden all treasures of wisdom and knowledge, no one can comprehend all this, that you have never sinned, nor have you ever lied; and being found in appearance as a man; you humbled yourself and became obedient, to the point of death, even the death of the cross.

3 There is one God and one mediator between the Father and us, and my Lord Jesus, that is you; who can truly understand, how majestic and brilliant you are, your intelligence is way beyond us, that you and your Father do share; deep calls to deep at the noise of your waterfalls, all your waves crashing over me; my heart filled with joy, my Spirit is alive, all because of you, I'm rejoicing for the light, my Lord.

4 You say my Lord, that whoever has my commands and keeps them is the one; the one who loves me, will be loved by father, and that you too will love them, that you will show yourself to them, Oh thankyou my Lord, I will wait on you again, I pray to you that the glory of the Lord be forever in my heart and soul; may the Lord forever enjoy what you have made, for all to see and enjoy, I'm rejoicing in your light my Lord.

5 I will rejoice in you always, I will pray without ceasing. And in everything in you my Lord I will give thanks, for I know and understand; that this is the will of God in, my Lord Jesus; now this is the confidence that we have as we pray to you, that if we ask and pray for anything according to your will, you will hear us, you answer, do not worry about anything, just pray, and ask God for everything, that we need, but always give thanks, I'm rejoicing for the light my Lord.

6 I see what God has done for me, amazing things, the words of my mouth are deep, fountains of wisdom, like a rushing stream, for with God, and all things are possible; for my Lord he says that when you pass through the waters, he will be with you, and through the river of waters, they will not overflow you, you will forget your troubles and remember it only as water goes by.

7 Again I write this new commandment to you, which thing is true in him, and in you; because the darkness id passing away and the true light how it already shines, we couldn't be surer of what we saw and heard, Gods glory, Gods voice.

8 The prophetic word was confirmed to us, you'll do well to keep focusing on it; it's the one light that you have in a dark time as you wait for the daybreak, and the rising of the morning star in your hearts, my child of the light; I'm rejoicing for the light my Lord.

9 Make sure that the light you think you have, is not actually darkness, so be sure; For if you are filled with the light, with , no dark corners, then your whole life will be radiant, as though a flood light were filling you with the light, for you were once this darkness, but you are now the light of the Lord, so walk now as a child of the light, I'm rejoicing for the Light my Lord.

10 The night is far spent; the day is at hand, let us therefore cast off, the works of darkness, let us put on forever in your life, the armour of the light, Oh I'm rejoicing for the light my Lord.

11 We here you my Lord, I know and understand, you do know are hearts well, you hear all our prayers, and we are trying hard, to live in your law well, the word of God is our life now, darkness has been hard to keep away,

12 However we do now understand, that we have struggled so much, but our love for you our God is keeping it at bay, watch over us Father, we will wear your amour of light, our armour of God, we love you so much, my Father, my Lord, I'm rejoicing in the light, my Lord.

41

Your Touch, I am Thankful, My Lord

1 The Earth how it trembled, and the Heavens they poured, then the clouds they opened and the rains they poured, the mountains quaked, the thunder roared, the clap of God's hands, Mount Sinai, is where it happened, it's the presence of my dear Lord, The God of Israel, blessed Oh Lord, I sing praises to you, you have opened my heart, how I do glorify you, your breath and your touch, I am thankful, my Lord for your love.

2 My Lord if I have now found favour in your sight, show me a sign, that it is you who talks with me, I ask you, do not leave me, I pray you, send your Angels to watch over me so my soul shall be like a watering garden to thee; so I shall sorrow no more, my Lord; but keeping focused on you, I know my Lord Jesus, he has Bourne all our grief, and carried our sorrows, for your love and your touch, I am thankful, my Lord.

3 Our Gracious Lord, much water couldn't even put out the flames of love that I feel for you; for all the floods couldn't even drown this deep devoted love that I have; for indeed you have made my days blessed, so loving, that even my age is as nothing before your eyes, for I am perfect to you, in every way; But you my Lord are my shield around me, you are my glory, the one who holds my head up high, your touch, I am thankful, My Lord.

4 The wondrous beauty that has surrounded me, feeling you touch are hearts the way you do, our soul feels glorified when I feel your presence, my soul is alive because of you; I pray my Lord let the fields be so joyful and all that is in it, all of the trees, the flowers and the forests can feel the touch of your breath, your touch I am thankful, my Lord.

5 Lead me now to calm waters, my Lord every morning you hear Oh my voice, every morning I tell you that I love you my Lord, and I will wait ever so patiently for that answer mu Lord, for you are great in my eyes, mighty and majestic, magnificent and glorious, so sovereign, so divine, all over the skies, and above the Earth, you have dominion and you exalt yourself, as my ruler, the ruler over all, your touch, I am thankful, my Lord.

6 We are witnesses of all things that you have done, I am a witness to all that you have done, for me and my life, My family, my God, you have saved me by your grace, for I do believe in you, I can't take the credit, for my believing for it's a gift from you my Lord, for your peace now rules my heart, which I was called in one body, your touch I am thankful, my Lord.

7 I am blessed for I do hunger and thirsty after righteousness, fill me Oh Lord, with this deep need, for your word, your love, so I will never thirst no more; to be a fresh, and bubbling spring, a spring within me, giving me eternal and everlasting life, For your way my Lord, your way my God, it's in the sanctuary who is so great a God, as our God, your touch I am thankful my Lord.

8 Can you discover the depths of God, can you discover the limits of the mighty one, from everlasting, to everlasting, and you are God. I confirm that your my God, and your beloved Son as the son of God, your my King completely in my heart my home for all time, it's the house of God, I'm secure forever, for great is my God; and greatly to be praised, your greatness unsearchable, my rock and my fortress, my deliverer my God, my strength in whom I trust, my salvation and my high tower, my devotion, my greatest love, your touch, I am thankful, my Lord, *AMEN and AMEN*

42
One Hope

1 There is one body and one Spirit, just as you were called in one hope, of your calling, one Lord and One faith; one baptism and One God, and one Father of all who is over all, and through all and in all, There is so much division, among believers in society today, it's important to do as much as we can, as Christians, believers in one God, to be in peace with others and to find that closeness with God, fellowship is a great start, The word of God is the truth, bringing closeness and love in your heart, one hope.

2 Unity it's such a big part of Gods heart, so making this a priority in your Spirit, by walking in life, when you walk in disunity with other believers, it not only grieves the one who truly loves God, because their Holy Spirit truly feels the grief, but it also grieves Gods heart, One hope, true love.

3 Why petty talk to cause you so much bother, avoiding arguments that get you nowhere; except talk that leads to nothing but conflict; I say to you, concentrate only on the things that build each other up, by walking in love and unity, for God so knows, one hope.

4 Life Is so short to be wasted on unimportant things that can lead to broken hearts, a broken heart will lead to unhappiness, unhappiness will lead you away from God, darkness will creep in and destroy you, destroy all that you love, so think about what really is that important, to take you away and destroy what you have.

5 Your one hope is in peace and Joy and strength and you will need this when darkness over takes you, your life will be a mess, your mind will play games, and God won't help you until you let him in, one hope is to call him, the comforter, will restore you and love will just flow in your heart, Gods grace and love will abound in you, and darkness, will be nowhere in sight.

6 One hope is God's love; your one Hope is our Lord Jesus Christ, One hope is your Spirit filled with his light, one hope is forgiveness, one hope is saved, of all your sins, one hope is Jesus, he Died to let you Live, your One hope is that you found him, One hope is to keep him, One hope is to live in God's word, one hope is to trust him, one hope is to believe in him, One hope is to believe he is the son of God, One hope is to believe that he died on the cross, your one hope is to believe that we have just One God, One hope is to believe that you believe that you are a beloved child of One God, One hope is to believe that you can rely on God, One Hope is to pray and to live in the word; of God.

Amen and Amen

43
Follow me in Love

1 Listen to me, you who know right from wrong, cherish my law in your hearts and do not be afraid of peoples scorns, or their slanderous behaviour and talk, for its the one who gets wisdom who loves life with God, the one who will cherish understanding, for in the understanding, you will soon prosper, all in your life, for the one I am, the one I am is God, so follow me in Love.

2 It is better to trust in the Lord your God, than to put confidence in man, I say to you, have nothing to with godless myths and old wives tales, rather, put training in yourself to be godly, from my mouth to yours, you shall speak of all wisdom, the meditation of my heart, you shall be of understanding, for the mouths of the righteous will utter wisdom, and their tongues will speak only what is just.

3 Now therefore stand and see this good thing, which the lord will do before your eyes, for I will satisfy the thirst and fill the hungry with good things, for I am the Lord your God forever and ever; I will be your guide even unto death, follow me in love with no regrets. *AMEN*

4 Jesus he asked The Father, what is the kingdom of God like, and what shall I compare the kingdom of God, for I say to you, the kingdom of God is not meat neither is it drink, but it is of only righteousness and peace, and joy in the Holy Spirit, follow me in love.

5 Whoever does not take up their cross and follow me, is not even worthy of me, however I say to you this, whoever doesn't bear his own cross, and come after me, can't be my disciple nor have everlasting life with me, every man that has hope in him, purifies himself. Even as he is pure, but if any man, who comes after me, let him deny himself, and take up his cross, and fully follow me in love.

6 Oh my gracious Lord, you are the most handsome, the most handsome of all, gracious words scream from your lips, God himself has blessed you forever, follow me forever,

7 Oh my Lord we will follow you, for you are gracious and full of compassion, slow to anger, with mercy for your children, you are good to all, showering compassion, compassion on all Gods creations.

8 The blameless will be rescued, following you in love, but the crooked will be destroyed, the fear of the Lord prolonged days, but the years of the wicked shall be shortened, so do not be to wicked, neither be foolish, why should you die before your time, so follow me only in love, and forever, everlasting love, don't waste it on sins of the world, pick up your cross, living life fully in me, and the word of God will set you free.

9 I have come as light into the world, so that everyone who believes in me, will not remain in darkness, no one lights a camp, and hides it in clay pots or puts it under his bed, for all who do evil will hate the light, so there deeds may not be exposed,

10 But my children of the light Lord God is a sun and shield, giving grace and glory to them, they will walk upright, follow me in love, and see the kingdom of my father in Heaven;

11 Then shall your light break forth like the dawn, and your healing shall spring up speedily, your righteousness shall go before you, the glory of the Lord shall be your guarded door, for I give you sound teaching; do not abandon my instructions, hear the word of your Lord, and let your ears receive the word my child, and never forget the things that I have taught you, storing my commandments in your heart, follow me in Love.

44
My heart is a harp to you

1 My Father I wish to thank you; for today there is a supernatural transformation happening in my life, right now; and it is all because of you, my Father you are washing me of all wrong concepts of you, and washing me of all sins of not believing in your love for me, deep down I do believe, however I fear is of rejection, If I know that I have made mistakes, and that I have grieved you, believe me Father when I tell you that, my heart is a harp to you.

2 My Father I reject Satan and his terrible lies, and I will do this now and always, and I deeply hold and take a stand with my beloved Lord Jesus and his word; and I know that you my Lord love me and provide me with all knowledge of the word, you my God, sending your son, I thank you for your love today; I thank you for washing me clean, thoroughly cleansed of all iniquity, from my sins, I love you, my heart is a harp to you.

3 Beloved children, God is not up in the sky with a gavel waiting to judge us, Gods anger for sins was already taken out on our beloved Lord Jesus; God is simply asking us to come boldly before the throne of grace, and to have confidence in his love towards us, oh my gracious Lord, my heart is a harp to you.

4 Father God we thank you right now that your heart towards us is to bless us, oh my Father your desire is to be gracious to us, to show us your favour, my heart is a harp to you.

5 This is eternal life, which we may know you, our only true God, and our Lord Jesus Christ, whom you have sent, your purpose for creating us was to have a relationship with us, and you my Father sent your son to die for us,

6 You done this because of your love for us; and I understand that when Jesus died for us, he did not die to only save us from the pit of hell, he did not just die to forgive us of our sins, but he did die to marry us, my Lord, my heart is a harp to you.

7 My Lord, My Lord God, compassionate and Oh so gracious, slow to anger and abounding in loving-kindness' and truth; blessed are they which are called unto the marriage supper of the lamb, I chose you out of the world, for whoever believes in him should not perish but have everlasting life, my heart is a harp to you.

8 No one has seen Father except the one who is from God, only he has seen the father, but as many as received him, to them gave power to become the children of God, even to them that believe on his name, my heart is a harp to you.

9 These are written, that you might believe that Jesus is the Christ, the son of God, that believing you might have life through his name, verily I say to you, I tell you; that the one who believes in me, has eternal life; sing to the Lord, bless his name, tell of his salvation, from day to day; talk of his wondrous works, make music to the Lord with a harp and the sound of beautiful singing, pleasing to the Lord your God, my heart is a harp to you.

10 Let the word of the Lord Jesus dwell in you richly, in all wisdom, teaching and admonishing one another with Psalms and spiritual songs, with grace in your heart to the Lord; the kingdom of Heaven doesn't consist of talk but only of power, truth, love, peace, and joy, faith and hope, trust, God be in it, to you, dwelling in you forever in Christ Jesus' name, my lord we will repent, we will pray Amen, My heart is a harp to you.

45
My Lord you are my Warrior

1 I the Lord will fight for you and you have only to be silent, my Lord you are my strength and you are my protection shield, my heart it trusts you, my soul it longs for you, I know that you are with me helping me, my heart it leaps for joy, and when I sing I praise you, my Lord you are my warrior.

2 Worthy are you to me, my love, my God, to receive glory an honour and power, for you created all things, including myself; and by your will they existed and were created, when I am weak my gracious one, help me, Lord my god, save me according to your unfailing love, for my Lord, you are my warrior.

3 Two people, better than one, as you made Adam and Eve, so we can help each other and succeed, but a companion of fools shall be destroyed, oils and perfume, they make the heart glad, so a man's counsel, is also sweet to his friends, be wise and honest without greed and sin nature, above all keep loving one another, earnestly since love covers a multitude of sins, my Lord, you are my warrior.

4 Happy is he that has the God of his help, whose hope is in the Lord his God, live as People who are free not using your freedom as a cover up for evil, but living as servants of God only, having been freed from sin, you become slaves of righteousness, standing fast, therefore in the liberty, where with our Lord Jesus he has made us free and be not entangled again with the yoke of bondage, my Lord you are my warrior.

5 For I say to you, if the son sets you free, you will be free indeed for all generations come, and generations go, but the Earth it will never change, as God also never changes, he set the Earth on its foundations, it can never be moved, for everything there is a season, and time for every purpose under Heaven, My Lord you are my warrior.

6 A time to be born and a time to die, a time to plant and a time to be uprooted, a time to suffer and a time to be healed, a time to move on and a time to rebuild, a time to cry and a time to laugh, a time to grieve and a time to find God, and a time to have everlasting life, to say to my Lord, you are my warrior.

7 A time to cast stones, a time to gather stones together, a time to embrace and a time to reframe from embracing; a time to seek and a time to lose, a time to keep, a time to cast away, a time to tear, and a time to sew and a time to keep silent, and a time to speak, a time to hate, and a time to love, a time of war, and a time for peace, a time for joy and everlasting love, my Lord you are my warrior, at last.

8 Submit to one another out of reverence for our beloved Lord and saviour Jesus Christ, for he that loves not, knows not God; it is God that is pure love, keep your life free from the love of money, and be content with what you have; for I the Lord, said I will never leave you nor forsake you, Oh my Lord, you are my warrior.

46

And Peace be with you

1 Do all that you can to live in peace with everyone, do not accuse anyone for no reason, when they have done you no harm; for he that loves not, knows not God, for God is pure love,

Depart from evil, doing only good, seek peace and pursue it, with all of your heart and your soul; as a beloved child of God, a devoted believer, devoted to the word of the Father, and peace be with you.

2 Let us pursue what makes for only peace and for mutual up building; for blessed are the peacemakers, for they shall be called children of God, rejoice in hope, being patient in tribulation, be constant in prayer to your beloved Father and his son in Heaven above, and peace be with you.

3 Ask and it will be given to you, seek as you have and you will find it, knock and I say to you, it will be opened for you, as I understand and know that you delight in the Lord your God; the Lord your God will give you all your hearts desires, keep praying without ceasing, and peace be with you.

4 In nothing be anxious, but in everything, by prayer and petition with thanksgiving, let your requests be made known to father God, for in all your ways acknowledge me, and I shall hear you directing your paths, cast all your anxieties onto me, because I care for you, and peace be with you.

5 I your Lord am good, a refuge in times of trouble, I am always with you, for compassionate I am, for those who put love and trust in me, I will deliver and rescue; I work all signs and miracles, wonders beyond belief, in Heaven and on Earth, for I the Lord takes pleasure in people, I will beautify the afflicted ones, with salvation, and peace be with you.

6 If you listen and obey God, you will be blessed with prosperity throughout your life, all your years will be pleasant, for I your Lord takes pleasure in you, when you fear God, and in those that also put hope in his mercy,

7 for all things were made in him and without him was not anything made that was made, for God created all things great and small, created man kind in his own image in the image of God, he created you; and peace be with you, my beloved children.

8 Don't ever forget to be always doing good including sharing; for with such sacrifices God is well pleased, sharing with the Lords people who are in need, practicing always hospitality, be not forgetful; to entertain strangers for these may already be entertaining Angels, the unawares to you from the kingdom of God, peace I give to you, and peace be with you.

9 I say to you each one must give as he has decided in his heart, not reluctantly or under compulsion, for God loves a cheerful giver, be kind to one another, tender-hearted, forgiving one another as god in Christ Jesus forgave you, bearing one another's burdens, listening and caring, and fulfilling the law of Christ, and peace be with you.

10 Listen to me; the ones who are strong ought to bear the weaknesses of the weak and not to please oneself; but being merciful just as your Father is merciful, be completely humble and gentle, and patient, bearing with one another in total love,

11 I say to you, you will understand if you listen to all my teaching in the word, peace be with you, imitate me, therefore in everything you do; because you are my dear children, my love and my peace, I will leave with you.

12 Listen to me beloved, the ones who are strong ought to bear the weaknesses of the weak, not to please oneself; but being merciful just as the Father is merciful, be completely humble and gentle, patient, bearing with one another in love, you will understand if you listen to all my words, peace be with you, imitate me therefore in everything that you do, because you are my beloved children and I do want to welcome you, my love and my peace I leave with you.

47
The Spirit of Life
has been given to you.

1 In Christ, you are all children of God through faith; it is the Spirit who gives life, the flesh it is no help at all, the word that I have spoken to you, you are Spirit, the spirit of life, has been given to unto you.

2 As the Father raises up the dead and gives them life, even so the son gives life to whom he will, all who are led by the spirit of God are children of God, the Spirit of life, has been given unto you.

3 These are written that you may believe that our Lord Jesus is the Christ, the son of God; and that in believing; you may have life in his name; there is no fear in love, but perfect love, casting out all your fears, because fear causes torment, havoc, disruptions, and heartache, all of these the work of darkness, he that fears is not made of perfect love, when worry weights only a person down.

4 however I say to you that a grounded person has encouraging words to say, that can bring happiness and a smile to cheer any person up, for the Spirit of God that I give to you does not make you timid, but only the power, love and self discipline, the Spirit of life has been given unto you.

5 Oh my Lord, how we have all sinned, do to us whatever seems good to you, but in this I do ask, for you to please be gracious and patient, and deliver us up, we pray to you, this day, oh great God of Israel; do not forsake us, for we love you, we respect and honour you, and we do not serve no other gods but only you.

6 Oh my great one, you are my strength, you are my true Father, I am your child, save me oh Lord, bring me back to complete righteousness, pure in your eyes, the life of Spirit has been given unto you, Oh thank you, my Lord.

7 I was thrust into your arms at my birth, and you have been my God, my Father, my grace, my deliverer, my hope, my faith, and my divine teacher, from the very moment I was born, you my Father are love, and I will remain in love, for loving you is easy, when you have shown me, what real love is,

8 It's not the kind of love that many think, its divine inner love that you show outwards, a love that you abound in us, my Lord; transforming us into new creatures in Christ, I do understand that you loved me first, Grace and peace to you, that you have given to us, the Spirit of life has been given unto you.

9 I have suffered much my Lord, but you have brought me back to you, while working in me; you have done so much, miracles in my eyes, and my Lord no one can ever change my understanding, that my God, my Father, my Lord Jesus Christ, worked miracles in me, preserve my life my Lord according to your words,

10 For my soul clings to dust, Lord I ask of you to give me life, for I am yours, saving me forever from this sinful world; for I have sought your precepts and I do delight in your word, your laws, and in your ways,

I will not neglect your word or truths deliberately, the spirit of life has been given unto you.

11 Oh gracious Lord make me go to the path of commandments for it is there that I delight in your work, your ways, I will never forget your laws, once trained in your ways; for it is with them that you have revived me, changing my life, while directing it to you and your words;

12 Oh gracious Lord, how you have done wonders to me, I know I need more work, but I declare your strength, to whom ever you bring to my door, your secret Angels, bringing light upon my walls, the Spirit of life has been given unto you.

13 My praises and my blessings I send to you, oh my Lord, my God of Israel; who alone has done many great and wondrous, marvellous deeds and I declare right now, that there is no other like you, my God you are great among your beloved and loyal believers, and mighty is your name.

14 Your children sing to you in prayers, worship, and blessings, for your loved and worthy to be praised, the fruit of the Spirit is love, its joy, its peace, its kindness, its goodness, its faithfulness, it's all which you bring to us, oh bless us oh gracious one and our Holy Spirits, for the spirit of life has been given unto you, a gift from our Father, *AMEN and AMEN.*

48
Praised

1 from the rising of the sun, to it's going down; from the east to the west; the name of my gracious Lord he is to be praised, we serve you oh Lord with gladness in our hearts, there is no one like you, and I know there never will.

2 Let us all bow down to you, come before you and sing, will our hearts my Lord with your love, fill our Holy Spirits that has been given to us; we know and perceive, and recognise, understand with approval my Lord, that you are our God, our God that deserves to be praised.

3 Entering into your gates with thanksgiving and a thanks offering and into your courts, with praises lets be thankful and I say to you with blesses and affection, I'd praise and say to you, Oh thankyou my beloved Lord; for I worship towards your Holy Temple and I would praise your name out allowed, so everyone would hear who I am praising; my beloved Lord Jesus, I'd shout.

4 Your name is loving and of kindness, for your truths and faithfulness that you have given, so my lips they shall pour forth with praises, love and thanksgivings for the wonderful Lord that I've grown to love and adore; and renewal of trust from my heart, when you teach me your ways and statutes, with praises how sweet are your words to my taste, I thank you and I love you, your praised in my heart, thanksgiving I give to you, when I say to you, goodnight.

5 We will lift up our hands to you oh Holiness, I will confess and praise you my Lord with my whole united heart I will glorify your name, forever more; for all times blessing you exalting in your strength, remembering how you have turned my life around, your power it amazes me, my heart trusting and relying in you, I confidently lean on you, for you have upheld me in my integrity setting me in your presence forever more; you have laid your hands upon me, telling me to keep going as I draw on your strength, I hear you, I obey you, as I try my best, I praised you since the day I have found you, my beloved Lord forever blessed do I feel every day, I might moan and groan at times but I am thankful for you.

6 I believe in my heart that those who wait, expect and look for having hope in the Lord, you will feel great changes and be renewed, will find the strength and the power, lifting up your wings, mounting up close to God, reaching to the Heavens above; like an eagle to flight, gazing up at the sun, running and not feeling weary, walking without feeling faint; working hard without becoming tied, for you will have Lord Jesus by your side, praised and blessed you will feel, loved and content, rejoicing and singing to him, your my rock you will say to him, your works perfect you will praise him; your my hiding place you will feel protected in him, your my shield your praised, my beloved grace your unfailing love will last forever in me.

7 I give praises to my Lord I have been crucified with Christ; in Christ I have shared his crucifixion, for it is no longer I who live, but my Lord Jesus Christ the Messiah he is the one who lives in me, I live in the body, the body that now lives in faith, for it's the son of God who loves me, giving himself up for me making all his ways known to me, by the word and the love of God; for my Father in Heaven he sent you, to save all from their sins, dying on the cross, because you love us, taking all of our sins to you within, granting me the courage and the Spirit of wisdom, revelation, and insight to mysteries; secrets of the deep and intimate, and knowledge of Christ within, praised and blessed I give to you, your love will endure in me, forever.

8 For faith comes by hearing, what is told and what is heard, coming from the lips of Christ, the Messiah himself, given through love; so pursue it with faith and love, peace and harmony, in fellowship with Christians who call upon the Lord, out of a pure heart, which is the best love of all; for with the Lord nothing is impossible and no word from God, shall be without power, or impossible of fulfilment, praised be the Lord, your faithfulness, almighty, lifting all believers up to our gracious Lord Jesus Christ, *Amen*.

49
My God I Worship you

1 Holy Holy Holy is the Lord God almighty, and four living creatures, individually having six wings, eyes covering them all over within and underneath even their wings; day and night they never stop saying, who was and who is and who is to come, my God I worship you, Holy is your name.

2 One cried to another saying Holy Holy is the Lord of hosts, the whole Earth is full of his Glory, oh give to the Lord due to his blessed name, I worship the Lord in the beauty of his Holiness, and in his Holy array, singing my God, I worship you, and I bow down to you, in your name I glorify you.

3 For he is our God, and the people of his pasture, the sheep of his Holy hands, and today if I hear his voice, sweet words it would be to my ears, a heavenly calling, that I'd be waiting to hear; worthy are you, our Lord our God to receive the glory and honour that you've placed in my heart; God he is Spirit (a spiritual being) those who worship must worship in Spirit and in truth, reality my Lord, my God, I worship you, fully.

4 I will bless the Lord at all times, and praises will continually come out of my mouth, in a loud voice I will say to you, salvation is due to our God, whom is seated on the throne, to the Lamb we owe our deliverance a song, I'll sing a reflective poem, I will write, I will sing of the mercy and loving- kindness of the Lord; forever with my mouth I will make known, your faithfulness from generation I will flow through to my child-ren, to hear the words of our Lord, day in and day out, blessings only worthy to our God.

5 For in obedience to God's word I offer to you all of my prayers and thanksgivings; for all that you have done for acknowledge them as blessings, blessings done over my life, in the name of my Lord Jesus Christ, I am blessed because I believe in, I trust in, I rely on the Lord; placing all of my hope and confidence in the Lord alone, for he gives desires and secret petitions of my heart, I worship you, I devote my heart.

6 I am a child of God washed in my Lords blood, and totally forgiven as I work in his love; I walk in his obedience to his will concerning forgiveness, with the grace of God, and the strength of the Holy Spirit; I allow my Lord Jesus as my mentor to keep teaching me in the word,

7 To walk in love, and to be a light for the lost, a living testimony of Christs mercy, willing to forgive, and not to be fretful; or resentful to never hold a grudge, in obedience to god's word, I will dwell in God's grace, and his love will forever live in me; and my God I will worship you, to be a devoted child of Gods.

50
Holy Spirit and Wisdom

1 Let my mouth be filled with your praise, and with your glory all the day; you turned the rock into a pool of water, a hard rock into a spring of water, like the tears that have rolled down my face.

2 You thrill me oh Lord, with all that you have done for me, I sing for joy because of all that you have transformed into my life and my heart it thanks you, my soul it is grateful, my Holy Spirit its saturated in love and wisdom.

3 The whole Earth is filled with awe at your wisdom and wonders; where the morning dawns, where evening fades, you come forth with songs of joy, if you are wise and understanding Gods ways proves it by living an honourable life, by doing good works with the humility that comes from wisdom.

4 Bear with one another and if anyone has a complaint against another, forgive each other just as the Lord has forgiven you, so to you also must forgive, always be humble, gentle and patient, accepting each other in love, letting your gentleness be known to all, the Lord Jesus is at hand.

5 The discretion of a man makes him slow to anger, and his Glory is to overlook a transgression, therefore as Gods chosen people, Holy and dearly loved, clothing yourselves with compassion, kindness, humility, gentleness and patience.

6 By the Lords divine power, God has given us everything we need for living a Godly life, we have received all of this by coming to know Jesus, the one who called us to himself, by the means of his marvellous Glory and excellence.

7 Submit therefore to God, resisting the temptations of darkness, and he will flee from you, as many as walk by this rule, peace and mercy be on them, and on Gods Israel, for the wise the path of life leads upwards, in order to avoid Sheol below.

8 You shall always love the Lord your God with all of your heart and soul, and with all your might; Glory and honour are in his presence, strength and gladness are in his place, tell everyone about Gods power for his majesty shines down on Israel, his strength mighty in the Heavens.

9 Ascribe to the Lord, oh Heavenly beings; Ascribe to the Lord, Glory and strength; Beloved you are Gods children now; and what you will be has not yet appeared, but you will know that when he appears you shall be like him, because you shall see him in all his glory as he is, Amen.

10 The Spirit himself bears witness with our Spirit, that we are children of God; and because we are Gods children, God has sent the Spirit of his Son into our hearts, prompting us to call out, Heavenly Father; therefore anyone who rejects his instructions does not reject a human being but God; the very great God, who gives you his Holy Spirit.

11 Now the Lord is the Spirit, and where the Spirit of the Lord is there is Liberty; so wait patiently for the Lord, being brave and courageous, yes I say unto you, wait patiently for the Lord your God.

51
Direct your Heart to God

1 Be strong in the Lord and take heart all you who hope in the Lord, and may the Lord direct your heart to God, and the love of God; and into the patience of Jesus Christ.

2 No one can serve two masters, for either he will hate the one, and love the other, or else he will be devoted to one and despise the other, for you cannot serve both God and money; you must therefore direct your heart to God,

3 For such people are not serving our Lord Jesus Christ, but only their own appetites, by smooth talk and flattery, they deceive the minds of the naive people; so therefore I say unto you since we are receiving a kingdom that cannot be shaken, let us give thanks by which we offer to God an acceptable worship with reverence and awe, love and thanksgiving.

4 Jesus said a Prophet is not without honour except in his own town, among his relatives and his own home; he who receives a prophet in the name of a prophet will receive a prophet's reward, he who receives a righteous man will receive a righteous man's reward.

5 My voice you shall hear in the morning oh Lord, in the morning I will direct it to you and I will look up in awe; My Lord I will hear what God the Lord will speak, of peace to his people and to his saints, direct your heart to God.

6 The things which you have learned, received and heard and saw in me, I say unto you that the peace of God will be with you, though the Lords mercies are not consumed because his compassions fail not, they are new every morning, direct your heart to God; Oh how great is your faithfulness.

7 The Lord God has made everything beautiful in its time, the Lord god has also set eternity in their Hearts, yet so that man can't find out the work that God has done from the beginning, even to the end; they are new every morning, Oh how great is your faithfulness; direct your heart to God.

8 But God he is faithful, who will not allow you to be tempted about what you are able; Oh Lord, you are my God, I will exalt you, I will give thanks to your name for you have worked wonders, plans formed for me long ago; with perfect faithfulness.

9 I will sprinkle clean water on you and you will be clean; I will cleanse you from all impurities and from all your Idols, with Joy you will drink deeply from the fountain of salvation.

10 With my soul I have desired you, in the night; yes, by the Spirit within me, I will seek you early; for when your judgements are in the Earth, the inhabitants of the World will learn righteousness, Direct your Heart to God.

11 The Lord is my light and my salvation, whom shall I fear; The Lord is the strength of my life of whom I shall be afraid, my Lord cling to me, keeping me safe and ever so close to you, for you are my light, as I direct my heart to you, shine upon me ever so bright.

AMEN

52
Protection of Light

1 Show me oh gracious Lord your protection of love, I may not always recognize the service that you provide out of this love; but if I listen closely as you tell me about all that I do, I do thank you my Lord Jesus for your protection of light, as I couldn't achieve nothing without you.

2 I bow down to you Oh mighty one, when I feel deeply your Holy Presence, in my private time, I will reach out to you, as my tears flow as I wash your feet; telling you my heart and my deep love and affection for you; knowing that you have always been working on me all the time, knowing that you knew that I would find you again, my only wish is that I had turned to you sooner, my protection of light.

3 It's what really counts now isn't it my Lord, knowing I would turn to you, when your love was going to abound in me and my love abound back to you, my Holy Spirit within, ready and waiting for my Lords protection of light.

4 I know that you have a purpose for me, waiting patiently for me to call upon thee; I know your love all along, feeling your presence time after time, your beauty my Lord Jesus; so deeply touching my heart, it's hard to resist someone who is so permanently deep in my heart.

5 Your essence is contagious, righteous and gracious and full of loving kindness; like a fever covering oneself; as I sweat it's a feeling that I cannot explain, I can only call it a power that you have given me to embrace, the protection of light; My Lord Jesus and I both together in My Holy Spirit within.

6 My Lord I am locked in you forever, throw away the key, completely trapped My Lord Jesus and me, fully under your control your love pressing deep within, holding and teaching me and embracing what you have given me; the fear of losing you is now slipping further away; each time I think of you, I know that you are around, we won't let each other go for we have found each other again, it's a protection of light now, that will never go away.

7 My Lord Jesus thank you for keeping me safe; and turning to me when I have needed you the most, I cannot live without you and I have come to far now, I am deeply in love with my Lord Jesus Christ; he is my protection of light, from Heaven above.

53
A Tender Heart

1 I say unto you, do not forget to be doing good, by sharing; for with such sacrifices God will be well pleased, sharing with the Lords people who are in need; it's a learning to practice hospitality,

2 I say unto you; if anyone has material possessions and sees a brother or sister in need but has no pity on them, how can the love of God be in that person, if you have not a tender heart.

3 Each one of you must give as he has decided in his heart, not reluctantly or under compulsion; for God so loves a cheerful heart, and a cheerful giver to be kind to one another as God in Christ Jesus forgave you; a tender heart, you must have in you.

4 I say unto you, you must bear one another's burdens so to fulfil the law of your beloved Jesus, for we who are strong ought to bear the weaknesses of the weak, being at all times merciful, just as your father is merciful, for he is wanting in his children, to have a tender heart, to be completely humble and gentle, patient, being with one another in loving kindness.

5 Imitate God, therefore in everything you do; because you are my children and I do watch over you, a tender heart will bring you close to me, loving your enemies and to do only good, and to lend a tender hand; expecting nothing in return and your reward will be ever so great; doing all that you can to live in peace with everyone; do not accuse anyone for no reason, when they have done you no harm.

6 He that loves not knows not God; For I your God am love, lets pursue what makes for peace and for mutual up building for I say unto you blessed are the peacemakers for they shall be called the children of God; Judge not and you will not be judged, condemn not and you will not be condemned; forgive and you will be forgiven; for with what judgement you judge you will be judged, judgement will be merciless to one who has shown no mercy, mercy triumphs over judgement, it shows a tender heart.

7 God sent his son into the world, not to judge the world, but to save the world through him, a tender heart I have had, to not judge but to only give a second chance; to save the world of all its sin.

8 There is only one law giver and judge, the one who is able to save and to destroy; but you, so who are you really to judge your neighbour , God is the righteous Judge, a God who feels indignation every day.

54
Flourish in the house of God

1 I your Lord Jesus, would rather stand at the threshold of the house of my father than to dwell in the house of wickedness, for it is those who are planted in the house of the Lord that are the ones that will flourish in the courts of our God.

2 Let us come before his presence with thanksgiving; let us shout joyfully to our Lord with prayers of Psalms, let us flourish in the house of God.

3 Oh my gracious and wonderful Lord, all shall be abundantly satisfied with the abundance of your house, for you will make us drink of the flowing rivers of your pleasure; flourish in the house of God, for my soul it yearns for you, I feel faint when my heart; it aches, for the courts of my Lord, my heart and my flesh it longs for the living God.

4 I know in my Holy Spirit, that you have made known to me the ways of life, how you make me full of gladness with the feeling of your presence; to open up ancient gates, and open up ancient doors and let the King Lord Jesus' glory enter.

5 Ascribe unto my God the glory that is due to his name, bring to him an offering worthy of the king that he is, and come into his courts being joyful and peace loving while you flourish in the house of God.

6 Generous to a fault as you give your love unto your children, with favour, therefore since, we are receiving a kingdom which cannot be shaken; let us have grace, by which we may serve our beloved God; acceptably with reverence and godly fear, for our God he is a consuming fire,

7 Oh God, show me your ways, my beloved Lord and saviour, Jesus, teach me your paths of righteousness', as my heart and soul follows you, let me flourish in the house of God, all the days of my life.

8 Let all that I am praise the Lord, Oh my God, Oh my soul; Oh how I love thee all the days of my life; how great you are to me, for you in my eyes are robed in honour and majesty in my house, your house; and in my eyes who covers yourself with the light as with a garment, that stretches out the heavens like a curtain that hangs with such grace and beauty.

9 My prayers and praises are to you my Lord; in an acceptable time, Oh Lord God in the multitude of your mercies I ask that you hear me as I pray for forgiveness, as I repent for all of my sins, past, present and future, for in my heart I do not wish to disappoint you for I seek only your grace and love and your tenderness in the truth of your salvation and to flourish in the house of God.

10 I will be of good courage, for you my Lord will strengthen my heart, I do put all of my hope in you, faith and trust; I believe in you with all of my heart and soul, I understand now that I can do all things through you my Lord, you have given me strength through love, grace and patience,

11 Oh gracious one you have waited for me to fall to my lowest point knowing that I would turn to you for help; understanding now what is real love, my true family in Heaven, my Father and my Lord Jesus Christ, to forever flourish in the house of God.

12 I see how you have made everything beautiful in its time, he who sits on the throne says, behold I am making all things new, I say to you, therefore if anyone is in Christ Jesus he is a new creature, and the old you has passed away, now behold I also say to you this; new things have come, I will make you innocent, and radiant like the dawn, and the justice of your course will shine like the noonday sun, unto you.

13 I will say unto you, I cause you to walk by the rivers of the waters in a straight way in which you shall not stumble, your soul shall be like a well watered garden, and you shall sorrow no more, when Jesus Christ was revealed as Gods son by his baptism in the water and the shedding of his blood on the cross, not by water only, but by water and blood;

14 Surely I say that Jesus has Bourne our grief and carried our sorrows, my Lord and saviour, how there is no one like you, and never will be; there is no God but you and the Father there is no rock like our God, flourish in the house of God.

15 My Gracious God; though we were spiritually dead, because of the things we have done against God, he who has given us a second chance to have a new life again, I say this to you now, that I am ever so thankful to be a new creature in Christ Jesus, and for all the changes that you have made to my life and family.

16 I am your disciple and a follower of Jesus Christ and my Father in Heaven, I do love you both with all my heart and soul; forever and ever I will pray and praise you, to flourish in the house of God, AMEN

55
You Need only Listen

1 I the Lord your God will fight for you, you need only listen, and have only to be silent; open your heart to the truth, for I your Lord are your strength and protection shield; My heart Oh Lord it does trust in you, and you have helped me in my most troubled times, you have lifted me up in many situations that have arisen, and my heart it leaps for joy just knowing that you guide and listen to my calls and cries, and with my prayers and songs I praise you all day, every day.

2 The Lord he is my warrior, and God is his name, worthy are you our Lord and God; to receive glory, honour and power, for you need only listen, and the Lord your God will hear your prayers, he will rescue you.

3 Oh save me my Lord for the waters they come upon my soul, and I do hear you, I know that you guide, praise and show me the way, we just need to open up and see, that you are always by our side; reaching deep inside our Holy Spirit which is our strength and our power where our Lord Jesus Christ resides.

4 I am your servant, my God! Having been freed from sin, I am a slave of righteousness, and I stand fast therefore in the liberty where Jesus Christ has made us free, and be not entangled again with the yoke of bondage; you need only listen; to be freed from all ungodliness to stay in the grace of God; and to heed the word of truth, if the son sets you free, you will be free indeed.

5 I was brought at a price and I glorify God in my Spirit, which is god's, however God he will demonstrate his own love for us in this while we were still sinners; this is why Jesus he died for us, Now to our King, eternal, immortal, invisible; to God who alone is wise, being of honour and glory forever and ever, you need only listen.

6 I say to you my God that your way is perfect, for the word God is tried, you are my shield unto us, we take refuge in our Lord Jesus Christ and I put my faith and trust in your unfailing love, and as my heart it rejoices in your salvation, and I understand that he who trusts in riches will fall, but the righteous shall flourish as a green leaf of the olive tree, for God's way is the only perfect way, all the Lords promises prove truth, and those who trust in their own wits are just fools; and you need only listen for those who walk in wisdom they shall come through safely.

7 Every word of God is pure and he is a shield to all who put their trust in him, who among you fear the Lord and obey the word, let the one that walks in the dark who has no light, trust in the Lords name and rely on him, to guide you,

8 Let's see if your idols can save you; when you cry to them for help, why a puff of wind can knock them down, if you just breath on them, they fall over, but whoever trusts me will inherit the land and possess my Holy mountain, you need only listen.

9 For to this end we toil and struggle, because we have hoped set on the living God, who is the saviour of all people, especially of those who believe in, trust in and relying on our Lord; where do you put your faith? When all does not go to plan, how do you think; what are your emotions, and where does it lead you; where do you take it, when you need only listen, where does your truth take you, what does your Holy spirit tell you, because God is leading you again you need only listen, for deep calls to deep.

56
"Revelation" the Divine Mystery

1 Revelation is a powerful word, how magnificent it is when you read thy word of God; it's about Jesus Christ, which God gave to him; the testimony of Jesus, when John bore witness to the word of God, a vision of love given by John.

2 Blessed are those who read, those who hear the word of this prophesy; for it is written and the time is near, for our beloved Lord Jesus the faithful witness, the first born from the dead, the ruler over all of us; our king of the earth.

3 He is our messiah our King; who has washed us from all of our sins, and in his son, and in his own blood; that loves, beyond what we can give; freedom given to us formed us into a kingdom, a royal race, priests to God our father to him glory; dominion forever and ever, the divine mystery, thankyou God, Amen and Amen.

4 Behold Jesus is coming with clouds and every eye will see; even the ones who pieced him, everyone who loves him; mourned for him; who is, who was and who is to come, the almighty Lord Jesus, who we dearly love, the beginning and the end, the divine mystery of Christ.

5 Being loved, being washed, being freed from all sins, how mighty is your power my Lord, to give all of this to me, and to all of your beloved children, who have turned to you just like me, with deep love in their hearts to never deny you; Revelation, the divine mystery that is beyond our comprehension, and many beliefs; revelations we have all had, when we are open to believe and our Lord, he speaks.

6 Many do not understand or know when you are reaching out to lend a hand; to give us divine wisdom from the mightiest of all; you my Lord Jesus Christ, revelations given in our deepest dreams, that all of us have had, divine interventions' you see many do not understand what has just been given to them.

7 Revelation throughout scripture, divine power from the beginning to end, all knowledge to be given; from all God's children, to listen and to learn, to reach out and to grasp it to hold it ever so tight; bringing it deep into our hearts, where it can never be lost.

8 Its Gods given protection to his beloved children who became lost, he will not let us go now; not without giving up a fight, the knowledge given from the beginning to the end: revelation is powerful; revelation the divine mysteries, which are given to us,

9 Jesus had revelation from the beginning, when he was born from a human womb; he was given revelation by God while in his mother's womb, mysteries and knowledge a prophet, a king, a teacher to all, he is our God the almighty one.

10 Jesus; he had foresight, revelation, he had done miracles for all to see, he is powerful beyond belief, but not to the ones who truly believe, I believe in my King, my Lord and my saviour, from the beginning to the end; he died to save us and to come back again, to rid the world of all evil, bringing peace to all again.

11 Revelation and your white throne your white horse, my king and my God, as you're seated at the right hand of your father, someone who is very important to you and to me, in every way, and father, your son in whom you are well pleased,

12 Your son my God and my beloved Lord Jesus, closely standing by you as you sit on your throne, thank you for my sight, loving you both with all my heart and soul; I can never forget the revelation, the divine mystery given by God.

13 Your beauty is radiance in my sight and my heart you have just made my room brighter, tonight; yes I have noticed my Lord, my light brighter, with these words spoken, revelation and truth given by Gods words, divine presence my Lord.

57
By the power invested in me (What the word, really means)

1 Behold what manner of love has the father bestowed on us, that we should be called the children of God, for are we not Gods masterpiece, he has created us anew in Jesus Christ, so we can do good things, he has planned long ago; to know the love of Christ which passes knowledge that you may be filled with all the fullness of God, what the word really means.

2 Lord God, your loving kindness is great above the Heavens, your faithfulness reaches to the sky, beyond even our knowledge and comprehension, Lord you have established peace in us, all that we have accomplished it's because of you; it's what you have done for us, now may the God of grace fill us with joy and peace in believing, so that we will abound in hope, by the power invested in me, by the power of the Holy Spirit.

3 I have waited patiently for the Lord, and he inclined unto me, and he heard my cries, for he has brought me out of a terrible place in my life, setting my feet firmly upon a rock, firmly in his loving kindness and grace, he brought me to my understanding of what the word really means as he establishes my steps.

4 I have learned in what state I am, to be content, I know how to be abased, and how to abound, by the power invested in me, if anyone thirsts, let him come to me and drink.

5 I say unto you he who believes in me as the scripture has said, out of the heart will flow rivers of living water, therefore anyone in Christ, the new creation has come, the old has gone, the new is here, in the beginning God he created; for everything was void without form, in darkness, with no light, no life existed until the love and the spirit of God was hovered over the face of the waters, and God called for light to form upon our Earth, for God is light, for there is only good in the light, and so he separated darkness from the light for again it is light that is good, for the light also brings goodness bringing seasons and goodness to creation and the living, for if all is in darkness, there is no life, to the created, Gods creation made two great lights, the greater was always to rule; rains covering like a mist over the Earth, helped everything; grow, life and light which is good, by the power invested in me, what the word really means.

6 Darkness has never had a place from the beginning its an empty void, no life can take place in nothingness, never ending darkness brings unhappiness, coldness, blindness, no peace, emptiness, only goodness and the light of God can help you see, what's in front of you, the lit pathway, filling the void, that darkness cannot penetrate, for light overpowers darkness, trusting in what you can see in the goodness of the light, of what the word really means.

7 I want only the children of the light to see the goodness of the light what is really in your sight, darkness is untrustworthy, your blinded, mislead, by what you can't see in front of you, the word of God is the truth and he says only goodness about the light; I the Lord your God do not praise, trust or put faith into darkness, so it cannot be seen, therefore it cannot pray on the goodness of the light, those who have eyes let them see, those who have ears, let them hear; by the power invested in me, let the light shine forth.

58
For I am a Just God

1 Fear not for I am with thee, says the Lord your God, who makes a way, a path through mighty sea's, for behold I am doing a new thing; Now it springs forth, do you not perceive it? Sing to God, singing praises to his mighty name for if you confess your sins, I am faithful God; and just to forgive you of your sins, to cleanse you from all unrighteousness, for I am a just God.

2 For all have sinned and fallen short of the Glory of God, but I say unto you that all who call on the name of the Lord, will be saved for he is the atoning sacrifice for our sins, and not only for ours but also for the sins of the whole world, for I am a just God, a fair and loving Father.

3 Listen unto me, did I not say in scripture that the wages of sin is death, but the gift of God is eternal life, through Jesus Christ, my beloved son; give all your worries and cares to me for I am a just God, do you trust and do you obey and keep faith, through the blood of Christ Jesus.

4 I tell you even so that there will be more Joy in Heaven, over one sinner who does repent, than over ninety nine righteous people who need no repentance, have you not repented with all your heart and soul, for I am a just God who knows all your prayers.

5 The light makes everything visible this is why it is said; awake Oh sleeper, rise up from the dead, and Christ will give you light for his lightening, enlighten the world; the Earth it saw and it trembled, your world is a lamp to my feet, and a light to my path, for I am a just God and I will wait, for the love of my child.

6 The Heavens proclaim his righteousness and all the people see his Glory, the Heavens declare the Glory of God, for I am a just God and the firmament that shows his handiwork when you open your eyes to the beauty that it holds.

7 I know the works and your thoughts, the time is coming to gather all nations and tongues and they shall come and see my Glory for in the beginning I created the Heavens and the Earth, and I your Lord God, I am a just God; follow me to the end, Glorify my name, love me as I have loved you and you will see the kingdom of Heaven.

59
The knowledge and Wisdom of Christ

1 In the year 1945 in Egypt was the understanding new ways of the Gospel; the beginning of Christianity; riding a camel a man came upon a magical sight, as he dug around a boulder to which he was drawn; against the face of a cliff, which the huge boulder had fallen, the month being of December, the month Christ was born.

2 He discovered something buried, it was a large storage jar sealed at the mouth, hoping that one day it would be found; as the man he "paused" worried; that it may be cursed with Jinna (Spirit) that it could harm him if it was released upon him.

3 Then his flesh it took over, recalling stories of hidden treasures in the ground; his love of money did overcome him; as the fear of Jinni disappeared from his thoughts; he took his staff lifted it high into the air, he smashed that jar, and a golden mist it did fill the air; floating before his eyes and disappearing into the air, a magical golden mist that had no fear; not the Spirit of Jinni anyway, that was well clear.

4 But what was discovered was much greater than gold, a library of the Gospel that has scriptures about Christ our Lord; they are the Gospel of truth, the Gospels of Thomas, Philip and john, and there was also James the brother of our Lord Jesus Christ, all of them disciples how followed our Lord; then there was the great invisible Spirit which is the Holy book itself.

5 However it really started decades ago, in the year 1896 in January, Akhmin, Egypt, I believe; buried in a cemetery where curses became legendary stories, where the Egyptian magic began; and affecting the lives of those working on all the codes; these were the Texts of Mary Magdalene, the secret book of John and the Gospel of our Lord Jesus Christ, the acts of Peter and only fragments of Thomas was found,(not to be mixed up with the Gospel of Thomas) do you know and understand?

6 The Gospels became born, pure truth and knowledge, knower, personified wisdom and Genesis accounts, an enlightening way of life and knowledge, the good news, the revelations of Christ is the Gospel of Paul, his is the Gospel of the cross; Given by Christ our Lord, the Gospel of Mark is the earliest of all, the beginning of the Gospel of Jesus Christ; Now the secret book of James; the brother of our Lord and saviour Jesus Christ, James was righteous and a leader of the Church in Jerusalem.

7 The Hierarchy of Angels seems to anticipate the fully ranks of powers, like the texts in the Holy Book, the Holy book of the great invisible Spirit and the secret book John, and its plot climaxes in the counts of the Angel Baruch,

8 Coming to Jesus of Nazareth who remains faithful to Baruch; and ascends to the good, then finally the round dance of the Cross, the song taught to his disciples, the Liturgical song of Jesus Christ; in order to explain what suffering is and how to escape it as well.

9 I your Lord say unto you, people must come to knowledge of oneself; this is what leads to salvation, when you know yourself, then you will be known, and then you will understand; that you are the children of the living Father God; I have taught my disciples to know themselves and that they should save themselves; for knowing oneself is coming to salvation through oneself, and creative thoughts are not primarily through faith.

10 Knowledge is to address human ignorance and to bring about enlightenment, people in this world of morality- this underworld are confused and have grown forgetful, they have fallen asleep and have been seduced by the deceptive pleasures and pain of the world,

11 becoming mixed up in this world of death, and they no longer remember who they are they have forgotten they are children of the divine, with the light of the divine within; opening their minds and to think; and in this way they can experience insight, afterthought and salvation, for I Jesus am the source of wisdom and knowledge, not first and foremost the crucified saviour.

12 I say unto you whoever drinks from my mouth will become like me; I myself shall become that person and the hidden things will be revealed to that person, the realm of truth- if you have seen Christ and have become Christ, you have seen the Father and have become the Father and the person who receives the name of God in the anointing oil (Chrism) is no longer to be a Christian, but is Christ- for I am in you and you are in me, just as the Father is in me and in you; with no crookedness at all, the kingdom is inside and out, the inner may be like the outer and the outer like the inner.

13 The Cosmic powers through which the soul must pass on your Celestial Journey are also the inner dispositions that a person must overcome, darkness, desire, ignorance, wrath, for the emanations and expressions of the divine one are mental characteristics and capabilities, mind (nous) forethought(Pronoia) thought (Ennoia) insight(Epinoia) wisdom(Sophia) and even mindlessness (Aponoia).

14 The fullness of God the divine realm above truly is within for what is the innermost is the fullness, and there is nothing further within, If the fullness is within so is the kingdom within, follow that, those who seek it will find it, I am the light that is all over things I am all from me; all has come forth, and to me all has reached, split a piece of wood and I am there, lift up a stone and you will find me there.

15 How miserable is the body that depends on a body and how miserable is the soul that depends on these two, shame on the flesh that depends on the soul, shame on the soul that depends on the flesh; if you do not fast from this world you will not seek the kingdom of Heaven, finding ones humanity and becoming truly human, ones true self; for you become sick and die; you love what deceives you, whoever has a mind should understand.

60

For God is our refuge

1 For to this end we toil and we struggle because we do have our hope set on the living God; who is our saviour of all people, especially of those who believe; Oh how great is your goodness which you have laid up for those who fear you, which you have prepared for those who trust in you, in the presence of the sons of men, we put our trust in you Oh Lord at all times, pouring out our Hearts to all, like an endless waterfall, for God is our refuge.

2 Oh God, my God, in whom I trust; let me not be ashamed, let not my enemies triumph over me, I trust in you my Lord, I said, you are my God, you are our refuge; vindicate me, my Lord, for I have led a life as best to please you; I have repented as not to flatter you, I have been washed clean from my sins, by the blood of the lamb.

3 I will greatly rejoice in you my God, my soul shall be joyful in you my Lord; for one thing I ask from you my Lord, "this only" do I seek, that I may dwell in the house of the Lord all the days of my life, Then will you call upon me, I will listen to you, Oh God almighty, how God is our refuge.

4 You shall seek me and find me, then you shall search for me, with all your heart and soul, the Lord is close to all who call on him; Yes, to all who call on him in truth, but without faith it is impossible to please him, for him that comes to God must believe that he is, and that he rewards them, that diligently seek him, Oh my Lord, for you are God, for God is our refuge.

5 We delight also in our God, and he will give us our desires of the heart, your righteousness is like the great mountains, your judgements are a great deep ocean, Oh purify me, with hyssop and I shall be clean as water, wash me and I will be whiter than snow, for you God our my refuge; Oh come close God, and God he will come close to you; wash your hands Oh sinners and purify your hearts, for your loyalty is divided between God and the world in which you live.

6 Show me your ways Lord and teach me your paths, guide me in your truths and teach me for you are God my saviour and my hope is in you all my days long; so we will wait on the Lord and be of good courage and he shall strengthen my heart, wait " I say" on the Lord. AMEN

61

God of Israel

1 God's blessed people, protected from the beginning of time, the Love of God has kept him close to their hearts, he has chosen Kings and people to lead, Abraham to his son Jesus Christ, reigning for many of thousands of years; a royal bloodline, well pleased by our God, our God of Israel, whom we love very much.

2 He has ruled over us, he is our Lord God, a God to worship, a God to trust, for he has also given us life; to worship and to praise, Israel is his love he is the God of Israel, and his land we must protect, for they have suffered they have been moved, thrown out of their own land, which angered God, we must forever make a stand, and our God of Israel we must embrace.

3 Israel forever more; your love for them so grand, the feast of tabernacle my God, it's a blessing from your Holy land, to worship you Oh God, for all that you have done, for your blessed my Lord, God of Israel, Holy is your name.

4 Holy, Holy is your name, God of Israel they call, pray and bless him, the feast of tabernacle, for 2 days, Oh God of Israel we will sing praises to you all day long, as we bless your Holy name, we bow down to our knees, God of Israel, hear our prayers, protect your land and your people oh Lord; and all of Gods children, who love Israel as well; our beloved Lord Jesus who is coming back soon; a thousand years of peace as Jesus he wins and rules; God of Israel my gracious Lord, Holy is your name, my blessed God of Israel as I bless and praise you *AMEN*.

62

Hope does not put us to Shame

1 For as the Heavens are higher than the Earth, so are my ways higher than your ways and my thoughts, being confident of this very thing, that he who has began good works in you, will complete it until the day of Jesus Christ,

2 For all your works we thank you, Lord; and your faithful followers they will adore and praise you, let the trees of the forests sing, let them sing for joy before the Lord, for he comes to judge the Earth, as hope does not put us to shame.

3 No good thing will he withhold from them that walk uprightly, Oh my gracious Lord God, how blessed is the one who trusts in you, they will hold their hands up in the air, in blessings to you, as we trust in the Lord God, you have an everlasting rock,

4 My Lord and my kindness, my love, the love that you have brought upon my life, shows me that your kindness and love shall never depart from me; neither your covenant of peace be removed, says you my Lord, who has mercy upon us, as hope does not put us to shame.

5 For the Angel of the Lord stays close around those who fear him, and he will deliver them up;' I say to you everyone who confesses me, the son of man also will confess before the Angels of God, even so, I say to you there is Joy in the presence of the Angels of God, over one sinner that repents, hope does not put us to shame.

6 Oh praise the Lord, from the Heavens above; praise him in the heights of the skies, praise him all the Angels, praise him all his hosts; praise him sun and moon; praise him all you stars of light, and as I give praises and thanks to my Lord God, with all my heart and soul, I will tell all who listen about your marvellous works, as hope does not put us to shame.

7 And hope does not put us to shame because Gods love has been poured out into our hearts, through the Holy Spirit, which has been given to us, and hope does not put us to shame, for behold what manner of love the Father has given to us, that we should be called the children of God; for who in the Heaven's can be compared to the Lord? Who among the sons of the mighty can be likened to the Lord, for is it not God who has made everything beautiful in its time.

8 I ask that all my thoughts be pleasing to Jesus, for I do rejoice in my hearts for my Lord; see all the birds of the skies, how our gracious Lord has taken care of them, as he does us; for he says that are we not more worth and of more value, I praise you my Lord because I am wonderfully made; and I know that full well, how hope does not put us to shame, for again I am fearfully and wonderfully made.

9 We do need to understand we have this treasure in our early vessels that the exceeding greatness is of the power; may it be of God and not from ourselves? You are the Lord and there is no other, for your right hand Oh Lord is gracious in power, as your right hand it smashes the enemy, and now I will pray, let the power of my Lord be great, just as you have spoken, for hope does not put us to shame, for you my God are my strong fortress, and you make my way perfect.

10 You have given me power when I have felt low, increasing my strength because your great power and by my outstretched arms, nothing is hard or impossible with you; as hope does not put us to shame, as we continue to speak of the glory of thy kingdom and talk of your mighty power; as my heart will forever be overflowing with a good theme; as I recite my composition concerning you my gracious King of Kings, and my tongue it is the pen of a writer, all given to me by you, Oh my gracious Lord and saviour.

11 You are fairer than any of the sons of men; as grace is poured upon your lips, therefore God has blesses and praised you forever for you are the Christ forever and ever; you are pure and all will have hope in you our Lord Jesus Christ as we keep ourselves pure like you, for great and marvellous are your works, almighty and righteous and true are your ways, you're our true King of all nations, as hope does not put us to shame.

12 Therefore as Gods chosen people Holy and dearly loved, as we clothe ourselves with compassion, kindness, humility and gentleness, patience, loyalty to your Holy kingdom; for God he does not like envy, and love it does not brag; it is not proud, so let all that you do be done out of love, being merciful, even as your father is merciful to you, for every good and perfect gift is from Heaven above, coming down from the father of the heavenly lights, who does not change like a shifting shadow.

13 I say unto you that the fruit of the Spirit it is love, joy, peace, longsuffering, kindness, goodness, faithfulness, gentleness, and self control, against such things, I say to you there is no law; for peacemakers are children of God, hope does not put us to shame, if any of you lack wisdom, ask God who gives to all generously without reproach, and it will be given unto you; create in you a pure heart; and a new steadfast Spirit within you I will give, Fear not for I have redeemed you, I have called you by your name, you are mine.

14 What matters I say to you, that it is not your outer appearance, neither the styling of your hair, neither the jewellery that you wear, or your clothing; but it is your inner disposition that matters to me the most,

15 cultivate inner beauty, the gentle gracious and kindness, that is what delights in, for I your Lord will give you strength, I will bless you with peace, for hope does not put us to shame. *AMEN*

63
Rushing Waters

1 Look for the Lord until he comes and pure goodness is on you like a spring of water, as you anoint my head with oil; and my cup it will overflow, for he who does believe in me as the scriptures says, out of his heart will flow rivers of living waters.

2 I pour out my heart like water as in prayer to the Lord, to be baptized in love, In the name of the Father and of the son and of the Holy Spirit; as we pray to you amen, as wise words are like deep waters, wisdom flows from the wise like a bubbling brook, and the mouth of the righteous flows with wisdom, as the perverted tongue is cut out; a spring of rushing waters over me, I believe my God he is around.

3 A spring of water it washes over stones as it wears them down and the rushing waters wash away the dirt, as in the same way that you can destroy all hope, as rushing waters washes over me, test me in this way says the almighty Lord, see I won't throw open the floodgates of Heaven and pour out so much blessings that there will not be room enough to store it; for he who believes in me as in the scriptures has said, from within him will flow rivers of living waters.

4 Do you not know how the clouds are balanced those wondrous works of Jesus, who is perfect in knowledge, as you open willingly your hand and satisfy the desires of every living thing; the things in which you have learned and received and have heard and saw in me; these do I say to you that the God of peace will be with you for the power of the just is like the shining sun that shines ever so brighter onto the perfect day, as a spring of rushing waters, shining like a glass like gaze.

5 You have shown me the way of life and you have filled my eyes with rushing waters, my heart with joy as all of your presence is upon my life; my God, my God show me my days; what is the measure of my days; let me know how frail I really am; so you can strengthen me, as I give you my full praise as a spring of rushing waters cleansing my frailty,

6 For my Lord you are my strength and my shield, my heart trusts in you, and I am helped, as my comfort has been sent by you; weeping may linger for the night, but Joy comes with the morning sun.

7 From the ends of the Earth, I call upon you, I call as my heart grows faint, lead me to the rock, that is much higher than I; as I call upon you my God; who is worthy to be praised, so shall I be saved from my enemies, by Gods grace, for your light has come and the Glory of the Lord is risen on me from love which flows between us like rushing waters.

8 A spring of rushing waters flows through me, because of the Lords great love, we are not consumed, for his compassion will never fail, Oh how gracious you are to me Oh Lord; according to your loving kindness, according to the greatness, of your compassion, blotting out all my transgressions, the Lord has appeared of old unto me saying, yes I have loved you with an everlasting love, therefore with loving kindness have I drawn you, behold what manner of love, that I should call upon only the children of God.

64
Oh High God almighty in hope I do trust

1 Above the voices of many waters, and the mighty breakers of the seas, Oh God almighty, how I love thee, when you pass through the waters, I will be with you and through the rivers, they shall not overflow you, my Lord how you establish peace for us, for all that we have accomplished, it's because you have made it happen for us, Oh high God almighty in hope I do trust.

2 I say unto you now that may the God of hope and love start filling you with all the Joy and peace in believing, so that you will abound in hope, by the power of the Holy Spirit, and you will keep whoever's mind is steadfast and in perfect peace, because the Lord God he trusts in you, Oh high God almighty in hope I do trust.

3 At night I will learn to be in peace as I meditate on you, I will lie down and sleep, for you alone my Lord you will keep me safe and sound; and as I wait patiently for the Lord; you have inclined unto me and your love for me as you have heard my cries; Oh high God almighty in hope I do trust; for I will always praise you as long as I live, and in your Holy name I will lift up my hands to you.

4 The one who believes in me as the scripture has been told, it is out of the believers heart will be the flow of living waters, it's there for anyone that is in Christ, and a new creature that you have become, for the old you has gone, and the new you will stay; If you trust believe and fear God, the Holy Spirits righteousness will never fail you; for God almighty will never fail you; Oh high God almighty in your hope do I trust.

5 For God has always remembered his covenant, forever the word which he commanded, to a thousand generations; for he sent redemption unto his people, he has commanded his covenant forever, holy and awesome is his name, his love and his faith I will bow down, In faith, trust and believing;

6 I hold out my hands for the love in my heart for you my Lord; as I wipe my tears from your feet with my hair, Oh high God almighty in hope do I trust; as in your name Oh God, so is your praise to the ends of the Earth, your right hand is full of righteousness.

7 You my Lord you give us strength, lifting us up when we realize that you do make everything fall into place, it's our faith that can become weak, it is us not you, that lets us down; please help stop our flesh from becoming weak; faith and believing in you, for you the Lord will bless his beloved children always with peace, and I will hear what God my Lord will speak,

8 For you will speak to us only of the truth and of peace; and you will show me the path of life, in your presence in fullness of Joy, and in your right hand there are pleasures forever more, Oh high god almighty in hope I do trust.

9 My Lord your voice is upon all the waters, the God of glory thunders, my Lord you are over many waters, I will sing to you praises my Lord God to your Holy name; singing loud praises my Lord "yes" to you alone who will ride the clouds; you cover the skies with clouds as you supply the Earth with rains, as it makes all things beautiful grow, the peace of you my Lord, it surpasses all understanding; as you guard our hearts with your love for us; and though our mind and our Holy Spirit, where our Lord, our god resides, Oh high God almighty in hope I do trust.

65
My Peace I leave with you

1 May the peace of God, which surpasses all understanding, guard your hearts and minds through Lord Jesus Christ; the work of righteousness will be peace, and the effect of righteousness, quietness and assurance forever, worship God who made the Heavens and the Earth, the seas and the springs of water, my peace I leave with you.

2 I say unto you let nothing be done through selfish ambition or conceit, but in lowliness of mind, let each esteem, others better than himself, these things I have spoken unto you, that in me you may have peace, in the world you have tribulation, but be of good cheer, for I have overcome the world, my peace I leave with you.

3 Problems they come and they go, and sometimes it feels never ending, for I tell you this, I have fully satisfied many weary souls, and I have replenished every sorrowful soul; that they may know from the rising of the sun to its setting, that there is none besides me, as my peace I leave with you, for I am the Lord; and there is no other.

4 Oh hear me my Lord, when I cry with my voice, I ask of you, to have mercy upon me, and answer my prayers, for I do not have the answer to my problems, and suffer confusion, when you said, seek my face, my heart said unto you, your face my Lord I will seek, you said in an answer my peace I leave with you, behold, I am with you always, even to the end of age, I thank you my Lord, Amen.

5 You speak and tell me; keep your lives free from the love of money, and be content with what you have, for God he says, never will I leave you, and never will I forsake you, my beloved child, I am your God I am your refuge and your strength; A very present help in troubled times, do you not know still, that I am aware of what's happening around you, do you not know that I will pull you free, as my peace I will leave with you, I love you my Lord, Oh Lord my strength.

6 I do understand my gracious Lord, in the days of my troubles, you will keep me secretly in my pavilion, In the covert of your tabernacle, you will hide me, you will lift me up on a rock, as you will not allow my foot to be moved as you keep me, I know i will not slumber, behold he who also keeps Israel close to their hearts shall neither slumber nor sleep, he will give you at all times, come follow me, who thirsts shall drink in accordance with the riches of God's grace.

7 My God who is rich in mercy, because of his great love for us even when we were dead in our trespasses he made us alive together with our Lord our saviour, Jesus Christ, God sent him from on high, he took me, he drew me out of many waters; and I say unto you Oh my Lord Jesus, for it is my grace that you have been saved, through faith, as this is not from yourself, it is a gift from God, my peace, I leave with you; be confident of this very thing, that he who has begun good works in you, will perform it until the day of Jesus Christ.

8 Be renewed in the Spirit of your mind, and you put on the new person in yourself which was created according to God, in true righteousness and holiness, my peace I leave with you,

9 I will command my Angels concerning you, to guard you in all your ways, Oh my Lord, thank you and let me hear your loving kindness in the morning when I awaken, let me feel freshness and splendour all day long; for I whole heartedly put my trust and faith in you; teach me the way in which I should walk, for to you I lift up my soul.

10 My precious Jesus, I long for you, as you hold me and the world in place, but I know in my heart I belong to you, and I need your love Lord, as you take me as I am, just like the flowers need the rain, as you guide me, leading me to your hands, for you healed me of all my pain, washed me of all my shame, I belong to you now my precious and wonderful Lord, as your peace you leave with me.

66

I'll open Heavens Gates

1 Your right hand, Oh Lord is gracious in power; your right hand Oh Lord smashes the enemy, and now I pray, let the power of my Lord be great, just as you have spoken, Oh my Lord God your my strong fortress how you make my way perfect, you smash the enemy when he interferes and he runs in fear; bringing peace to my home, your love for me is perfect in every way, my home above when you say to me, I'll open Heavens gates.

2 You can stir up the seas with your mighty power, and with your understanding, you can break up the storm, Oh how great is our Lord his power is absolute, and his understanding is way beyond our comprehension as he teaches us in his way to understand, why we must suffer; turning to him for his love and help; and he will tell you, I'll open Heavens gate's.

3 Our Lord Oh how mighty, he gives power to the faint, and it's to them that have no might, that his love and compassion he will increase strength, Lord God it is you, by your great power and by your outstretched arm how nothing is too hard for you; how they shall speak of the glory of thy kingdom, your Angels how they speak of power, you God are my God, earnestly I will seek you! I'll open Heavens gates.

4 My beloved Lord and Saviour, with my whole heart I have sought after you; I ask of you please hear my deep loving prayers, don't let me wonder away from your commandments, I seek only your protection and love, give ear to my cries, give ear to my prayers, for I do not have deceptive lips; but only of a kind and caring heart of which you have given me, I'll open Heavens gate's.

5 I say unto you; the sacrifice of the wicked is an abomination to God, but the prayers of the upright is always Gods delight, I'll open Heavens gate's to the righteousness of Gods light, for he is far from the wicked, but he hears the prayers of the righteous, seek the Lord while you can find him; call on him now while he is near you, live in peace and love as Christ he loves us; and he gave himself up for us, a fragrant offering and sacrifice to God, God the almighty.

6 I devote myself to you, and I devote myself to prayers with an alert mind and always a thankful heart, I will rejoice forever more, and I will pray without ceasing, In my heart you deserve my praise, for I devote myself to you, and I devote myself to prayers with an alert mind and always a thankful heart, I will rejoice forever more, and I will pray without ceasing, In my heart you deserve my praise, for all that you have given me, so in everything I give thanks for you are telling me that it's the will of my Heavenly Father, in the name of my Lord Jesus Christ, who says I'll open Heavens Gates.

7 What can I truly say to such a clear message from God himself, for all the mistakes that I have done, that God can still send you all his love; how my heart aches with Joy for his deep understanding and compassion, to save all his beloved children, who call out to him in troubled times, all answers are truly given, just reach deep inside and you can feel him; live in me and I will live in you, abide in me and I will abide in you, and I'll open Heavens gate's.

67
How great is the Lord, my God

1 My Lord, My God, how the world in which we live, fits into your hand, that's so hard to imagine, so I see in my eyes, how powerful you are; as I think to myself; how great is the Lord, my God.

2 You can control the world in which you live, but you gave us a chance, to totally believe, to turn to our creator, our Saviour to save us from all of our sin's, to be born again as devout Christians and to return to your kingdom, how great is the Lord my God; and thank you for saving my life.

3 Our world that you created is becoming a real mess; even with all of its beauty, which we have forgotten to see and to embrace, for many have forgotten who created it all, even the ones that do take a look at its beauty and do see it all, how sad my great one, that so many forget, our world wants to eliminate religion out of most off our schools; changing our children's futures with no knowledge of scripture at all; parents do not tell children, how great is the Lord, my God.

4 Too many leaders and to many wars and to many opinions from them all, how we truly need you my Lord; you are the power, you are the glory, you are the only decent one; your pure love, pure power;

the only truth that has been written for all; the Holy Bible, knowledge to be given to you when you reach out for the Lord; my Lord Jesus we do need you to come back soon, I will tell as many as I can, how great is the Lord my God.

5 I do feel powerless that I cannot change the leaders of our world, for I am only a grain of sand; in this world of so many; and my opinion will not change what they will say and do; for they even crucified my Lord Jesus, my King and yours, the only thing that I have is what you have given me to write; changing the minds of many, bringing people back to the kingdom of you my God; and to strengthen the faith of all believers, to turn even closer to you, when I explain to them, how great is the Lord my God.

6 All that is promised, 1000 yrs of peace, it's hard to comprehend when our world and what we have made it is so full of sin; you gave us a chance by sending us your only beloved son, and I praise and love you for that my Lord, for you have turned my life around; back to you and the word of God; and I will never ever forget what you have done; I do slip up, but you are always there, to say to me, get back on your feet, my Spirit alive, that is my God within; how great is the Lord my God, who has saved me.

7 I may not understand for so much is not for me to know, but the wisdom that you have given me, is breathtaking my gracious Lord; to open my eyes to understand about the world, an eye opener; when you truly find, the real love of the Lord, my God.

8 Can anyone: not discover the depths of God, can anyone discover your limits, for they are beyond anyone's thoughts and comprehension, off how vast is the universe that continues to just grow, forever and ever; how great is the Lord my God, to give us such wondrous beauty when we look up and look around; to be awestruck and still not fully comprehend; the power and the wonder of our almighty God.

9 You're always there to all who call upon you; always there to pick us up when we fall; always there to give us wisdom, love peace and happiness and joy, to give us power and strength when we can except that is there; to all of your children, who love you with all their heart and their soul; and to except that you are the greatest gift to us all, and how truly great is the Lord my God.

10 Listen to me all of you who know right from wrong, and cherish my laws in your hearts; and do not be afraid of peoples scorn or their slanderous talk, for its the one who gets wisdom who loves life; and the one who cherishes understanding, will soon prosper,

11 For I your God says cursed is the man who trusts in man, and makes flesh his arm; and who's heart will depart from me, for I say unto you, it is better to trust in the Lord than to put confidence in man; to learn also from God and to understand; how great is the Lord my God.

12 Train yourself to be Godly; and have nothing to do with Godless people, myths and tales, for only the mouth of the righteous will utter wisdom and their tongues will speak of what is just, now stand and see this great thing; which I your Lord will do before your eyes, for I will satisfy the thirsty and fill the hungry with good things.

13 This God is our God; forever and ever, he will be our guide even unto death, blessed are they who do hunger and thirst after righteousness for I say unto you, you shall be filled, Lord rescue me from evil people, protect me from cruel people, deliver my soul, Oh save me for thy mercies sake, how great is the Lord my God.

14 How great is the Lord my God, who will never leave me, Oh God almighty where is there anyone as mighty as you, Lord faithfulness is your very character, your way my Lord is in the sanctuary who is so great; our Lord Jesus Christ.

15 Who is like you Oh God among anyone; none, for you are majestic in Holiness, awesome in your ever deeds, forever doing wondrous things in all who seek you, you are God alone.

68

So shall my words be

1 Set a watch my Lord God, before my mouth, keep the door of my lips, safe before me;' because so many people were coming and going that I didn't even have a chance to eat; then my Lord he said unto me, come before me, by yourself to a quiet place and get some rest; so shall my words be.

2 If anyone among you thinks they are religious and does not control their tongue, but deceives his own heart, their religion is useless; for when words are many and transgression is not lacking; but the prudent are restrained in speech, minds can be like a snake pit, how do you suppose what you say is worth anything when you are so foul minded, it's your heart, not the dictionary that gives meaning to your words, so shall my words be.

3 A word fitly spoken is like apples of gold in pictures of silver, people who are not proud will inherit the land and will enjoy complete peace, I will give peace and you shall lay down in the land, and no one will make you afraid, you will keep peace perfect, all who trust in you all those thoughts are fixed on you, so shall my words be.

4 So shall my words be, that goes forth from my mouth, it shall not return to me void, but it shall accomplish what I please and it shall prosper in the things for which I sent it; when deep calls to deep at the noise of your waterfalls, for all your waves and billows have gone over me, and God shall wipe away all tears from your eyes.

5 Who ever has my commandments and keeps them, loves me and the one who loves me will be loved by my Father, and I too will love them and show myself to them, so shall my words be, you will keep in me perfect peace, whose mind is stayed on you, because he trusts in you.

6 Let the peace that I your Lord Jesus who gives control to your thinking, because you were all called together in one body to have peace, always be thankful, always have a pure love in your heart, always be repenting for all your wrongs; then I know what is true in your heart, for the peace of God which transcends all understanding, and will guard your heart, so shall my words be, and your minds in Jesus Christ.

7 Peace I leave with you, my peace I give you; not as the world gives, give I to you, stop letting your heart be troubled, neither let it be fearful; the way of the righteous is smooth; Oh up right one, make the path of the righteous level, listen unto me, the way of the righteous is like the first gleam of dawn, which shines ever so brighter until the first full light of the day.

8 In all things I gave you, an example, in so labouring you ought to help the weak, and to always remember the words of the Lord Jesus; that he himself said, it is more blesses to give than to always receive, each one must give as he has decided in their hearts for God he loves a cheerful giver; giving generously to the poor, never grudgingly for the Lord your God, will bless you in everything that you do, do you really want for anything, have I not provided.

9 I say unto you, let the words of your Lord Jesus dwell in you and your house and in you; richly in all wisdom, shall you be, teaching and admonishing one another in psalms and hymns and spiritual songs, singing with grace in your hearts to be Lord your God.

10 Oh my heart is fixed Oh God my heart is fixed; I will sing and give praises to you all day long, you are never far from my heart, for you are good to me, let us all come boldly to the throne of our gracious God almighty; there we will receive his mercy, and we will find grace to help us when we need it most; as my grace is sufficient for you.

11 For my strength is made perfect in weakness, for my Lord God is a sun and my shield, for you give grace and glory; and no good thing do you withhold from those who walk uprightly, as we make our way straight for the Lord, as you put breath into me, and make me live again, for forgiveness of our sins and for the love in our hearts for you, my beloved Lord, my beloved Saviour, so shall my words be. Amen and Amen

69

I will pour out my Spirit on you

1 God he has poured his love out richly to us, the Holy Spirit, through our Lord and Saviour Jesus Christ; for his hope it will never disappoint you because God he has poured out his love to fill our hearts, his given love through the Holy Spirit, that God our Father has given us, he who believes in me as scripture is written, out of his heart will flow rivers of living water, behold my beloved one, I will pour out my spirit on you, I will make my words known to you.

2 And it shall come to pass afterwards that I will pour out my Spirit on all flesh, your children shall prophesy and they shall dream and shall see visions, for it is the spirit that gives life; the flesh is of no help at all, these words I speak to you are of spirit and life.

3 The spirit of God has made me the breath of the almighty God who gives me life; the Lord he brought me forth as the first of his works, before his deeds of old; I was formed long ago at the very beginning when the world came to be; the mighty one has spoken, God; in whom you also trust after you heard the word, the truth; the Gospel of salvation in whom you also after believed; then you were sealed with that Holy Spirit of promised, I will pour out my spirit of you,

4 For it's by grace you have been saved, through faith, and that not of yourself, it has been said unto you before that it is a gift from God, not as a result of works, just so no one will boast, my Lord you do give me so much strength; and I ask of you to lead me down the path that is right, for the good of only your name, for that I praise, I glorify and worship all that you have done, no need for boast, for without you we are truly nothing.

5 The steps of the good are only ordered by Lord God, and he then delights in his ways, you show me the path of life, and in your presence there is fullness of joy, and in your right hand are pleasures for evermore, I will pour out my spirit on you, be still and know that I am God.

6 The wisdom that comes from Heaven is first of all the pure then the peace loving, considerate, submissive, full of mercy, and the ones of good fruit, impartial and sincere; how kind are you my Lord, how good are you, so merciful is this God of ours who says I will pour out my Spirit on you, I will come to you, you were sent to heal the heartbroken to help teach, to preach also deliverance, you our Lord Jesus Christ, I say unto you, I am the Lord who heals.

70
Stepping out in faith believing

1 I say unto you that if you are wise and understand Gods ways prove it by living an honourable life, by doing good works with humility that comes with wisdom; the discretion of a person makes them slow to anger, and their glory is to overlook a transgression;
My Lord I will hear what you speak, for I understand that you will speak peace to all your children and to your saints, stepping out in faith believing.

2 I say unto you that it is not the spiritual that is first, but that of the physical, and then the spiritual, the first man was from Earth (Adam) a man of dust, the second man is from Heaven (Jesus Christ) in him we have redemption through his blood and the forgiveness of sins; according to the riches of his grace, washing away all guilt and making you clean again; if we confess our sins, the Lord God he is faithful and just to forgive us of our sins and to cleanse us from all unrighteousness.

3 So come now and let us reason together say I your Lord; though your sins are as scarlet, they will be as white as snow, though they are red as crimson they will be like wool, I have removed your sins as far from you to the east from the west; and stepping out in faith believing let my prayers be set before you as incense, the lifting us of my hands as the evening sacrifice.

4 Therefore let all the faithful pray to you while you may be found, surely the rising of the mighty waters will not reach them, you can pray for anything and if you have faith, you will receive it, stepping out in faith believing.

5 Believe me that I am in the Father and the Father is in me; otherwise believing because of the works of themselves, truly, truly I say unto you, he who believes in me, the works that I do, he will also do, and greater works than these he will do, because I go to the Father.

6 The same anointing that was on and in Jesus is on and in his people today! He says the same works that I do, my people will do; when you have faith; as a believer to put your hands on people as you pray for them, you are going to see results; Praying for those around you, taking authority over the enemy, finding courage to step out of your comfort zone to see God move through you; stepping out in faith believing.

71
Everlasting God

1 Everything in the Heavens and on Earth is yours, Oh Lord and this is your mighty Kingdom, we adore you as the one who is over all things, your are the rock, our rock; for your works are perfect and your ways are justice, for you God are able to make all grace abound: and always having sufficiency in everything; you may have an abundance for every good deed, the everlasting God, that we need.

2 Our Lord is the everlasting God; the creator of the ends of the Earth, he does not faint or grow weary his understanding is unsearchable, call on me in your days of trouble, and I will deliver you, and you will honour me, Help me oh gracious Lord, to open my eyes, so that I may see wonderful things in your law, letting the words from my mouth and the meditation of my heart be acceptable in your sight, oh my gracious Lord almighty who is my strength and my redeemer.

3 I have loved you with an everlasting love, an everlasting God who is there for you always; for I have drawn you with loving kindness, for I your God will hold your right hand, saying to you, fear not for I will help you; I ask you then my Lord, to listen to me when i pray and call upon you, as I bring my requests to you and wait expectantly, and I will hear what you my God, the Lord will speak of peace and you will bring peace unto your people.

4 For the kingdom of God is not eating and of drinking but of righteousness and peace and Joy in the Holy Spirit; be still I say unto you that I am your God, I am your everlasting God, stand still and consider the wondrous works of God, for he has said unto me, my grace is sufficient for you, for my power is made perfect in weakness.

5 My grace and peace be yours in abundance in the knowledge of God and of Jesus Christ our Lord, for you have been my help and in the shadow of your wings I will sing for joy as I say Oh praise God and let us lift up our hearts with our hands to God, in the Heavens, I will bless you while I live, I will lift up my hands in your name, my everlasting God.

6 They that really know your name will put their trust in you, for you Lord have not forsaken me, for I my Lord did seek you according to your name, I was broken hearted and you comforted me, Oh my Lord so is your praise to the ends of the Earth; your right hand is full of righteousness for the Lord is close to the broken hearted and he rescues those who's spirit is crushed, submit yourself then to God,

7 Resisting darkness, when you are suffering and being tormented by the devil for your God says he will leave; he will flee from you, call upon me and love me will all of your heart and soul, you are a child of God and the devil will come after you because of your love for your God, be strong and keep faith believing and you will not suffer from the torment of darkness of your thoughts, learn what is godly and what is not.

8 My everlasting God, by the rescue of you as we present our bodies as a living sacrifice, Holy and acceptable to God, which is your reasonable service, as you say unto us, do not be conformed to this world, but only to be transformed by the renewal of your minds, that we may prove what is good and acceptable and the perfect will of you, my everlasting God.

9 My Holy Lord God who has made everything good and nothing should be refused if it is accepted with thanks, for you are worthy our Lord and God, to receive glory is accepted with thanks, for you are worthy our Lord and God, to receive glory and honour and power for you created all things and by your will they were created and have their being, all the earth bows down to you, they sing and praise your Holy name.

10 My everlasting God I will give repeating thanks to you Oh my Lord, praising you to everyone, as I say to them blessed is the Lord of Israel, for he has visited and redeemed his people, greater love has no one than this, that someone lays down his life for his friends and loved ones; as God has given them eternal life and they shall not perish, no one will snatch them out of my hands says the Lord God; he has redeemed all sinners who repent and become a new child in Christ, redeemed from sin, even as the Father has loved me, I also have loved you, remain in my love.

11 For if you keep my commands you will remain in my Love, just as I have kept my Fathers commands and remain in his love and if you call on the Father who without partiality Judges according to each ones works, conduct yourself throughout the time of your stay here in fear knowing that you were not redeemed with corruptible things like gold and silver, but with the precious blood of Christ as of a lamb without blemish and without spot.

12 So it is with Christ's body we are many parts of one body and we all belong to each other for I say to you there is neither Jew nor Greek, slave nor male or female, for you are all one in your Lord Jesus Christ, so make every effort to keep yourself united in spirit, binding yourselves together with peace again, I say to you that if two of you agree about everything that they may ask, it shall be done, for them by my Father who is in Heaven. Amen.

72
Full of gladness in your presence

1 For a day in your courts my Lord is better than a thousand outside; I would rather stand at the threshold of a house of my God, than to dwell in the tents of wickedness, my God make me full of gladness in your presence; for those who are planted in the house of the Lord shall flourish in the courts of our God.

2 We shall be abundantly satisfied with the abundance of your house, for you will make us drink of the rivers of your pleasure, my gracious Lord you have made known to me the ways of life and you will make me full of gladness, in your presence.

3 My father since we are receiving a kingdom which cannot be shaken, I ask for you to give me grace by which we may serve only you, acceptably with reverence and godly fear, for you my God are a consuming fire, I ask of you to show me your ways my Lord and teach me your paths, make me full of gladness with your presence.

4 Oh my Lord, my God how great are you to me as you are robed with honour and majesty, full of gladness in your presence, I will be as you are gracious and your loving kindness you bring into my life.

5 My prayer is unto you, Oh my Lord in an acceptable time, Oh God in the multitude of your mercy hear me in the truth of your salvation, Oh hear me Oh my Lord, for your loving kindness is good full of gladness in your presence turn to me according to your multitude of your tender mercies.

6 I say unto you, I will make your innocence radiant like the dawn and the justice of your cause will shine like the noonday sun, I am confident of this that the one who began a good work among you will bring it to completion by the day of Jesus Christ; full of gladness in your presence I will be my gracious Lord; as you fill my Holy Spirit with love, joy and peace.

7 He has told me, Oh mortal one, what is good, and what does the Lord require of you, but to do justice and to love kindness and to walk humbly with your God; blessed are the ones who don't walk in the council of the wicked, nor stand on the path of sinners, nor sit in the seat of scoffers; the path of righteousness, I will give to the ones who walk in the same path who love me with all their hearts and soul, full of gladness in your presence.

73
I call him my Saviour, my Lord God

1 When you call on me I will answer you, when you need me; I will provide your every need. According to your riches and glory, when you are in trouble I will prepare a table before you and in the presence of your enemies you will be comforted with peace and joy that I will give you, and your enemies will ask themselves who is that; that is taking care of the one that I want to destroy, I call him my Saviour, my Lord God.

2 I will say unto them he is the Lord my God, he is wonderful, he is my councillor, he is the mighty God, he is the everlasting Father, he is the prince of peace, he is the God who created Heaven and Earth.

3 He is the one who holds a mountain in a scale, he is the one who keeps the hills in a balance, he is the one who conquered death, hell and the grave, he has been called the lion in the tribe of Judea, he's been called the fairest of 10'000, he has been called the lamb of God for sinners slain; but I call him my Saviour, my Lord, my redeemer, who is faithful and true, he is my rock, he is my fortress, he is my shield, he is my strong tower, he is faithful and almighty, he is all knowing,

4 Oh magnify the Lord with me, all who will hear my prayers to our almighty Lord and Saviour, and exalt his name together, Oh what a mighty God we serve, I call him my Saviour, my Lord God.

5 For the Lord God his word does not return void, for the one thing that I have learned is that the Faster I trust in him the further that I will go, and the delay between me receiving his blessings and Gods willingness to pour it out, it's the time it will take for me to trust, that his promise is true, so we must trust in the Lord with all our heart and soul, I call him my Saviour, my God.

6 It's so easy to say all this my Lord, but how is it that it's so difficult to sometimes do, for I do know in my heart, my Holy Spirit, that I truly love you I ask why; is it because trust is deteriorating so badly in our world today, we do not trust, family and friend, nor neighbours, people that we work with, everyone is suspicious and have motives, the public is even suspicious and doesn't trust the government and what they say that they will promise people and everyone knows that they do not keep all their promises, however the government in turn does not either trust the public.

7 The more I am able to put my trust and faith in you my Lord and my Saviour, the further I will be able to go; for you have already proven to me, that I can trust in you, I have prayed and you have given to me, I've wished for things in my mind hoping for changes in my life and you have heard my thoughts and provided and without me even realizing straight away, until you have come forth and told me that you have provided that my prayers have been answered; your goodness has been poured out for trusting; and my heart trusting by turning to you, I call you my saviour, my Lord God, I trust in you.

8 Trusting my Lord is a development with 2 fundamental elements (consistency) for one; If you can find this in someone you can have and find trust, and then there is (capability) for when you have someone who is capable then you can trust in them, and when you have someone who has both of these qualities then you can truly have faith and trust in them; and when someone has either one or the other they sometimes do not know if they are having a good day or not, for they are not capable of making their mind up or consistent on making up their mind on how it will turn out, and then they become disappointed.

9 My point my Lord is that you are there for us to help, for you are our God that we are serving and you are consistent, you are capable, you are the same yesterday, today and tomorrow, you do not change and we need to learn to trust in you my Lord for you are forever; everlasting to everlasting.

10 You said my Lord that you're consistent goodness and mercy and it will follow us all the days of our life; that your angels will walk before me clearing a pathway in front of me and every door that was closed, you my Lord would open it and I know that every storm that has fallen before me you have calmed it, in your mighty name all enemies will be crushed before me, so I say to you this day, that the God I serve I can fully trust, I praise and I glorify your Holy name, I bow down to you, as I call you my Lord and saviour, my God, I say these things to you with all my heart and soul.

11 Your consistency to me Lord is comforting and it is also a warning, because if I look back at what you have done, I can build expectations on what you can still do for if you can bless me and my family and all whom you have blessed in the Holy Bible who have put trust in you; I call him my saviour, my Lord God, for you have shackled every sin from out of our lives setting us free from bondage and addictions, and everything that binds us,

12 I call him my saviour, my Lord God; I can comfort and declare that I love and put my faith believing and all my trust in you; work consistently in us with our sins, freeing us, shackle them, past, present and future; as we drink from the Holy cup of our Lord Jesus Christ as I sing praises, calling upon him as my Saviour for my new life as a devout Christian, my King of Kings, thank you and Amen.

13 As I call him my saviour, my Lord God, words of our Lord God can change and turn your life around, Why do people give up and turn away from you my Lord, getting caught up in this world with what man has done, but I find it hard to understand for all that I have done I find that so much of my old self seems to have just faded away; and that's because of you my Lord, the trust and the deep faith that now I couldn't imagine my old ways anymore.

14 How you make my heart feel, how my tears just flow freely down my cheeks, it is you my Lord my Holy Spirit within, I've never known before, what I now feel for you today; how It is now my true calling; that will never go away, and I don't ever, want it to my Lord, for my Holy Spirit would just never be the same; a huge part of me would be gone, but never lost to this world, ever again, for I now belong to you God, for I know that you will never let me down; you'd never let me go, never to this world now; my Lord and my Saviour, my Holy one.

AMEN and AMEN

74
At your Touch

1 My Lord the Earth trembles at your glance; the mountains smoke at your touch, you will show wonders in the sky above, and signs on the Earth beneath, blood and fire and smoking vapour; why you do not know what will even happen tomorrow, what is your life? for you are mist that appears for only a little while, and then it will vanish; for the grass it also withers and the flowers they will fall, but I do say to you this, the word of God endures forever.

2 I am the rose of Sharon, and the lily of the valleys, for I your God have made everything beautiful in its time, at your touch, I will comfort and touch your life; call upon me for am I not your workmanship, created in Christ Jesus for good works.

3 Pour out your unfailing love on those who love you, giving justice to those with honest hearts, for this cause everyone who is Godly shall pray to you in a time when you may be found, surely in a flood of great waters they shall not come near, for even much water cannot put out the flame of love, floods cannot drown love, at your touch, my Lord I have found perfect love.

4 You are worthy Oh my Lord My God; to receive glory and honour and mighty power, for you have created all things and your pleasure they are and were created, at your touch you have healed all pain, transformed lives by your love and grace, My God, My God; you demonstrate your own love for us in this; while we were still sinners, as Jesus Christ, he was sent to die for us all.

5 Now to the King, eternal, immortal, invisible, to God who alone is wise being of honour and glory, by your touch forever and ever, for you my God, your way is perfect, the word of God is tried, you are my shield, unto all who takes refuge in you, as I offer sacrifices of righteousness and put trust in my Lord, and I put trust in your unfailing love, My heart it rejoices in your salvation, at your touch, I am shown the way.

6 Oh how great is your goodness, which you have laid up for those who fear you, which you have prepared for those who trust in you, in the presence of the sons of man and at your touch, your miracles are breathtaking, never forget by those who receive them, always remember by the ones who hear about them, as your grace and love pours over all who are witnesses.

7 At you touch, my Holy Spirit is transformed, at your touch, my life will never be the same, at your touch my heart it becomes alive, when you have heard my cries for mercy, the Lord he accepts my loving prayers, for we do not know what we should pray for, as we ought to, but the Spirit himself makes intercessions for us, with groaning which cannot be uttered, we need the Lords strength we need to seek his face, forever more at your touch, my Lord, we need to embrace.

8 At his touch, he who searches the heart it knows, what the mind of the Spirit is, because he makes intercessions for the saints according to the will of God, live in me and I will live in you, abide in me and I will abide in you.

75
Remain in me

1 Behold I am with you and will keep you wherever I go, I can never escape from your Spirit, I can never get away from your presence, my presence shall go with thee, and I will give you rest; behold I will come and I will dwell in the midst of you, says I your Lord God, remain in me.

2 For I say unto you for where two or three gather in my name, I am there among you, remain in me, as I remain in you, as no branch can bear fruit by itself, for it must remain in the vine, neither can you bear fruit unless you remain in me.

3 Those who say they live in God should live their lives as Jesus did, do not take your Holy Spirit from me, for I am with you always even to the end of age, Holy, Holy, Holy is my name, remain in me.

4 I hear you my Lord Holy and worthy are you, I will remain in you, our Lord and God the Holy one to receive the glory, the honour and the power, for you created all things, including me, my Heart it overflows with a good theme, I recite my composition concerning you, my King of Kings.

5 Remain in me, love is patient and it is kind, love doesn't envy, and it isn't proud, then at resurrection of the righteous, God will reward you for inviting those who could not repay you, let all your things be done with charity, let all that you do be done in love and compassion, faithfulness and trust.

6 Remain in me for long ago the Lord he said to Israel, I have loved you, my people with an everlasting love, with unfailing love, I have drawn you to myself, remain in me, for you are peacemakers with seeds of peace and you shall reap the harvest of righteousness.

7 Remain in me and be merciful, even as your Father is merciful, for every good and perfect gift is from above, coming down from the Father of the heavenly lights, who does not change, remain in me and be the fruit of the Spirit as love, joy , peace, long suffering, kindness, self control, gentleness, for against such there is no law, remain in me and I will remain in you, for blessed are the peacemakers, for they are called the children of God.

76
(Spiritual Influences)
The Enemy of the Mind

1 For I say to you that your struggle is not against flesh and blood but against the rulers, against the powers against the world forces of darkness, against spiritual forces of wickedness, the enemy of the mind.

2 In heavenly places the fight that we are in is invisible; the majority of our conflicts are not between flesh and blood, the real battle ground is in the arena of the mind, the thoughts are a manifestation of the Spirit realm and we need to warfare in our thought life against the enemy of our mind.

3 Don't be passive about your thoughts allowing just anything to captivate your thinking process, practice a supernatural awareness in your mind, by rejecting thoughts that are not from our Lord, spiritual influences, that can tear your life upside down, making you feel insecure in yourself, darkness tearing you away from your Lord God, a liar that is the enemy of your mind.

4 Our Lord God is a pure loving God who would not interfere, neither give you ungodly and unhappy insecure thoughts; he would never want you to feel insecure, unloved, depressed, and having anxiety, he would not have your thoughts confused, these things and thoughts are spiritual influences of the enemy of the mind; My Lord God of a pure heart, give me a new steadfast mind and Spirit within me.

5 Take charge and control for you are a new child of Christ, listen to your Holy Spirit within, what's right and what seems wrong, what's of God and what is not; for the Godliness within you what is truth and loving kindness, what is right and what to really do by trusting in God for the guidance and the pathway to take, the enemy of the mind, with God's love and peace he will cast it away.

6 For we are a fragrance of Christ to God, among those who are being saved; and among the darkness of the ungodly, those who are perishing, It will be that whoever calls on the name of the Lord that will be saved, for those who believe do enter into rest those who have taken captive, the enemy of the mind, will have peace, and my peace I will give unto you.

7 Depart from evil, the enemy of the mind and do good, seeking peace and pursue it; for he that satisfies the longing soul, and fills the hungry soul with goodness, and these three will remain in love, faith and hope, but the greatest of these is love, let the peace of God rule in your hearts to which also you called in one body; and be thankful, for the bread of God is the bread that comes down from Heaven and gives life to the world.

8 This is the will of God the Father who sent me, that everyone who sees the son and believes in him may have everlasting life, and I will raise him up at the last day, for I am the bread of life; whoever comes to me will never be hungry again, whoever believes in me will never be thirsty, I have come so you will have life, and that you may have it more abundantly.

9 Your life shall be for a prize to me unto you, because you have put your trust in me, says I your Lord God; for most certainly I tell you that he who believes in me has eternal life, I tell you, shut out and rebuke the spiritual influences that enemy of the mind; and keep your faith and believing in me and the enemy will flee from you, remember abide in me and I will abide in you, live in me and I will live in you.

10 For it's the law of the Spirit of life in my Lord Jesus who made me free from the Law of sin and of death, the witness is this; That God he gave us eternal life, and this life is in his beloved son, our Lord and our Saviour Jesus Christ; for just as our Father raises the dead and gives them life, even so the son gives life to whom he is pleased to give it.

11 Therefore I say to you, do not worry about your life, what you will eat, nor about your body and what you will put on, for in the way of righteousness is life; and in its pathway there is no death, for when I who is your life shall appear, then you also shall appear with me in glory, and the enemy of the mind will have no hold over you, for I am in you; I will delight myself in your statutes, I will not forget your words.

12 For the one who dwells in the shelter of the most high will abide in the shadow of the almighty; I have hidden your words in my heart, that I might not ever sin against you my Lord, keep me my gracious Lord as the apple of your eye, hide me safely under the shadow of your wings, keep out and protect me from the enemy of the mind, as I rebuke the influences and replace them with the love and joy of my Lord God.

13 The word is near you, in your mouth and in your heart- that is the words of faith which you preach and my words will never pass away, before you came forth out of the womb; I sanctified you, for I knew the thoughts that I think towards you, says I your God; and not of evil, to give you: but of hope and a future.

14 My gracious one, I can never escape from your spirit, for I am lost without you in my life; I can never get away from your presence as

I need you every day, if I ascend into Heaven you are there, if I make my bed in hell, behold you my beloved Lord will be there, for my Lord your loving kindness indeed never ceases, your compassion will never fail me, as you lift me up.

15 May Gods love be gracious to us as he blesses us and makes his face shine upon us, your words are a lamp unto my feet and a light to my path, as I put my trust in you my Lord with all of my heart and my soul; as I lean on you for strength and understanding,

16 In all your ways I acknowledge you as you direct my paths for the fear of God is the beginning of knowledge, but the foolish despise wisdom and instructions; but he who listens to me shall live securely and will be at ease from the dread of all evil, and the enemy of the mind; those who have ears let them hear. *AMEN*

77
Touched by God And Abounding in Love

1 Your righteousness is like the highest mountains; your justice is like the great deep, deep calls to deep at the noise of your waterfalls, and your waves they rush over me, may the God of hope fill you with all the joy and peace in believing so that by the power of the Holy Spirit you will abound in hope; touched by God and Abounding in love.

2 I say un to you that your faith should not stand in the wisdom of others, but only in the presence and the power of God, for it is God that has made his wonderful works to be remembered, the Lord he is so gracious and fulfilling in his compassion for you,

3 Touched by God and abounding in love, visit me my Lord with your salvation. Turning to me and having mercy upon me, as you always do to those who love you in your name and because of our great trust in you, my God, through our beloved Lord Jesus Christ.

4 Touched by God and Abounding in love, when I your God says unto you, don't worry about anything, instead pray about everything, tell me what you need and thank me for all that I have done, and loving me with all your heart and your soul; so that you can approach Gods throne of grace an confidence, so that we may receive mercy and find peace and grace to help us in our time of need.

5 We come to share in Jesus Christ our saviour if indeed we hold our original conviction firmly to the very end, for faith is the confidence that what we hope for will actually happen; it gives us assurance my great one about things we cannot see, for we do walk by faith and not by sight, I want to be touched by God and abounding in love.

6 God you are my refuge and strength, a very present help in my times of trouble, your comfort gives me so much hope and faith, to be touched by God and abounding in love, I can do all things through you my Lord Jesus for it is you who strengthens me, power through your Spirit, in your inner being.

7 Beware beloved, I say unto you, do not also believe every spirit, but I say to you this; test the spirit to see whether they are from God, for many are false prophets that have gone out into the world, for they are not from me your God, they must be cut down for they are false Christs and they will rise and they will show signs of wonders to seduce if possible, even the elect; for these false prophets do not serve the Lord your God.

8 But listen and learn for I am with you, stay in Joy and in hope, being patient in affliction, stay faithful in your prayers, encouraging one another, building each other up, just as you are doing now; keep the confessions of your sins going admitting to them to me in prayer for I your God are listening, praying also to one another and believing that you are healed; for the prayer of a righteous person has great power as it is working, to be touched by God and abounding in Love.

78
My Heart

1 My heart has heard you say to me, come and talk with me, and my heart it responds, my Lord I am coming for I do delight myself in you, and my Lord i shall walk in grace and faith as you give me the desires of your heart, my heart is fixed Oh God my heart it is fixed as I sing praises to you all day long.

2 Let your heart therefore be perfect with God, our God to walk in his statutes and to keep his commandments as from this day forth, for you shall love the Lord your God with all of your heart and soul.

3 Thanks be to God for his unspeakable gift, his name will be called wonderful councillor, mighty God, everlasting prince of peace; my heart it exalts in him, my soul longs for him, as my heart and my flesh cry out for my living God.

4 As your name deserves Oh God, you will be praised to the ends of the Earth; your strong right hand is filled with victory; lift me up for my heart and soul needs you, you have showed me the way of life, you have granted me the joy of your presence and the pleasures of living with you forever, my heart it rejoices in you, blessed are you by me my Lord and saviour, I have so much joy in my life and in your presence.

5 You have granted me life and favour and my Lord you are caring, and that care has preserved my Spirit for it is you who blesses the righteous Oh Lord you have surrounded me with favour like a shield, blessed is the one who hears you Oh Lord; watching daily at your gates waiting at the posts of your doors for their my Hearts happy and longing to see your beauty.

6 The Spirit it gives life and the flesh it counts for nothing, the words of God you have spoken to me; they are filled with the Spirit and life blessed be the God and Father of our Lord Jesus Christ who has blesses us with every spiritual blessings in Heavenly places in Christ;

7 Reach down from Heaven and rescue me for you drew me out of deep waters and filled my heart with peace and joy, forever will I remain with you, my beloved Lord, Jesus Christ, Hallelujah and Amen.

79
My God, My Strength

1 I love you Lord, My God, My Strength; into your arms at my birth that was the day I became your child; that was the day that you became my God, my God you are love and I remain in love, I remain in you, and you remain in me; I love you because you loved me first, you gave me life, my God, my strength.

2 As I take good heed unto myself; that I do love you my Lord, my God, Oh Lord my strength, for there is no fear in love, but only perfect love that casts out fear, for fear only involves torment, however a loving God brings forth love, peace, joy and happiness, I your Lord God says unto you; thou shalt love your Lord your god, seek the kingdom of God above all else and live righteously; and I will give you everything you need, Oh God my strength, you have given me the greatest gift which is finding you, and now is our salvation nearer than when we believe.

3 My Lord I ask of you, how shall we escape if we ignore so great a salvation? I say unto you, honour the Lord your God from your wealth and from the first of your produce, for I am the first and I am the last, apart from me, there is no God; Oh God my strength, you are my God, and early will I seek you, for my soul it thirsts for you.

4 Those who love me I will deliver, I will protect those who know my name, when you call on me, I will answer you, I will be there for you in your troubled times to give you back your peace, by rescuing you for you have honoured me and I will honour you with long life I will satisfy you; I will give and show you my salvation, peace and grace, from God our Father and your Lord and saviour Jesus Christ is my name, My God, My strength.

5 My God, My Strength, now therefore as I pray to you, for I have found favour in your sight, I pray that you show me your ways, so that I might know you deeper and deeply, so deep is calling to deep, for I know that you withhold no good thing from those who do what is right, for sin shall no longer be our master; because we are not under the law, but under grace for under your fullness we all shall receive grace upon grace.

6 My Lord how your love and grace abounds in me and how your love and grace picks me up when I fail and fall short, yes I do think of you always as my shortfalls and the grace flows over me like a beautiful waterfall,

7 Never letting me stray of your pathway for very long, my God my strength; I love and need your embrace day after day your truths keep me ever so close to your spirit, for you are my rock and my fortress, for your names sake, you do lead me and guide my ways.

8 My God, My strength, you do ordain peace for us, for you also have done all our works in us, lighting our pathway and crushing darkness, which makes us fail when we lose our strength, I ask of you, My God my strength, Oh my God of peace crush Satan under my feet, do this my Lord for my family and me, By the grace of my Lord Jesus Christ to be with me always.

9 I say unto you, that I have come as light into this world, so that everyone who believes in me will not remain in darkness, if you are filled with light with no dark corners, then your whole life will be radiant as though a floodlight where filling you with light, for no one lights a lamp and hides it; so seek only of peacefulness, be touched by Gods grace believe in me and be filled with light so then your light shall break forth like the dawn,

10 And your healing shall spring up speedily, your righteousness shall go before you, the glory of your Lord God shall be your rear guard, My Lord, My God, My Strength and My Shield, my heart has trusted in you since finding you and you finding me, although I was never lost in your sight; I am helped therefore my heart greatly rejoices with my prayers and songs, I can only thank you , no wonder my heart is glad and rejoices and my body rests safely in you.

11 My God, My strength, My Lord, you are my home, my church, my temple, my safety, my God, my strength, my rejoicing, my peace, my happiness, my heart, my Holy Spirit within, my light, my health, my joy, my love, my wonder, my beauty, my salvation, my righteousness, my glory, my prayers, my guidance, my rock, my fortress, my helper, my pathway, my blessings, my deep waters, my victory, my refuge, my abounding love, my confidence, my forgiveness, my compassion, my mercy, my wisdom, my soul, my fear, my shelter, my delight, my spiritual teacher, my everlasting life, my awareness, my self control, my unfailing love, my patience, my rest, my transformation, my kindness, my mind, my body, my living drink, my divine wonder, my living bread, my sacrifice, my holiness, my touch, my breath, my eternal king, my great invisible spirit, my justice, my vapour, my creator, my workmanship, my good works, my rose of Sharon, my lily of the valley, my saviour, my conqueror, my redeemer, my meditation,

my anointing, my purity, my fruit, my morning star, my almighty, my understanding, my trust, my faith, my believing, my knowledge, my everlasting love, my faithfulness, my power, my perfectness, my gift, my provision, my preservation, my wholeness, my healing, my eyes, my hearing, my thoughts, my robe, my gratitude, my strong right hand, my word, my truth, my beginning and my end, my treasure, my miracle, my insight, my divine within, my consciousness, my innermost fullness, my Lord within, my father in heaven, my rewarder, my blood of the lamb, my God of Israel, my king of kings, my humility, my steadfast spirit, my willingness, my desire, my shining sun, my spring of water, my fragrance, my deliverer, my sanctuary, my perfect peace, my inheritance, my Holy Kingdom, my heavenly places, my deliverance, my cleansing, my discretion, my eternal life, my consuming fire, my comforter, my lion of Judea, my strong tower, my disciplinarian, my heavy heartedness,

You are all of this and so much more; you are my Holy one,

You are my Lord, Jesus Christ
Amen and Amen

80
Bathe me my Lord

1 Bathe me in your power my Lord,

Bathe me in your truth my Lord,

Bathe me my Lord in your Holy Spirit,

Bathe me my Lord in your righteousness,

Bathe me in your light my Lord,

Bathe me in your hope,

Bathe me in your army of Angels,

Bathe me in your peace my Lord,

Bathe me my Lord in your Holiness,

Bathe me in all your Joy,

Bathe me my Lord in your Holy place,

Bathe me in all your happiness,

Bathe me my Lord in your wondrous glory,

Bathe me for I need you, and your strength,

Bathe me will all your Passion,

Bathe me my Lord with wisdom,

Bathe me my Lord with the power of your Holy Blood,

Bathe me my Lord with your broken body,

Bathe me my Lord with all faithfulness,

Bathe me with love and praise,

Bathe me with the light of your presence,

Bathe me my Lord with all your miracles,

Bathe me with the fruits of the vine,

Bathe me from redemption,

Bathe me my Lord with deep rushing waters,

Bathe me my Lord with the book of life,

Bathe me my Lord with courage and compassion,

Bathe me my Lord in protection from all evil,

Bathe me my Lord with eternal life,

Bathe me with your constant love,

Bathe me my Lord with your stronghold,

Bathe me my Lord with answered prayers,

Bathe me my Lord with your shinning face,

Bathe me my Lord with gladness,

Bathe me my Lord with your security,

Bathe me my Lord with mercy,

Bathe me my Lord with your gentle loving kindness,

Bathe me my Lord, with faith believing,

Bathe me my Lord with the Law of commandments,

Bathe me my Lord with the Holy robes of righteousness,

Bathe me my Lord, for I am a believer of God,

Bathe me my Lord with the truth, the words of God,

Bathe me my Lord, with contentment and peace,

Bathe me my Lord with compassion,

Bathe me my Lord with forgiveness,

Bathe me my Lord for the forgiveness of all my sins,

Bathe me my Lord with repentance,

Bathe me my Lord with your Holy Hands,

Bathe me my Lord, with the Love of God,

Bathe me my Lord, my beloved Lord Jesus Christ.

Bathe me my Lord as I say to you thank you for hearing all my Prayers.

Bathe me my Lord as I pray always to you,

Amen and Amen

81

Do all that you can to live in Peace

1 Do all that you can to live in peace with everyone; do not accuse anyone for no reason, especially if they have done you no harm, for he that loves not knows not God, for anyone who knows God knows that he is love.

2 Let us pursue what does make for peace and mutual up building, for blessed are the peacemakers, for they shall be called the children of God, rejoicing in hope, being patient in tribulation, be in continuous and constant prayer, for when you ask it will be given unto you, seek and you will find, knock and the door shall be opened to you, do all that you can to live in peace.

3 As you take delight in the Lord, he will give you your Hearts desires, pray without ceasing, in nothing be anxious, but in everything by prayer and petition, with thanks giving, let your requests be made known to God, do all that you can to live in peace.

4 In all your ways acknowledge the Lord, as he directs your path; cast all your anxieties and your doubts of him, because he cares for you;

for our Lord he is good, and a refuge in your troubled times, for he cares for those who put all their faith, trust and hope in him, abide in me and I will abide in you, live in me and I will live in you, do all that you can to live in peace.

5 Put your trust in the Lord and he will lead you in the right way; he will protect you from all evil, you will feel safe and sound; you know that you are saved, a child of God, wrapped safely in your fathers loving arms, do all that you can to live in peace, in the clouds of heaven, you will find your sleep and your peace.

6 Our Lord he takes pleasure when he saves a beloved child, beautifying the afflicted ones with salvation, but if they listen and obey God they will be blessed with prosperity throughout all of your years, all of your years will be as pleasant as can be, to live in peace, showing God that you love him, putting all your faith, hope and trust in him.

7 Let me live in peace Lord, show me the way; I say unto you, I set my rainbow in the clouds for it to be a sign of the covenant between me and the Earth, for you to do all that you can to live in peace and in harmony, do not suffer anymore, lean on me, and be in prayer; I will give you signs along the way, the sign of the son of man will appear also in the sky, and people will see the son of man in all his power and in all his glory.

8 I will gather all my children up bringing them into the clouds to meet the Lord in the air, and we will be with the Lord forever, no more suffering and your peace you will finally find, my Lord you are my light and my Salvation so why should I be afraid? I will do all that I can to live in peace, for you are my fortress, you are just wanting to protect me, from all danger, so why should I even tremble? My Lord God you are my refuge and my strength a very present help in trouble.

9 Oh my gracious Lord, how gracious you've been to me, as I long for you; be my strength I plea thee, I wake every moment during the night, thinking of you; for salvation in my stressed times, as you say unto me, be still and know that I am the Lord your God, do all that you can to live in peace, remembering child that I am ever so close to "Reach" giving all your cares and worries to the Lord your God, for he cares for you, so close to be reached, I will hear and obey you Lord, for you speak only off peace, ordaining peace for us.

82

I need your comfort my Lord

1 All my distress, I call upon my Lord, to wipe away tears, asking you why do they fall, these tears of mine, please explain my Lord; I am asking you is it me verses this world, I need your comfort my Lord, it's hard to explain, since I've found you my Lord, I don't need people anymore, in the world we live in, and the people we see, is it a test my Lord, to open our eyes and see.

2 Bathe me more my Lord in your glorious light, for I do believe in your word, the word and the truth of God, I feel selfish my Lord for you have done so much for me, is this why I feel I should fear you my Lord God, the guilt, the ramifications, the wrath and power of God; to be saved by my Lord Jesus, Father it's all that I have, I believe, I trust, I hope and have faith for what I feel, for what you have done, for what you have shown me, the love for you that I have, I need your comfort my Lord.

3 Its comforting my Lord when I feel your presence in my heart, your present in me every day and every night, I'll never forget what you have done for my life, and I do understand Lord that without you I am nothing at all;

However I do believe that children of God do they suffer more, but what always breaks them free is their love for our Lord Jesus Christ, you can feel really sad, but at the same time happy and content inside, for I know that is where you reside, my Holy Spirit, my God.

4 It's a different sadness my Lord, not like before, I do still cry though, but I cry more for my joy from my Lord, and the pain that is real, it's flesh complaining that is all; but there is nothing that is more important than the love that I feel for my beloved Lord God; I do understand that it is hard to get away from this world, But I can't bless people who annoy me my Lord, for they would curse me for using the words of God, but you are the judge you are the supreme power, why can't unbelievers see that you are a truly amazing God, to live in this world I need your comfort my Lord, in my prayers to you every day and every night, my God my Holy Spirit, where you will; in me reside.

5 All that you have done I feel truly blessed my Lord, you've given me so much and you have changed me and my life; because I needed and called on you, my beloved Lord God; my life was turning upside down, you came and blessed me in all that I needed, in business and in health; for all that had gone wrong, you've turned it all from negative to positive, oh thankyou my Lord, I understand and I know what you have done my Lord God, and I am writing this for you because you have placed in on my heart; your wonderful and you are amazing and I am so glad to have you, I truly now know that you are with me, and you will never let me go.

6 I don't want to let you go my Lord I only wish I had found you long, long ago, you are so deep inside me now, I would feel lost without you, and I understand Lord I will always struggle with this world, I will always have my Lord and I now understand why, I was always with you as I remember as a young child my Lord, I had seen vision as a baby that I remember my Lord, Now I realise and know why all the sins that had happened in my life, it was darkness trying to take me away from my God, and you waited my Lord, you waited too long, but that's how I feel because of my love for you my God, It didn't matter to you, did it my Lord, for time doesn't matter in Heaven above; you have me now, a saved child of God, repented and blessed because of my beloved Lord my saviour, Jesus Christ.

7 Heavenly music playing played for me to hear; acknowledgment from Father, angels singing, a blessing my Lord, knowing that you will help me every step of the way, all of your children who love you feel this way its knowing that they have repented, and are longing to be saved, to be in heaven for eternity; a long side you my beloved Lord,

8 But you haven't failed me only my flesh and this world; knowing though that you are with me now and will help pick me up when I fall and I call; it's a blessing from Heaven a gift from God, to show me and tell me that you are never far away; I say unto, keep your faith, your believing, and your love and trust in your God.

9 Thankyou my Lord, for coming through for me, to help me understand and to write this from me to you, to get me through what I am feeling right now and what I need to say to you; not wanting to fail you again; I needed you to understand that I'll love you always my Lord, but you just reminded me that you already knew that because, you already know what's in my true heart, and of course you do; my amazing God, my God of loving-kindness' and my God with the amazing heart, I just needed your comfort my Lord, my God.

83
My meditation of my Heart

1 Let the words of my mouth, and meditation of my heart be acceptable in your sight; Oh my Lord my strength, and my redeemer, I will meditate on your words, your precepts as my eyes are fixed on your ways of value, your paths of righteousness, the light of your life.

2 The way of the righteous is always smooth, Oh upright one, make my pathway of the righteous level, for the way of righteous is like the first gleam of the dawn, which shines ever so brighter, until it's the full light of the day, my meditation of my heart.

3 In all things; I gave you an example, that so labouring you ought to help the weak and to remember the words of the Lord Jesus, that he himself said; it is more blessed to give than to receive, my meditation of my heart, my Lord Jesus Christ.

4 The flowers are springing up, the season of singing birds has come, and the cooing of turtledoves will fill the air; the wilderness and the solitary place shall be glad for them, and the desert shall rejoice and blossom as the rose it's like the dew of Israel; he shall blossom like the lily, my meditation of my heart, the smell of the flowers in the air, the rainbow overlooks all the beauty everywhere.

5 I will fetch my knowledge from afar and will ascribe righteousness to my maker; the almighty is beyond our reach and exalted in power, in this justice and great righteousness he does not oppress, truly God will not do wrong, the almighty will not twist justice; my meditation of my heart, the loving-kindness' of God.

6 Let justice roll on like a river and the righteousness like a mighty stream, learn to be good; in Jesus' name; summon your power Oh God giving us strength for your divine power has given me everything, my meditation of my heart will give me eternal life, for great is my Lord, greatly to be praised.

7 I can never escape from your spirit I can never get away from your presence; if I go up to heaven I know you'll be there, to reach out your hand there'll be rejoicing, the presence of Angels everywhere that's your promise God, being a child of yours, my meditation of my heart, I love you my Lord Jesus Christ.

84
Being swift to hear

1 Oh my gracious Lord, how the Heavens will praise your wonders, and your faithfulness also in the assembly of the Holy ones, the Heavens proclaim the glory of God through our Lords mercies we are not consumed, because his compassion will fail us not; they are new every morning oh my Lord how great is your faithfulness, being swift to hear.

2 My God who is so faithful, who will not allow you to tremble above what you are able, and thank you be unto God who always causes us to triumph in Christ, and to make manifest the fragrance of his knowledge by us in every place, being swift to hear, come closer to your Lord.

3 How shall I come before you my Lord and bow myself before the exalted God that you are; shall I come before you with burnt offerings, now he who supplies seeds to the sower and bread for food who will also supply and increase your store of seed and will enlarge the harvest of your righteousness.

4 The Lord he will give me strength and to all his people; the Lord will bless his people with peace, being swift to hear, I praise and glorify you Oh gracious Lord; who holds my heart.

5 Great peace; have those who love your law my Lord for nothing can make them stumble for every good gift and every perfect gift is from heaven above; it comes down from the Father of lights, with whom there is no variableness neither shadow of turning, let everyone be swift to hear and slow to anger, slow to speak; walking upright for the Lord, true blessed children of the Lord God.

6 Be doers of the word and not merely heavens who deceive themselves, for blessed is the man who walks not in the counsel of the ungodly, nor stands in the path of sinners nor sit's in the seat of the scornful, but his delight is in the law of the Lord and in his law he meditates day and night, being swift to hear, remaining with your beloved Lord.

7 And all the works of the righteousness shall be peace, and the effects of righteousness with quietness and confidence for ever; Oh taste and see that the Lord is good, blessed is the man that trusts in him, blessed are the ones who believe and trust for these are the ones who are faithful to the Lord thy God; being swift to hear, as I grant you whatever you need.

8 Your works are swift, your comfort is grand, your loving kindness is joyous as we put our hearts into your word; our hearts into our Lord Jesus Christ, our belief is strong as we put our faith into you, our hearts will forever remain, where you do in our Holy Spirit my Lord' being swift to hear, blessed my Lord remain in me please, Oh my gracious Lord.

9 The kingdom of Heaven, is where we are longing to be, a real home my lord much better than the home which we now live; a real family so trusting, so loving and so kind; peace and no trouble, no one to hurt you all the time, being swift to hear, how we need your strength my beloved, my Lord Jesus Christ I place my heart and soul into your hands, to hold.

10 Being swift to hear; it is what I have learnt from you; our hearts and eye's always completely now fixed on you; we just can't seem to get enough of you, you are always on our minds, always looking over our shoulders, just wondering where you are; but we do know that you are there, and we do want to be good, only on our best behaviour, just to please you my Lord.

11 We do feel like little children knowing that we must behave, like children not wanting to be in trouble, by our heavenly father "our dad" do you understand; do you know how we feel, we want to behave, for we deeply love you father and our Lord Jesus; the son of man; being swift to hear, your teaching us well; in our belief and all our trust, which comes from who we rely on the most, our Lord Jesus Christ.

12 How you make me feel, as the more that you take my heart, no one can take me away from my beloved God; my tears are of pure love, drawing me even closer to you, as I write for you more, knowing that your holding my hand, you touch my soul like no one has ever done before my Lord; you hold my hand as my pen is writing your words, being swift to hear my words from my beloved Lord, your truly God, how blessed I feel knowing that you are by my side, I praise you Oh Lord as I say to you AMEN.

85
"Gods way"
It's perfect in every way

1 for all we have done to transform our lives, I praise you my Lord God with all of my heart, I will glorify your Holy name forever; our lives glorious for the perfection of beauty, as God shines forth onto us for who is God, except the Lord? And who is our rock, except our God, a God so worthy before us, whom we bow down to, and to receive glory and honour and power, our creator of all, our king eternal, immortal, invisible to God who alone is wise, Gods way it's perfect in every way, glory to God, forever and ever.

2 Gods way it's perfect in every way all the Lords promises are true, he is our shield of love and our protection, don't trust in yourself and be a fool, walk in only wisdom; and God will bring you safely through, every word of Gods is true for to this end we will only toil with trouble and struggles, because we have our hope set on the living God, who is our Lord and Saviour Jesus Christ, our Saviour of people especially when we believe, that's our Gods way it's perfect in every way.

3 Oh how great is your goodness which you have laid up for those who fear you; which you have prepared for those who trust in you in the presence of the sons of men; trusting in the Lord at all times, pouring our hearts out to him, God is our refuge; Gods way is perfect in every way, my soul shall be joyful in my Lord God; as we pray with our love for him and in our hearts every single day and night.

4 For my Lord God he is awesome I cherish all that you have done; my heart explodes with excitement when I feel your presence so near; when in the word of God my eyes fill with tears, my Holy Spirit alive, all because of my Lord Jesus Christ, a teacher and a healer, when you believe and trust in his love; he will always be with you, but call on him when you must, he is waiting for you to call and to put your whole trust in him, that is why he has saved you, so let God do his job, he will work on you, he is a loving God, for God's way it's perfect in every way, just remember saved and loved child of our Lord Jesus Christ.

5 The peace of God which passes all understanding shall guard your hearts and your thoughts in Jesus Christ; so what do you benefit if you gain the whole world, but lose your soul? So this is the witness that God has given to us "eternal life" and this life is in his beloved son, he is my beloved my Lord and my Saviour Jesus Christ, and Gods way it's perfect in every way, do not ever lose sight, for our Lord he is wonderful and so ready to forgive, and abundantly in mercy, to all who call upon him.

6 My Lord you make known to me, the path of life, you fill me with joy every single day and night, for my Lord you are pure, and as I put my hope in you; I shall keep myself pure like Christ, as the peace of my Lord rules my Heart, forever more; Gods way it is perfect in every way, gracious and full of compassion, as he showers this compassion on all his creations, giving breath to everyone, I am the Lord your God; I have called you in righteousness, to take you by the hand and to keep you, let my words dwell in you, for I am, who I am; The Word of God.

AMEN

86

I am the door, the doorway to Heaven

1 I your Lord say unto you, I know my own and my own will recognize me, as my Father knows me, and I know my Father, am I not a giver of my very own life and did I not lay down for you, know and recognize my voice and the voice of Father so you can know and recognize the difference of the voice of deception, for if you know Gods character by learning, reading and following the bible, you will then understand how God has lead others out of deception leading you to safety, I am the door, the doorway to heaven, I am the Lord your God.

2 Understanding God is to understand and know what we have heard is something that God would say; for God he does not contradict his word, but your wisdom and common sense should prevail, if you however truly believe, truly belong to the Lord God he will give you peace, give you knowledge to know his voice, from voices of deception, so not to be deceived, so you can be safe and have the confidence by believing that your Father in Heaven is guiding you to follow him in the right direction, for our Lord will let us know either to go forward or to wait, I am the door, the doorway to Heaven, I am the Lord your God.

3 I say unto you I have no intentions to let my children down, nor to allow deception to interfere in what I want for my children, however put in an effort for me, listen and follow in the word, so you do not stray, stay on the pathway so not to get into trouble or to be deceived, I your Lord am the Good shepherd and I do know my own, my own will recognize me, I am the door, the doorway to Heaven, I am the Lord your God.

4 You are born my sheep and I am your shepherd he who enters my door is the shepherd of the sheep, the watchman opens the door for the man, and the sheep listen, I will call my own sheep by name and lead them out, my sheep will hear me and they will follow, they trust me and are guided by my voice, I will lead them through the door, they will be saved "will live" I will come to you and you will find the pasture in Heaven, for I am the door, the doorway to Heaven, I am the Lord your God.

5 Deception will come in to destroy you; I am your Lord Jesus the good Shepherd and I only want to save you, so come and take my hand as I lead you on your way, follow my voice, the pathway to righteousness, I am the good shepherd trying to save my good sheep, the word is the way, the only way to be led; open your eyes and wipe away those tears, I am the light showing you the way, I am the door, the doorway into Heaven, I am the Lord your God.

6 My sheep they sometimes stray when they fail to understand, my sheep sometimes get lost when they do not believe in God, they try but cannot find their way, they are sometimes blind to this world, but I will wait I am patient; more patient than my beloved sheep; and they will fall into place when they open up their eyes and see, stop struggling with darkness, look for my light and just believe, for faith comes with faithfulness, those who have ears let then hear, those who have eyes let them see, I am the light, I am the door, the door way to Heaven, I am the Lord your God.

87

To forever live in Eternal life

1 Verily, Verily I say unto you he that believes in me will have everlasting life, I am your Lord God, I am the resurrection and the life; he that believes in me though he were dead, yet shall life; and whosoever lives and believes in me shall never die, believe in this to live forever in eternal life.

2 Behold I show you a mystery, we shall not all sleep but we shall all be changed in a moment in the twinkling of an eye at the last trump, for the trumpet shall sound and the dead shall be raised incorruptible, and we shall be changed, for this corruptible must put on in corruption, and this mortal must put on immortality, to forever live in eternal life.

3 When this corruptible shall have put on in corruption, and this mortal shall have put on immortality, then shall it be bought to pass the saying that is written, death is swallowed up in victory, and this is the promise that God has promised us, Eternal Life; to forever live in eternal life,

4 For since by man came death, by man also came the resurrection of the Dead, these things have I written unto you that believe on the name of the son of God so that you may know that you have eternal life, and that you may believe on the name of the son of God, and to forever live in Eternal Life.

5 Marvel not at this, for I say unto you that the hour is coming in which all that are in the graves shall hear his voice, and shall come unto the resurrection of life, and they that have done evil unto the resurrection of damnation.

6 For I the Lord himself shall descend from the Heavens with a shout, with the voice of the Archangel, and with the trump of God, and the dead in Christ shall rise first; to forever live in Eternal Life.

7 Therefore are they before the throne of God, and serve him day and he that sits on the throne shall dwell among them, they shall hunger no more neither shall they thirst anymore, neither shall the sunlight on them, neither the heat, for the lamb which is in the midst of their throne shall feed them, and shall lead them into the living fountains of waters, and God shall wipe away all the tears from their eyes, and forever live in eternal life.

8 Oh God who so loved the world that he gave his only begotten son, for who believed in him, that will not perish, but by the promise of God will have eternal life.

9 So also is the resurrection of the dead, it is sown in corruption, it is raised in corruption, it is sown in dishonour, it is raised in glory, it is sown in weakness, but it is raised in power, it is sown in the natural body, and raised in the spiritual body, there is a natural body and there is a spiritual body.

10 However if the spirit of him that rose up our Lord Jesus Christ from the dead dwells in you, he that rose up our Lord Jesus from the dead shall also quicken your mortal body by his spirit that dwells in you.

11 And our God who will wipe away all of our tears from our eyes, there shall be no more death, neither sorrow nor crying, nor pain, from all the former things that have passed away; for the wages of sin are death, but the gift of God is Eternal life through our beloved Lord and saviour Jesus Christ.

12 Oh my Lord though after my skin; worms will destroy this body, yet in my flesh I see only you, my God, whom I shall see for myself, and my eyes shall behold your beauty, and not another, for this is no body but my Lord and my saviour, who has done more for me than any other, saved me and comforted me like no other, though my reins be consumed within me.

13 For I say unto you, my child, for it is he that soweth after his flesh, seeking of the flesh reaps only corruption, but the one that soweth of the spirit shall of the spirit reap life everlasting, to forever live in eternal life, and it's the many that sleep in the dust of the earth that shall awaken, some to everlasting life and some to shame and everlasting contempt, for all will be judged.

14 The dead men shall live together with my dead body shall they arise, awaken and sing you that dwell in the dust, for the dew is as the dew of herbs and the Earth shall cast out the dead, for they will not leave my soul in hell neither will they suffer the Holy one to see corruption but to forever live in Eternal life,

15 But is now made manifest by the appearing of our Lord and Saviour Jesus Christ, who has abolished death, and has brought life and immortality to light through our scriptures, the Holy Bible, and this is the record that God has given to us to forever live in Eternal life, and this life is in his son.

16 I understand and know my Lord that if our Earthly house of this tabernacle were to dissolve; we have a building of God and a house not made with hands Eternal in the Heavens; for in my Father's house are many beautiful mansions if it were not so I would have told you, I go to prepare a place for you, and if I go and prepare a place for you, I will come again and receive you unto myself, that where I am there you may be also to live forever in eternal life.

17 For they shall be accounted worthy to obtain that world and the resurrection from the dead, for they are neither married or given in marriage, neither can they die no more, for they are the children of God, being the children of the resurrection, I say to you my sheep they hear my voice, and I know them and they follow me, and I give them eternal life, they shall never perish, neither shall any man pluck them out of my hand.

18 Who so ever eats my flesh and drinks my blood, I say unto you they shall forever live in Eternal life, I will raise them up at the last day, those who have eyes let them see, those who have ears let them hear, let thine ears hear a word behind thee, saying this is the way you walk in it, when you turn to the right hand and when you turn to the left,

19 For this God is our God forever and ever he will be our guide even until death, a man's heart decides his ways, but the Lord directs his steps, the steps of a good man the Lord he orders, and the Lord he delights in his ways.

88
Trust in Wisdom And Gods love and Grace

1 For your Lord God he is a son and a safe covering; he will hold back nothing good from those who walk in the way that is right, oh my Lord my God, how happy are those who walk and trust in wisdom and Gods love and grace.

2 I say unto you trust in the Lord and always do good so you can live in the land that was provided for you; and I can feed you for without me you are nothing, so be happy in the Lord, and I will give you your hearts desires, I will hear your prayers for you give your way over to me, trust in wisdom and Gods love and grace, trust in him also, and he will give unto you, for your loyalty and faith.

3 Do not trust in your own understanding as you do for it will account for nothing, it will only cause you grief and confusion, thrust in the Lord your God with all of your heart and your soul, I say unto you have I ever truly let you down, agree with me in all your Ways, for I will make your paths straight, how happy are you when you do understand that I have answered your prayers, you have not turned to the proud or to the followers of lies for you recognize putting all your trust in wisdom and Gods love and Grace.

4 A believer who puts faith and trust in the Lord are like mount Zion which cannot be moved, but stands steadfast forever, the work of being right and goodness will give peace from the right and good work will come quiet, trust forever as you are now children of God, because you have put trust in your Lord and saviour Jesus Christ, your trust in wisdom and Gods love and grace.

5 But as for you, always hold on to what you have learned and know it to be true, remember where you have learned them, you have known the Holy writings since you were a child; they are able to give you wisdom that leads to being saved from the punishment of the sins of the world in which you live, the heartache and all the grief you are facing; for putting your trust and faith in your Lord and saviour Jesus Christ, for I say unto you, trust in wisdom and Gods love and grace.

6 For your God he is a loving and caring God, he so loved the world that he gave his only son to whoever puts trust in Gods son, they will not be lost but they will have life that lasts forever, I say unto you that all the earlier preachers spoke of this; trust in wisdom and Gods love and grace for everyone who puts their trust in Christ will have his sins forgiven through my name.

7 The Holy writings say "see" I put in Jerusalem a stone that people will trip over, it is a rock that will make them fall, but the person who puts all their love and trust in the rock who is I your Lord Jesus Christ; will not be put to shame, live in me and I will live in you.

8 He gave the right and all the power to become children of God to those who receive him, He gave all this to those who love and put trust in his Holy name, my gracious and loving Lord, I trust in wisdom and Gods love and grace; I will love you forever and all the days of my life, all that you give me to say and write gives me faith believing, love and trust in wisdom, to write with fellowship with my Lord God.

9 I say unto you, whoever puts trust in Gods son, is not guilty and whoever does not put trust in Gods son in him is guilty already; It is because he does not put his trust in the name of the only son of God, for he who puts his trust in his son has life that lasts forever, he who does not put his trust in the son of God will not have life, but only the anger of God, which is on him.

10 The Holy writings say; "see" I lay down in Jerusalem a stone of great worth far more than any amount of money, anyone who puts his trust in him will not be ashamed, trust in wisdom and Gods love and grace, so I say unto you put your trust in your Lord Jesus and you and your family will be saved from the punishment of sin; I came to the world to be a light, anyone who puts his trust in me, will not be in darkness.

11 I say unto you that I am the bread of life, keep coming to me, Oh my children of God and I promise you; you will never be Hungry you always put your trust in me and I promise you; you will never be thirsty, trust in wisdom and Gods love and grace, for sure, I tell you, you do this and you will have life that lasts forever.

12 For the one that does not have wisdom I ask God for it, seek and you will find, ask and you will have, for God he is always ready to give to you; God he will never say that you are wrong for asking, he will teach you about his ways, My Lord God you are so kind and understanding, your faithfulness never lets us down, your promise is to never leave us, your words and your pathways are from righteousness as you teach us your ways of truth, so we can walk in your pathways of righteousness, to never stray, for the law it will go out from Zion and the word from you my Lord from Jerusalem, Amen.

13 I say unto you I will show you the way as I show and continue to teach you, in the way you should go; I will tell you what to do with my eyes upon you, for God he has given wisdom and much learning and joy to the person who is good in Gods eyes.

14 Then you will understand the fear of the Lord, and find what is known of God, for I your Lord gives wisdom and much learning and understanding and this comes from my mouth, for I your Lord stores up perfect wisdom for those who are right, I am a safe covering to those who are in right standing in there walk, trust in wisdom and Gods love and grace.

15 "see" you want truth deep within the heart, and you will make me know wisdom in the hidden places, I your Lord Gods son has come, to give you understanding to know me; who the true god is, you are joined together with the true God through I your Lord Jesus, I am the true God, I am the life that lasts forever.

16 I will give you honour and faithfulness; and thanks to you my Lord and my true God, who has told me what to do "yes" even at night my mind it teaches me "for it was God who said" the light will shine in darkness, for he is the one who made his light shine in our hearts; this brings us the light of knowing, Gods shining- greatness which is seen in my Lord Jesus Christs face Oh as I put all my hope and my trust in wisdom and Gods love and grace.

17 Sinful people who will not change do not understand what is right and fair, but it is those who will look to you, my Lord Jesus who understands all things, who can take and turn you in an instant, I can just stop everything and pray turning to you for help and knowing in my heart that you are really there, and that you will answer all prayers not just mine and acknowledge, Jesus oh who has answered me; you gave me all my hope, you listened, you love and you care; you have helped me on many occasions, have changed my life around, bringing peace into my life,

18 I have so much to be thankful for, my heart truly aches for you, because of my faith and my trust in you, nobody could ever change my heart and take you away from me, I understand that when I call upon you, you will hold my hand, your compassion and your love is undeniable, deep with love' and that is how I feel, trust in wisdom and Gods love and grace, and you too can have something truly amazing, your Lord God forever and ever in eternal peace and love.

19 I will never be ashamed to tell anyone about your love and what you can do, your miracles working every day within us, It is only our ignorance that doesn't see, we cannot acknowledge what we refuse to see; blind you may say that our eyes cannot perceive; what you have done for them, we see only what we can, understand and comprehend, when it is you my Lord that deserves all the credit, for all the miracles that you have done; we really don't understand,

20 It's the power of Lord God, the power of believing, the power of the word of God, the power of your people, "the Jewish first" the apple of your eye, how I am glad I have found my Lord, to believe I have life and eternal peace above; for all who obey; your children who trust and believe; for the opening up of your word which gives light it gives life; and understanding to the child like, who have faith believing in God,

21 For the word of our Lord it is a lamp that can lead your way, follow the light and you will find the word and the Lord and you will be safe and saved; you my Lord Jesus are the teacher for all, give me your hand Oh my Lord and never let me go, you are my teacher, I am in fellowship with you, train me give me wisdom, give me the word my Lord, words that can punish, to keep us in the word and the light my Lord, the way of life to be shown; trust in wisdom and Gods love and grace.

AMEN MY LORD AMEN

89
Trust in the Teacher I am

1 I say unto you as it is written behold; I lay in Sion a stumbling stone of offence and whosoever believes on him shall not be ashamed for as many who received Jesus to them he gave power to become the sons of God; even to them that believe in Jesus name.

2 He that believes in Jesus is not condemned, but he that believes not is condemned already because he has not believed in the name of the only begotten son of God, he that believes has everlasting life; wherefore also it is contained in scripture, behold I lay in Sion a chief corner stone elect, precious and he that believes on him shall not be confounded,

3 I am who come a light into the world that whoever believes in me shall not abide in darkness; I say unto you this I am the bread of life, come to me and never be hungry, believe in me with all of your heart and your soul and you shall never thirst again.

4 believe in your Lord Jesus Christ and you shall be saved and your house; for the promise is unto you and your children and to all that are afar of, for even as many as the Lord our God shall call. And all your children shall be taught of the Lord, and great shall be the peace of your children.

5 For I will pour water upon the one who is thirsty and floods upon the dry ground, I will pour my spirit upon thy seed and my blessings upon thy children, verily I say unto you whoever shall not receive the kingdom of God as a little child shall not enter therein, and the Lord took them up in his arms, put his hands upon them and blessed them, all thine children blessed by the Lord thy God, in the name of the Father and the son and the Holy Spirit.

6 Lo children are the heritage of the Lord and the fruit of the womb, is his reward, as arrows are in the hand of a mighty man so are the children of the youth for whom the Lord your God loves, he corrects, even as a Father the son in whom he delights, thou shall also consider in the heart that as a man chastens his son, so the Lord thy God chastens thee, therefore thou shall keep the commandments of the Lord thy God, to walk in his ways and to fear him.

7 A merry heart does good it is like medicine, but a broken spirit dries the bones, let your conversations be without covetousness' and be content with such things as you have, for he has said, I will never leave you, nor forsake you; a sound heart is the life of the flesh, but envy it rots the bones, but godliness with contentment is great gain,

8 For I know him, that he will command his children and his household after him, and they shall keep the way of the Lord to do justice and judgement showing to the generations to come, the praises of the Lord and his strength; and wonders of the Lord your God, that's been done, your children and your children's children might know them, arise and declare them to your children, so they might set there hope in the Lord your God and not to forget the works of God, but to keep his commandments.

9 You shall teach to your children, speaking to them when you sit in your house and when they walk your way, when they lay down and when they wake and get up, take heed to yourself and keep your soul diligently that you not forget the things which your eyes have seen and to not depart from your heart all the days of your life, but teach your child, and your child's child and their children.

10 Gather people together and I will make them hear my words and they may learn to fear me all of their days, that they shall live upon the Earth and that they may teach their children, train up your child in the way they should go, so when he is old, he will not depart from it.

11 Correct thy son and he shall give you a rest and he shall give you delight into your soul; you fathers provoke not your children to wrath, but bring them up in a nurturing and admonition (firm warning or reprimand) of the Lord your God.

12 Peace, peace, peace, to him that is far off to him near, says the Lord your God, I will heal him and let the peace of God rule over in your heart, to which also you are called in one body and be you thankful.

13 I will hear you my Lord God as you speak we will speak peace unto your children and people and to your saints which pass understanding we shall keep our hearts and minds in Christ Jesus.

14 As the works of righteousness shall be of only peace and the effect of righteousness with the quietness and assurances forever, thy faith has saved us, we shall walk and live in peace in your Holy name; I say unto you my peace I leave with you, my peace I give to you, not as the world gives, give unto you, let not your heart be troubled, neither no more be afraid.

90
The New Life,
the Word Fellowship in Christ

1 Hear my word, if anyone is in Christ, your new life, the creation; has come upon you, the old new is gone and the new you is hear, prove by the way that you live that you have repented of your sins and that you have turned to God, the new life, the word, fellowship in Christ.

2 As you are newborn, do not continue to copy the behaviour and customs of this world, but let our Lord God transform you every single day into a new person by changing your ways and the way that you think, learning and behaving the way Gods will is, that he wants for you, which is good, pleasing and perfect, the new life, the word, fellowship in Christ.

3 You have been taught now to put off your old self, which is being corrupted by its deceitful desires, to be made new in the attitude of your minds, being transformed to have the mind of Christ, to put on the new self created to be like God in true righteousness and holiness, the new life, the word, fellowship in Christ.

4 I say unto you, in all circumstances, take up your shield of faith, with which you can extinguish all the flaming darts coming your way from the evil one; and I say unto you; take the helmet of salvation, and the sword of the spirit, of which is the word of God; praying at all times, in the spirit with prayer of supplication, the new life, the word, fellowship in Christ.

5 To that end keep alert with all perseverance making supplication for all saints, now rejoice in the new life, the word, the fellowship in Christ, pray without ceasing in everything give thanks, for this is the will of God in Christ Jesus, given for you.

6 I say unto you, the new life, the word, fellowship in Christ, do not sin, control the way you now live, do not give in to sinful desires, do not let any part of your mind and your body become an instrument of evil, to serve sin; your thoughts, you cannot hide from me, I see what you do, I say unto you, instead give yourself completely to God for you were dead but now you have a new life; completely give, use your whole body as a new instrument to do what is right, for the glory of God, sin is no longer your master, you are no longer under the requirements of the law, instead you live under the freedom of God's grace, the new life, the word, fellowship in Christ.

7 So by no means are you to continue in sin, that grace may abound? How can you who died to sin, still live in it? Do you not know that all of us who have been baptised into Christ Jesus were baptised into his death? Buried therefore with Jesus by baptism into death, in order that just as Christ was raised from the death by the glory of the father, so to we might walk into the newness of life, the new life, the word, fellowship in Christ.

8 Submit yourself to God; resist all evil, for I say unto you he will flee from you, I say unto you when I your Lord God died, I died once to break the power of sin, but now do I not live, I live for the glory of

God, so you also should consider yourself to be dead to the power of sin and alive to God, through your Lord Jesus Christ; do not allow sin to control the way you think and live, do not I say unto you give in to sinful thoughts and desires.

9 The spirit gives life, these words I have spoken to you, they are full of the spirit and life, When the spirit of truth has come, I will guide you into all truth, I will not speak on my own authority, but whatever I hear I will speak and I will tell you things to come.

10 The helper is your Holy Spirit, it will teach you all things, and it brings to you remembrance, all things that I have said to you, that if you love me; you will keep my commandments, and I will pray the father, and he will give you another helper that he may abide with you forever- the spirit the truth, whom the world cannot receive, because it neither sees him nor knows him, but you know him, for he dwells within you, and will be in you, the new life, the word, fellowship in Christ.

11 And you will receive the power when the Holy Spirit comes on you, and you will be my witnesses in Jerusalem, and in Judea and Samaria and to the ends of the Earth, the new life, the word, fellowship in Christ.

12 The body is dead when Jesus Christ is in you because of sin, But the Spirit it is life because of righteousness, but if the spirit of God who raised Jesus from the dead will also give life to your mortal bodies through his spirit who dwells in you; Oh my Lord, my God, your word it is a lamp to guide my feet, and a light for my path, for every word of God proves true in my eyes, for your shield is to those who take refuge in you, the new life, the word, fellowship in Christ.

13 All scripture is inspired by God and I give it to you as a useful guide to teach what is true and to make you realize what is wrong in your lives, Oh thankyou our gracious Lord for it corrects us when we are wrong and it teaches us to do what is right, I say unto you, blessed is the one who does not walk in step with the wicked or stand in the way of sinners nor the way that sinners take or sit in the company of mockers, the new life, the word, fellowship in Christ.

14 But those whose delight is in the law of your Lord God, and those who meditate on my law day and night; for that person is like a tree planted by the streams of water, which yields its fruit in season, if you remain in me and my words remain in you, ask for whatever you wish and it will be done for you, for the word of God is alive and active, sharper than any two edged sword, it penetrates even to dividing soul and spirit, joints and marrow, it judges the thoughts and attitudes of the heart, the new life, the word, fellowship in God.

15 I say unto you that everything that was written in the past was written to teach you, so that through the endurance taught in the Holy scriptures of God and the encouragement; it provides you with hope, Heaven and Earth will pass away, but my words will by no means pass away, for with my whole heart I have sort you; Oh let me not wonder from your commandments my Lord, my God, for your words they are hidden deep within my heart; that I might never sin against you again, for its my wish to have the new life, the word, fellowship in Christ.

16 I say unto you, let us think of ways to motivate one another to act of love and of good works, and let us not neglect our meetings together as some people do, but I say unto you encourage one another, especially now, that the day of my return is drawing near, the new life, the word, fellowship in Christ.

17 For if we walk in the light as God is in the light, we have fellowship with one another, and the blood of Jesus the son cleanses us from all sin for as the body is one and has many members, but all the members of that one body, being many are one body so also is Christ; this it makes for harmony among the members in fellowship, so that all the members care for each other, for if one part suffers all the parts suffer with it, and if one part is honoured all the parts are glad, all of you together are Christs body, and each of you is a part of it, those who have ears let them hear, the new life, the word, fellowship in Christ.

18 Now all the believers devoted themselves to the apostles' teaching and to fellowship and sharing in meals including the last supper, and to pray; I say unto you to be devoted to one another above yourselves, beloved if God so loved us, we also ought to love one another, be kind and compassionate to one another, forgiving each other, just as in Christ God forgave you, we proclaim to you what we ourselves have actually seen and heard, so that you may have fellowship with us; and our fellowship is with the father and his beloved son, our Lord and Saviour Jesus Christ.

19 I delight greatly in my Lord, for my soul it rejoices in my God, for he has clothed me with the garments of salvation and arrayed me in the robes of righteousness for the wages of sin is death, but the free gift of God is eternal life through Jesus Christ our Lord, the new life, the word, fellowship in Christ.

20 I am not ashamed of the Gospel for it is the power of God for salvation to everyone who believes, to the Jews first and also to the Greeks, after this I heard what seemed to be the loud voice of a great multitude, in Heaven crying out, Hallelujah' Salvation and glory and power belong to our God, be encouraged my child, your sins are forgiven, the lord your God is merciful and forgiven, it is the power of God that brings salvation to everyone who believes.

21 The Lord he is my light and my salvation, whom shall I fear, for you my Lord are the stronghold of my life, whom shall I be afraid, The new life, the word, fellowship in Christ, I bow down my head in worship, I bow my head in praise, I bow my head in honour, as I pray and bless your Holy name,

91
We are one body, one in Jesus Christ

1 So it is with Christ's body, we are many parts of one body and we all belong to each other, so I say unto you make an effort to keep yourself united in the Spirit, binding yourself together with peace, again I say unto you, that if two of you agree on Earth about anything that they may ask , it shall be done for them by my Father who is in Heaven, do nothing out of selfishness, ambition or vain conceit, rather in humility, value others above yourself, for we are one body, one in Jesus Christ.

2 Oh my Gracious Lord, I am therefore a prisoner of the Lord; beseech you that you walk worthy of the vocation by which you are called; for as the body is one and has many members of one body, being many are one body; so also is my Lord Jesus Christ, we are one body, one in Jesus Christ; Glory to God in the highest, and of Earth, peace and good will, towards people.

3 For I say unto you, God isn't a God of confusion, but of peace, and of all the assemblies of the saints, so grace and peace to you from God; our Father and the Lord Jesus Christ, and let the peace of God rule your hearts, to which also you were called in one body, and to be thankful, we are one body, one in Jesus Christ.

4 And those who are peace makers will plant seeds of peace and reap a harvest of righteousness, mercy unto you and peace and love be multiplied, finally all of you be of one mind, having compassion, for one another, love as brothers, being tender hearted, being courteous for you have been my help, and in the shadow of your wings, I sing for joy, we are one body, one in Jesus Christ.

5 Let us lift up our hearts with our hands to God in the Heavens, let Heaven and Earth praise him, the seas and all that move in them, accept my prayers my gracious Lord and my words of love that I speak to you, as out of my mouth my words honour you, and my upraised hands as an offering, we are one body, one in Jesus Christ.

6 Oh my Lord you are the Lord of Lords and King of Kings and those who are with you are called chosen and faithful, Lord Oh Lord how excellent is your name in all the Earth, as I say unto you, I will bless you while I live, I will lift up my hands in your Holy Name, as my Lord says unto me, Jesus answered saying, will you really lay down your life for me? I say to you my Lord, we are one body, one in Jesus Christ, my Lord and my Saviour.

7 Blessing and honour and Glory and Power be to him, who sits on the throne, and to the Lamb, I say to you my gracious one, forever and ever as I honour the Lord for the Glory of his Holy name, I am nothing without you, I cannot live without you, I worship the Lord, in the splendour of his Holiness, rejoicing in the Lord, My God always, again I say rejoice, we are one body, one in Jesus Christ.

8 I say unto you, the mountains shall depart and the hills be removed, but my kindness shall not depart from you, nor my covenant of peace be removed, says I your Lord who has mercy on you, I hear your prayers and as I answer them to, stay in peace my child, I shall call on you, we are one body, one in Jesus Christ, for blessed as those, who believe and trust in the word. *AMEN*

92
Trust in my Lord God
And Peace within

1 The Lord has heard my cries for mercy; the Lord accepts my prayer, for we do not really know what we should pray for as we ought to; but the spirit himself makes intercessions for us with groaning which cannot be uttered, I say unto you seek God and his strength, seek his face forever more, trust in the Lord God and peace within.

2 Pray in the spirit at all times and on every occasion stay alert, and be persistent always in your prayers for all believers everywhere; now for the one who searches the heart knows what the mind of the spirit is, because he our Lord god makes intercessions for the saints according to the will of God, so trust in my Lord God and peace within.

3 I say unto you, if everyone among you is suffering; then pray, for when you are cheerful, sing praises; for I am always with you, therefore I say unto you, whatever things that you desire when you pray, believe that you will receive them and you shall have them, have I not already proven to you and given, trust in my Lord and peace within.

4 The effective fervent prayer of the righteous one avails much; calling upon me, "I will answer" I will be with you in your times of trouble, I feel your presence, I feel the change within me, I trust in my Lord God and my peace within that you have my Lord given me, I praise and honour you with all my soul, I love you my Lord my God.

5 How my heart rejoices in the Lord, the Lord he is making me strong, for I now have an answer for my enemies, I will be complete in rejoicing, and it's all because of my Lord God, the changes you have brought into my spirit, you have rescued me my Lord; it's my trust in the Lord and my peace within, you have given me wisdom and you have opened my eyes to see, showing me my God within.

6 You have heard my prayers my God, the words from my mouth, you've given me answers from heaven above; and there is only one I can believe and trust in; my Lord God, the one who truly loves me, I repent, you hear and forgive me, for its only you who knows my true heart, you have known my grief, when I have prayed to you, with the deepest of love in my heart, and your love and forgiveness, your righteousness Oh God, it reaches the highest Heavens, your kingdom above.

7 You have done such wondrous things in my life, and no one can tell me it wasn't from the love of God; who can ever compare with you Oh great one, I rejoice over you with joy in my heart, understanding clearly what you have done, I thirst for you every day, your word, your love, your wisdom, grant me these things in my Holy Spirit, my divine within me, my trust in my Lord God, and peace within.

8 You my Lord have swept away my offenses like a cloud; my sins like the morning mist, as you say unto me, return to me Oh child, for I have redeemed you, you have washed away all my guilt and made me clean again, for you gave your life to free me my Lord, freed me from every kind of sin; to make me your very own, I am now free to forgive and to not feel shame to not listen to others who will drag me down, to remember to trust only in my Lord God and peace within.

9 For it is you my Lord God whose name is excellent in my eyes, it's you my Lord that has transformed my life; changing me every day, you have set your glory above the Heavens, your love, my Lord reaches my heart, my soul, your faith embeds deep within me, and it is you alone; "God" of all the kingdoms of the Earth, no one is capable of what your hands can do, no one is capable of doing the miracles you can do; I praise you and thank you, for your works of wonders that you have done all over the world, from the beginning of creation, and the works that you have done in my life, I glorify your Holy name.

10 You've created me in a clean heart Oh my Lord God, renewed a right spirit within me, the fruit of the spirit, floats freely in spirit, it's love, it's joy, it's peace and so much more, in self control, as the kingdom of God it's more than what we do here, taking for granted; but righteousness, peace and joy in the Holy spirit can be perfected, be comforted of the same mind when God is present in your life, with love I trust in my Lord God and peace within.

Amen and Amen

93
We are Nothing without our Lord

1 The Earth is my Lord's and everything in it, the world is the Lord's and all who live in it, for it is by the Lord all things were created, and that are on Earth, visible and invisible, dominions, principalities or powers, all things were created through Christ and for Christ, we are nothing without our Lord.

2 My Lord you are great and powerful, you have glory and victory and my full honour, everything in Heaven and on Earth, and it all belongs to you, the kingdom belongs to you; you are ruler over everything great and small, you look down from Heaven and you can see the whole human race, we are nothing without our Lord, our Saviour Jesus Christ.

3 So as we praise and glorify, let us come boldly to the throne of our gracious God, there we will receive his mercy, and we will find grace, to help us when we do need it the most, my strength my Lord, I will draw it from you, I praise you, as you deserve my full love and glory for all your miracles of love that you have done to transform me my Lord, without your grace where would we be, in everything I shout praises, we are nothing without our Lord, Jesus Christ.

4 As God poured out richly upon us the Holy Spirit through Jesus Christ our Saviour, and this hope given it will never disappoint us, because God has poured out his love to fill our hearts, he gave us his love, through the Holy Spirit, whom God has given us, he who believes in me, I say unto you the scripture has said, out of his heart will flow rivers of living water, behold, I will pour out my spirit onto you, I will make my words be known to you,

5 And it shall come to pass afterwards that I will pour out my spirit on all flesh, your children they shall prophesy, the old they shall dream, dreams, and the young they shall see visions; For we are nothing without our Lord, for it is the spirit that gives life, the flesh it is no help at all, the words, I speak to you are spirit and life.

6 Our gracious Lord, the spirit of God has made me the breath of the almighty; it gives me life, I am nothing without my Lord, he who has brought me peace and comfort in my mind my body and soul, understanding and love, as I praise the name of God forever and ever, you have all wisdom and power, I was brought with a price, therefore I glorify God, in my body and in my spirit, which belongs to God almighty.

7 My king and my redeemer, thank you for saving and changing me, opening up my eyes, showing the lit pathway to fellowship with God, the word, the truth, a Christian, a child of the living God, I worship, I bless, I praise, I pray, I believe, I love, I trust, I hope, I rely on my Lord Jesus Christ, the only beloved son of our Father in Heaven, GOD

AMEN and AMEN

In my heart and my soul
Lord I give You control
Consume me from the inside out,
Lord, let justice and praise
Become my embrace
To love you from the inside out.

GOD always has something for you, a key for every problem, a light for every shadow, a relief for every sorrow and a plan for every tomorrow.

LOVE must be sincere
Hate what is evil;
cling to what is good.
Be DEVOTED to one another in LOVE
HONOR one another above yourselves
Never be lacking in zeal,
but keep your spiritual fervor,
SERVING the LORD.
Be joyful patient in faithful
in hope, affliction, in prayer.
Share with the Lord's people
who are in need. PRACTICE
Romans 12:9-13 HOSPITALITY.

94
The power of the blood of Jesus Christ

1 Through faith just as it is everywhere in the kingdom of God, faith is largely dependent on knowledge; for if knowledge of what the blood of Jesus Christ our king can accomplish is imperfect, then faith would then expect little and the more powerful effects of the blood are impossible.

2 For the life on the flesh is in the blood, and I have given it unto you, upon the altar to make an atonement for your souls, for it is the blood that makes an atonement for the soul, because the soul or life is in the blood, and because the blood is offered to God the father on the altar, it has redemptive power; the power of the blood of Jesus Christ.

3 Life is in the blood, the value of the blood corresponds to the value of the life that is it, for the life of a sheep or goat is of less value than the life of an ox, and so the blood of a sheep or a goat in an offering is of less value than the blood of an ox, the life of man is more valuable than that of many sheep or oxen, the power of the blood of Jesus Christ.

4 I say unto you, can you tell the value or the power of the blood of Jesus Christ, the soul of the Holy Son of God dwelt in that blood; the eternal life of the Godhead was carried in that blood, the power of the blood in its many effects is nothing less than the eternal power of God himself, what a glorious thought for everyone who desires to experience the full power of the blood of our Lord Jesus Christ.

5 However the power of the blood lies above everything else in the fact that it is offered to our father God on the altar for redemption, for when we think of blood as shed we can only think on the lines of death and death follows when the blood or the soul is poured out; death makes us think of sin, for death is punishment of sin; the power of the blood of our Lord Jesus Christ.

6 For God he gave Israel the blood on the altar as the atonement or covering for sin, this means that the sins of the transgressor were laid on the victim, and its death was reckoned as the death or punishment for the sins laid upon it, life is in the blood, the power of the blood of Jesus Christ.

7 The blood that was life, given up for death, for the satisfaction of the law of our father; and in obedience to his command; sin was so entirely covered and atoned; for that it was no longer reckoned as that of the transgressor, the transgressor (us) were forgiven; but all these sacrifices and offerings were only types and shadows until our Lord and saviour Jesus came, his royal precious blood was the reality to which these types pointed.

8 My Lords blood was in itself off infinite value because it carried his soul or life; but the atoning virtue of our Lord Jesus' blood was infinite also because of the manner in which it was shed; in Holy obedience to the fathers will, he subjected himself to the penalty borne, but the law was satisfied and the father was glorified, life is in the blood, the power of the blood of our Lord Jesus Christ.

9 Jesus Christs blood atoned for sin in that made it powerless; however it has a marvellous power for the removal of sin and opening Heaven for the sinner, whom is cleansed and washed and sanctified which makes fit for the sinner in Heaven, and it is because of the wonderful Jesus Christs blood that was shed, fulfilling the law of his father God, while satisfying it's just demands that the blood of atonement, and its power to redeem; accomplishing everything for in the sinner, that is necessary for salvation.

10 My gracious and wonderful Lord, we see something of the wonders that this power has accomplished, for we will be encouraged to believe that it can do the same for us; we believe, as our best plan is to note, how the scriptures they glory in the great things that have taken place, that the power of the blood of our Lord Jesus Christ, that life is in the blood.

11 Oh the wonderful power of the blood Of Jesus Christ, just as it has broken opening the gates of the grave and of hell beneath, and over the kingdom of Heaven; and all its magnificent glory above; life is in the blood, the power of the blood of Jesus Christ.

12 As the desire for holiness becomes so much stronger in us, should not the thought that the blood has more power than we know off and can do for us, much greater things that we have yet experienced causing our hearts to go out in strong desire; if there were more desires for deliverance from sin, holiness and intimate friendship with our heavenly father God it would be the first thing that was and is necessary for being led further into knowledge of what the blood can truly do.

13 As a believer and of a greater importance to receive full reconciliation for the power of the blood of our Lord Jesus Christ; it should obtain a deeper and more spiritual idea of its meaning and blessedness, for if the power of the blood in redemption is rooted in reconciliation it's the surest way to obtain a full experience of the power of the blood of Jesus, the son of the God.

14 It's the heart I say unto you that is surrendered in Christs Holy Name, in all the good works of Jesus Christ, God's Holiness that fore ordained reconciliation that is in the blood of Jesus Christ that ordained it and that the pardon results for it and above all in reconciliation God's objective is the removal and destruction of all sin; therefore the knowledge that we have of sin is necessary , for the knowledge of reconciliation; life is in the blood, the power of the blood of Jesus Christ.

15 The effect of sin upon God, in his divine nature he ever remains unchanged and he is unchangeable, but in his relationship and conduct towards us an entire change has indeed taken place, sin it is disobedience, a contempt of authority of god, for it seeks to God of his honour as God and our Lord, sin is determined opposition to a Holy and loving God, and it not only can, but it must, awaken his wrath.

16 Reconciliation means to cover, if we are to understand correctly we must also consider the Holiness of our loving God who fore-ordained it; God's holiness in his in-finale glorious perfection which leads him always to desire what is good in others as well as in himself, he works out what is good for others for God he knows our hearts all too well, he knew us before we were born; however he hates and condemns all that is opposed to what is good, the power of the blood of Jesus Christ, God's son, cleanses us from all sin, life is in the blood.

17 The believer who is now cleansed should have no more conscience of sins through the Holy Spirit, for we have

Received an inward experience, the blood of Jesus Christ which has fully delivered us from the guilt and power of all sin that we in our regenerated nature have escaped eternity from its dominion, however sin does still dwell in our flesh there is no escape from this while we are still in our fleshly bodies with its temptations, but listen unto me; It has no power to rule; because the conscience has been cleansed; there is no need for the least shadow of separation between us and our belief our full trust and faith in our Lord our saviour Jesus Christ, washed and cleansed in the blood of Jesus Christ.

18 Oh my Lord God we look unto you in the full power of redemption, our conscious which has now been cleansed by the precious blood that bears witness to nothing less than a complete redemption of the fullness of God's good pleasure, a pleasure he gives his beloved faithful believers who have called upon him; and if our conscience is now cleansed so also is our hearts of which our conscience is the centre, washed cleansed in the blood of our Lord Jesus Christ.

19 I understand God that a heart must be cleansed of an evil heart and conscience, so not only must the conscience be cleansed but so must the heart, including the understanding and the will within all our thoughts and desires, through the blood, by the shedding of which our Lord Jesus Christ delivered himself up to death and by virtue of which he entered again into heaven; the death and the resurrection of Jesus are ceaselessly effective, by the power of his death and resurrection, sinful lusts and inclinations are now slain, life is in the blood, the power of the blood of our Lord and saviour Jesus Christ.

AMEN

95
Faith is the power of Christ

1 Our faith may be strengthened by recognizing what the blood of Jesus Christ has already accomplished for us, for heaven and hell bear witness to this, faith will grow by training in confidence in the never-ending fullness of the promises of God, so let us heartedly expect that; as we enter more deeply into the fountain of Jesus Christs precious blood; for its cleansing, its life giving power, faith is the power of Jesus Christ, being revealed more blessedly to believers of Christ our saviour.

2 When we bathe we will enter into the most beautiful intimate relationship with God, with the purity of the water; giving ourselves up to its cleansing effects; calling on the baptism, calling on our Lord Jesus for purification of our bodies, The blood of Jesus is described as a fountain opening... an opening for sin and for the uncleanness' and by the power of the Holy Spirit which comes down through the Heavenly temple by faith, faith is the power of Jesus Christ.

3 As I place myself in the closeness with this Heavenly spiritual contact, as a stream washing over me, I yield myself to it, Letting it cover me, going through me, and as I am bathing in this fountain of beauty I'm being baptized in purity; it cannot with-hold its cleansing, and it cannot with-hold its strengthening power, therefore I must in simple trust, love and faith in our Lord Jesus Christ, turn away from what is seen to be able to just plunge myself into the spiritual fountain which represents the Lord and saviour Jesus' blood, with assurance that it will manifest its blessed power within me.

4 So let us with child like faith and hearts, persevering with expectant faith which is opening our souls to an everlasting experience of this wonderful power of our Lords blood, faith is the power of Christ, the spirit and the blood, but there is still yet another question as to reply that I need oh Lord; so that the blood of Christ may manifest its power onto me?

5 I say unto you this, Holy Scripture connects the blood most closely with the spirit, you need only have eyes to see; it is only where the spirit works that the power of the blood will be manifested, for faith in the blood produces such great results, there are three that bear witness in Earth, the spirit and the water and the blood; and these three agree in "one" for the water it represents baptism unto repentance with laying aside of all sins; and the blood refers to redemption in I your Lord and saviour Jesus Christ, the spirit is he, the one who will supply all power to the water and the blood, so also the spirit and the blood are associated, faith is the power of Christ.

6 How much more shall the blood of our Lord Jesus Christ who through the eternal spirit offered himself unto God, his father (our father) without spot (blemish) to purge our conscience; it was only by the eternal spirit in our Lord Jesus Christ that his blood had its value; for our Lords blood it has power, and it is always through the spirit that our Lords blood possesses its living power, in heaven and in the hearts of all who believe; faith is the power of Christ; our beloved Lord.

7 The blood and the spirit always bear testimony together; where the blood is honoured in faith or preaching, it is there that the spirit will do its work; and it is where Jesus works, for Jesus will always lead souls to the blood, the Holy Spirit cannot be given until the blood of our Lord Jesus our king was shed; this is the living bond between the spirit and the blood which cannot be broken.

8 In our hearts we must live as those who know that the spirit of God really does work within us deep within as a seed of life; for the Lord Jesus he will bring the hidden powerful effects of the blood to perfection, and we must allow our Lord Jesus Christ to lead us; faith is the power of Christ.

9 Through the spirit, the blood will cleanse us, sanctify us, and unite us to God, which all believers are to listen to Gods voice with his call to holiness, for we have been redeemed by the precious blood of Christ; to have the correct perception of what the preciousness of the blood of our Lord which is the power of the perfect redemption, the power of a new and holy life and it is this power that also applies to us, the precious blood of Jesus is about redemption and knowing before that we can experience its full power value, faith is the power of Christ, the shed blood to take away sin, the power of the blood to nullify the power of all sin.

10 My Lord Jesus may the desire for holiness become stronger in us, should the thought that the blood it has more power than we know of, and can it do for us greater things than we have yet to comprehend and experience, causing our hearts to go out in such strong desire; if however there were more desire for deliverance from sin for holiness, and having an intimate relationship with the Holiness of God, it would be the first thing that is necessary for being led further into great knowledge of what the precious blood of our Lord Jesus Christ's blood can do, the second thing my Lord will follow is that desire must become expectation.

11 Now as we do inquire from the word of God in faith of what the blood has accomplished this must be a settled matter with us that the blood can manifest its power, full power that is also in us with no sense of unworthiness or ignorance or that feeling of helplessness which causes us to have doubt; for we must have faith and know that the precious blood works in the surrendered soul with a ceaseless power of life, therefore surrender yourself to god the Holy Spirit, fixing your spiritual eyes and your heart on the blood of Jesus Christ, opening your whole inner being to its wonderful power.

12 Children off God take shelter under the ever continuing sprinkling of the blood of Jesus; the blood in which the throne of grace in Heaven is founded for it can indeed make your heart rejoice in the temple and throne of God.

13 I ask the Lamb of God himself to make the blood effective in us, the experience that nothing can compare with the wonderful working power of the precious blood of Jesus Christ our king and our saviour, life is in the blood, faith is the power of Christ.

96
Burning Passion

1 My desire and my burning passion is to pray to my lord, to have intimate talks always and for you to hear my heartfelt words so I can grow with you each day, as my Holy Spirit expands to learn with burning passion, for the deep love of my Lord.

2 The word of God evolving and filling me with the burning truth, opening my eyes and my heart with what is real, as the love and the compassion is taking over my body bit by bit; Oh my Lord please scrape away more ungodliness from me, my Holy Spirit is becoming overwhelmed, washed and cleansed with total love, the continuous burning passion, and my love and joy for my Lord Jesus Christ.

3 How I long to be standing in your presence my Lord; to not feel any shame or guilt, for your promise is that my sins have been forgiven, for I only want to rejoice for the transformation that you can bring to a loving child; I long to be one of your angels that sing praises to you, to be in your presence, to glow within; the burning passion flowing from deep within, the light of your angels, Gods love transforming.

4 My heartfelt words, so inspiring and with peace, that can only come from the Holy Spirit within, words from God, wisdom power and love, burning passion exploding from pure love, feeling your presence surrounding the air, to bring the word of God's love to keep the holiness deep within, to help us to grow to be in righteousness with Christ, tears that flow from the depths of the heart within, the love from a child the heart of the family in heaven above.

5 It's been a struggle my Lord can I tell you that please, I know I can't go back to the person I use to be; I can't even imagine I once was that person at all, I do have one regret is that I could have found you sooner my Lord; but I realize you didn't have that in your plans at all; I believe, I trust a burning passion for so much more, more of your love, more of your strength, more of your compassion, and more of your wisdom to teach about my beloved Lord Jesus Christ.

6 Lord make me more aware to keep love surrounding all our lives, to keep peace my Lord deeply inside, in our Holy Spirit; where you Jesus reside; burning passion given to us to learn, to open us up spiritually inside, for the love of our Lord who died for us, to change the law, to save us all, a burning passion of the purest love, given to us all by our Lord Jesus Christ.

7 I cannot deny how deeply I feel you within, my heart feels like it wants to explode; it's the power I know that you have given me; It feels like Lord that it has its own life, it thinks and it feels, its changed my life, its graceful its caring, it's the burning passion of Christ; watching every thought deep inside, the pathway of righteousness, my Holy Spirit is alive.

8 I passionately serve the son of God, my obedience of faith; my trust in the Lord, his power will defend, when darkness tries to sneak in, God will protect his children who truly trust and love him, and he will switch on the Holy light the pathway to him, the eternal path to the saved children in the end, a burning passion from knowing God his deeply given within.

9 Feeling my spirit full of acceptance, and coming to realization my Lord, your love is overflowing in my like a waterfall, a curtain of wings being embraced by God; I turned to you Jesus I needed this in my life; Oh my holy one above, I love prayer to you all the time, you fill me with so much love now, it's all of the time, we all need God in our life to turn us around, to feel the deepest love, that the world cannot give, our saviour is Jesus, we need to just call on him.

10 Our prince of peace, just one precious word from you, how it can make me speechless when I hear from you; you break my heart open is such a huge way, tears of joy rolling down my face, my arms stretch high to the heavens above, where you are seated, at the right hand side of God; a burning passion so deep within, oh hear my voice Lord, for I truly love you deep within; a Father from heaven with such love for his child, for once my Lord, I truly don't know what to say; for each prayer that you have given, takes my breath away, to give to the world and to save many souls.

97
By Gods design

1 I will give mercy to whoever I choose; I will show compassion to whoever I wish, regardless of whatever you want or however you try to earn it, it is entirely up to me says the Lord your God; to either show mercy or harden the heart of whomever I choose this is by Gods design.

2 For I your God are completely in control, do not forget I created all, but many of my children forget who I am, all humans I moulded out of clay, one may even ask, why did I make you this way, are you not then denying the right to the potter to make out of the clay; an ordinary pot, or something of beauty and elegance, is this not by Gods design.

3 However I your Lord God am extremely patient, loving and caring, do I not though have the right and power to unleash anger and wrath to those who deserve it; listen unto me, those who are rejected I say unto them that they are mine; to the ones unloved, I say unto them, you are my darling ones, and to the ones that have been told you are nothing at all, they will be renamed the children of God, by Gods design.

4 The passionate design of my heart, my Lord my God; and my constant prayers to you are for all fellow children, to experience salvation, to love and to change their ways, for many say they are deeply devoted to you; but many are so unenlightened, they are ignorant to the righteousness that you give, wanting to only just be excepted by you because of their own works, refusing to even submit to your path, they do not really know you, It's because of Jesus that God has transferred his perfect righteousness to all who believe, by Gods design, believe.

5 How Gods deep messages are close to all, as close as your heart that beats in you; beating in your chest with every breath, so what is Gods message, could it be the revelation of faith; salvation is the message that we should all teach, teach all who will listen that Jesus he lives, to publicly declare with the words from our mouths, that Jesus Christ is our Lord; and to believe it in your heart, and that God he raised Jesus from the dead, and if you believe, then you will be, truly blessed, salvation will be given in Jesus' name, by Gods design, you are saved and blessed.

6 Its the heart that believes the Holy Spirit given by God, all who believe and except Jesus as the son of God; the gift of righteousness by Gods design, moulded with great love with God's hands, the creator of all the giver of life, to rescue his children from darkness, to cover them in the blanket of love and light; we give thanks to our Lord as we bow our heads in prayer, our saviour our King, Jesus Christ is his Holy name.

7 Oh my Lord my God how loving that you are; how you have given us a chance time after time, how it breaks my heart how disappointed you are, we have all sinned so many times, with love, you have been patient; out your mouth giving us prayers, offering yourself to unbelievers to turn their hearts around, and even myself as little as I have done, but I believe now, I accept Jesus as the son of God; and I am glad I have given myself to you, with all of my heart; I believe and love you, by Gods design, I will worship and pray to you for the rest of my days.

8 By Gods design living happily together in spirit, truth and harmony; speaking blessings and love to all who have ears; let your inner most heart win over at all times, blessing those who hurt you all of the time, being kind I say, so let this hope burst forth within; bringing continuous joy in your Holy Spirit within, commune to me all that you can, I will get you through all your troubled times, I love you my children, I came to you to save, to bring you into a family with love; for eternity, to suffer no more, to have joy in your life, to walk every day, tall and with a smile.

98
Take control of my life

1 Gracious Lord as I bow down to you, one thing I ask for, is for you to take me by the hand; take control of my life, I beg of you, because you have heard my heartfelt prayers, you have witnessed my tears of distress, you know I haven't done the very best.

2 I need you Lord every single day, as I live and breathe in your touch, your word and truths; take control of my life, I need more of you, embrace me Jesus as I need your love; with the word of God, and your truth at last, like a magical waterfall, flowing over me.

3 Jesus takes care of you in every way; take Jesus in embrace the love he will give you every day, follow me he says unto you, run to your king, he will change your life's ways, I asked my Lord, bowed down with tears, as I prayed Lord I put my hope in you.

4 Jesus he heard my cries, he took control of my heart, he held me close, a long lost child, he said let go of your pain; feel no more guilt, I've been waiting for you, you called out to me, feel the light surrounding you that I am filling you within, don't listen to darkness just cast it away; don't let it filter in, only feel the pure love that Jesus gives, and you will feel safe, knowing he is next to you.

5 Take control of my life; fill me with love, my Holy Spirit alive because you have transformed my life, Oh how great it is to have Jesus Christ by my side, I feel at peace, for the first time in my life; tears rolling down my face, but it's not from pain, but from happiness within; where Jesus resides; he is holding my hand, that's deep love, its hope, its grace, it's our Lord Jesus Christ.

6 The word of God is the word of life, and his name is Jesus Christ; he is the only answer in your troubled times, so pick up the Bible, pick up the cross; the blood of Jesus is the blood of life; and blessed your life will be, when you truly believe.

7 All God wants is for you to love him in faith believing; God gave up his son to change the law; to give us life, Jesus died for us, he took all of our sins, to give all eternal life; as God promises to us is to stay fixed on him, believe in Jesus and believe in the word; It's not too much to ask for, to believe in the son of God; God's power, God's strength I worship you my Lord.

99
Strengthen my Spirit

1 I'm willing to receive the light you're bringing into my life; oh strengthen my Spirit, Jesus Christ, filling it with love and divine intervention, angels by my side filled with light.

2 I love the Lord, believing in him with all of my heart, my Lord strengthen my Spirit, it's needed my Lord; a breakthrough at last, for I was lost, and a loving God who has showed me the path, walk to the light, don't stray from me, walk towards the light, where you will find God.

3 My spirit lifted, so willing to receive; the supernatural works that's been done in me; a truly amazing God; who needs so much praise, so I do praise God everyday; I know what you have done for my life, my eyes are open, I feel the light; you strengthen my Spirit, I am truly alive, blessed by a God who wants only love for his child.

4 So much happier, my hearts rejoiced, spiritually filled, with love in my eyes, Oh my gracious God, I thank you so much, my Holy Spirit transformed, where my Lord Jesus resides; tell me Lord when I look up at the stars what I can truly feel is my home above; I feel alive when I look up at you, and I feel happy knowing that you can see me too.

5 Spiritual work to do for my God, the good within, the change in your life, the work of God strengthen my spirit indeed, the breakthrough from heaven, where God he lives, I needed the truth about our world, I needed real love from our Lord, where angels rejoice in the presence of God, stars are bright as they show you the way.

6 In fellowship with our Lord, the church of God, a real family it's a home with the Lord, come he calls come sit with me, learn the word, and I will show you the way; angels with wings wrapped around us with love, the protection of God enfolding us.

7 Oh praise the Lord, holy, holy is his name, a king of king as we bow down on our knees; we hold our hands up high to him, as we sing the song "hallelujah" our king; Oh strengthen my Spirit as we pray, we need our Lord our Messiah who reigns; I believe in your power Oh yes my God, I believe in the healing that you have done, an amazing God filled with love and light.

8 Oh God" strengthen my spirit when I feel low, keep me on the right path which follows my Lord, my tears overflow when I feel you near, deeply connect are me and my Lord, so much love, that you make me feel; and for all, that do come near me; your children God that you will not let go, your infinite love is for all, all spiritual children, true children of God.

100

My passion, my belief in our God

1 I say unto you that I have swept away your offenses like a cloud strongly in the wind; your sins vanishing like the morning mist return to me, for I have redeemed you, have guilt no more, washed and cleansed in the presence of our Lord, my passion, my belief in our God.

2 A loving amazing God true to his name, when totally committed in doing good deeds, for his deep love he makes you his own, our God on high who is the mightiest of all; my passion my belief in our God, who loves all his children and died to save all.

3 How your love reaches to the Heavens and your faithfulness it shows in the skies and the stars, they show their beauty and wonderful glory, sparkling at night for all to see; look up and see my wonder as it talks to you at night; my passion my belief in our God.

4 You alone are our God, our fascination, our almighty one, you alone have changed the way I now live my life, you alone are my passion my belief in our God, our creator our king over all; you alone who sends in the comforter, to his people and will have compassion on all his afflicted ones, my Lord you alone are the greatest of love.

5 Then this angel showed me this river; the river and its water of life, how it shines like crystal and flowing from the throne of God; the lamb the son of God, my passion my belief in our God, for all things were made through Christ; who's shed blood was spilt on the mercy seat, for life it's in the blood.

6 My passion my belief in our god, being found in the appearance of man, he humbled himself and he became obedient, obedient to the point of death, even to death on the cross; they didn't believe he was our king, a saviour to save us from our sins, not knowing that there is one God, and one mediator between God and us, and his name is Jesus Christ, our king of kings, our Lord of Lords our saviour, our Messiah, let's give thanks as we pray amen.

7 This Lamb he sits on the throne next to God and feeds all who are hungry for the word, the truth that will set you free, and our Lord will lead them to the living fountains of waters, and God shall wipe away all the tears from our eyes, my passion my belief in our God.

8 I say unto you, who shall keep also my commands, is the one who loves me, I say unto you the one who loves me; will be loved by my father, as I love you I will show myself unto you; remember my compassion my child, repent and all will be forgiven unto thee, you will be free, be sorrowful for all your wrongs, believing in God, receive the glory of the lord forever, and may the lord give you his peace, enjoying what he has made for all to see, my passion my belief in our God AMEN.

101

The life of every living thing, is in God's Hands

1 How precious do you think life is when the life of every living thing is in God's hands, when God gave breath to every living thing, does that not make you stop and pay attention, to be on guard; to stand up strong in your faith believing, to have deep love for God almighty,

2 When the life of every living thing is in God's hands, then all the Earth Lord shall worship you, singing praises to you all day long; for all that you have given, for all that you have done; you are the creator, our Father in Heaven, we send to you our faithfulness for all the good and the bad which we have done, for your mercy endures forever, you alone are the one we love, and in righteousness you look down from Heaven, hearing our pleas in repentance.

3 Blessed be God's glorious name forever, let the whole Earth be filled with his glory, and everyone who has hope in our saviour Jesus Christ, purifying them with his love, just as Jesus himself is pure, for his precious blood is life, Jesus his sacrifice was great to save us of all our sins, the life of every living thing is in God's hands, for whoever believes in the son of God has eternal life.

4 The words of the mouth are important, the words of the mouth are like deep waters, but the fountains of wisdom is a rushing stream and the deeper the word of God can be revealed, then the deeper the love will go, the rivers of living waters will flow from your heart, the deeper the wisdom, the deeper the word, the deeper the love, the deeper the truth, the deeper the calling of God will enter through, deep calling to deep, he will reveal all, the life of every living thing, is in God's hands.

5 When a tree becomes planted it is rooted firm, planted by the rivers of water that flow; passing through the rivers Jesus he will be with you planted firm, rooted deeply within; how deep is your love, how deep is your faith; I say unto you remember I write you a new commandment which is true in me to you; that darkness is passing away, the true light is already shining through, the life of every living thing is in God's hands, god's word, God's glory, God's voice, the prophetic word, now confirmed unto you.

6 You'll do well to keep focused on what I say, it's the one light you'll have in dark times as you wait, for daybreak and the rising of the morning star' keep my deep love in your heart at all times; as you remain focused on the word; keep focused on the path of righteousness, as I light your way, keep sin at bay; look into your heart as you feel the joy, for it is the joy I give for your belief in me, the life of every living thing is in God's hands.

7 You oh my God are the shield enfolding me; you are my glory abounding in me, oh search my heart for it is only you and your love you gave; what you will find, you alone know how I feel, you have brought me to calm waters; when I have cried and prayed, you've calmed the beast trying to take me away, repentance comes easy with Jesus by your side; as I was ashamed of all the sins that I had done; I meditate on all you love every night and every day, I live and breathe the word of God, to be filled with light as you stand by my side.

8 I believe in God, I believe in the word, I believe my Lord and Saviour is the son of God, I believe your blood was spilt to save us from all of our sins; and I thank you father, for giving us your precious beloved son, I give myself to you with all of my heart, as the life of every living thing is in God's hands, I glorify you both as I pray to you Amen and Amen.

102
Treasure of salvation, wisdom and knowledge

1 Like a woman who cries out close to giving birth, in pain and struggling, bearing down, so as we before you oh Lord, we call out to you in distress, therefore as we hear the word of God, we can therefore bear down and move forward and not stumble and go backwards, becoming snared, taken captive, oh Lord fulfil us, with your protection, give us your treasure of salvation, wisdom and knowledge.

2 Teach us oh Lord not to be arrogant for all we seek are your truths, not the truth of what this world believes, as the world it makes up lies to conceal the truth; concealing itself in deception; and for devout Christians this truth is hidden, not reaching us, so we call on the faith and our love in our Lord to reveal to us spiritual truth and guidance, treasure of salvation, wisdom and knowledge.

3 You say that he who believes; who trusts in you, relies on and adheres to you will not be disturbed or gives way in panic; you say oh Lord you will instruct us correctly teaching properly, you say listen and hear my voice, and you say listen carefully and hear all my words.

4 Lord speak to us in your softly spoken voice, instruct us what is right, give us visions of the light, the right path to take, for you my holy one, I love with all of my heart and soul, you say you wait expectantly and long to be gracious to us, the ones who long for you, these word oh Lord are uplifting to my Holy Spirit, I plea thee my Lord never leave nor forsake me, for your children long for you; your love is treasure of salvation, wisdom and knowledge, listen carefully and hear my words.

5 As we must learn the results of righteousness, for it brings us into quietness, confidence and trust forever; as we live in these peaceful surroundings with God we have the feelings of security in our dwellings; for this effect of righteousness is everlasting peace, as the fear of you Oh Lord is our treasure of salvation, wisdom and knowledge.

6 The knowledge we seek "Lord Jesus" gives us stability and it's this stability that you have given unto us, my surroundings you have blessed in our house of prayers, we bow down to honour you, our hearts they seek our God forever and ever.

7 Please always be patient with us as we try our best, as we live each day in your presence we seek only to please you, to do our work which you have chosen for us; and to serve our God to do only good, this is truly treasure of salvation, wisdom and knowledge, to think about others who suffer, to feed the poor, to give and not murmur on what we have done for others.

8 Our Questions to you are learning like a child, frustrations we feel at times towards a God that is full of love and compassion, and can our frustrations towards you Lord be even harmful to us, as you rule over all; have we even the right after all our sins to ask you for help are we even worthy enough, how many of these questions have we all not asked our saviour our God; in all our situations you still give us treasure of salvation, wisdom and knowledge.

9 Frustration from manmade laws that is taking away the law and words of God, taking away the truths that should teach our children today; these laws can save us from all of our sins and sins of our future children, for all the children of God would follow in then the laws of God would be placed upon their hearts, treasure of salvation, wisdom and knowledge; treasures in heaven is what all do seek; Our Lord Jesus Christ our saviour and our king.

10 A frustrated Christian who so loves the Lord, a frustrated sinner is what I once was; a loving Lord who took the sinner by the hand, a loving Lord transformed and turned your life completely around; a family transformed when God came into the home, then all heartache was completely gone; filled with the Lord is all that you did need, its trust and faith that only God can give; a blessed child is he that hears the word of God each day, a frustrated Christian who needs the love of the one, the one who gives treasure of salvation, wisdom and knowledge to stay perfectly grounded by the love of God.

103
Blessed are those
who are pure at heart

1 How much more should the blood of Christ cleanse your conscious from dead works, as to serve your living God; when the conscience is cleansed so is your heart, and once cleansed you should have no more conscience of sin, and blessed are those who are pure at heart.

2 Through the spirit we receive an inward experience that the blood of Jesus Christ has fully delivered us from guilt and the power of sin that we all in our regenerated nature have escaped entirely from its dominion, blessed are those who are pure at heart.

3 As sin still dwells in our flesh, its temptations have no power to rule over us, for our love and protection from our lord is our promise; our conscience is cleansed there is no need for the slightest shadow of separation between our God and us, for we are now looking up to God for this full power he will give in redemption, blessed are those who are pure at heart.

4 Now as our conscience is the centre; and if the conscience is cleansed, so is our heart cleansed including our full understanding;

our will, our thoughts and our desires, through the shedding of blood of our Lord Jesus Christ, for its exercises its spiritual heavenly power of the soul, blessed are those who are pure at heart.

5 The heart can abide every moment under protection, and the cleansing power of our Lord Jesus Christs precious Blood, it is not sufficiently recognized that purity of the heart is a loving characteristic of every child of Gods, and this is a necessary condition of fellowship with God; the enjoyment of his salvation and blessed are those who are pure at heart.

6 There is too little inner longing to be truly in all things; at times well pleasing to the Lord, for all the stains of sin, they trouble us to little; but as God's word it comes to us, with all the promises of blessings, these blessings that ought to awaken all our desires, believe that the blood of Jesus can cleanse us from these sins, for if you yield yourself correctly to its operation it will cease; our Lord can do great things for you; if you call on him for help, trust and faith is all you need to have a life in the kingdom about, all these blessing God can give you, they will be given to your heart, blessed are those who are; pure at heart.

7 Should you not desire ever hour, to always think of our loving God; to experience his glorious cleansing effect that he can bring to your life, to be preserved by our depraved nature which causes us to sin, as our conscience is constantly accusing us to have our desires awakened; too long for a blessing that only God can give; so put God to the test to work it out for you, he is waiting on your prayers, so do not fail him, for what God has faithfully promises us, is to be cleansed of all unrighteousness, and blessed are those who are pure at heart, for they shall see the love of God.

8 Cleansed and blessed a divine meaning, deeper and wider than you could imagine it to be; believe it's our Lord Jesus a power he gave, he washes and cleanses with his blood a sacrifice that he gave, for all his beloved children who have sinned and can be saved; it's a daily enjoyment of which you can confidently abide, for sanctification is union to be one with God; it's the fullness of blessings, purchased for us by the blood of our Lord, and blessed are those who are pure at heart and truly love God.

9 Now to understand what the sanctification of the redeemed is; we must then first learn what the Holiness of God is; he alone is the Holy one; for Holiness is the perfection of Gods nature; God's Holiness cannot bear sin, he desires what is supremely good; he is the Lord who sanctifies to make you his own, to make you Holy and to sever you from others, sanctification is always God's own work and blessed are those who are pure at heart, for they shall see God.

10 Where the blood is honoured in faith or preaching the Spirit works, where Jesus works, for he always leads souls to the blood; the Holy Spirit could not be given until the blood was shed; the living bond between the spirit and the blood of our Lord Jesus Christ cannot be broken, If the full power of the blood is to be manifested in our souls, we must place ourselves under the teachings of the Holy Spirit blessed are those who are pure at heart.

11 Believe firmly that Jesus resides in us, carrying on his works in our heart, for we must live as those who know that the spirit of God really dwells in us as a seed of life bringing the hidden powerful effects of the blood of Jesus to perfection, allowing our Lord Jesus to lead us through the spirit, the blood will cleanse us, sanctify us and unite us to God, believers listening to the voice of God, with his call to Holiness "be Holy for I am Holy" for you have been redeemed by the precious blood of Jesus Christ, blessed are those who are pure at heart.

104
Will you pick up the cross and follow me

1 Do you believe in me, and do you love me, will you pick up the cross and follow me; oh hear me Lord, oh hear my prayers as I give myself unto you every day; I picked up the cross and I will follow you every step and in every way, as I ask of you my Lord Jesus to cast all of my sins away.

2 Let me flourish like a living tree, near living waters, as I once was a withering shrub, all alone lost and dying, until one day you heard me, my cries and my distress; you lead me to you, you had mercy on my soul, you found me worthy to be saved my Lord, to become a child of God; for I had no happiness nor did I have peace, no joy at all, an unrighteous sinner was me; a loving God who said; will you pick up the cross and follow me.

3 You came to show me what real love is, the day you said; will you pick up the cross and follow me, this overwhelming love I feel for you has completely transformed my life; I am no longer a withering shrub I am blooming from head to toe, the Joy in my life has been given to me; by my Lord and saviour Jesus Christ; the cross of Jesus and his blood that was shed; it's given me new life by the word made manifest; I am now alive with my Lord God, oh Hallelujah and AMEN

4 You are now the Lord of my life, my Lord Jesus Christ; I have now been crucified on the cross, as my values have changed my desires have too; sadness has gone away, all tears now shed, are my deep love for you; the day those amazing words said learn the word of God, will you pick up the cross and follow me.

5 I now have a personal experience with the son of God, It's a relationship that I will never let go; he lives in me, every day of my life, the Holy Spirit given, when you pick up the cross and follow him, we are now connected mind, body and soul, a spiritual connection between me and the son of God.

6 Do you know God, do you know what you feel inside, to know the difference in every way; in how you think in how you feel, trust in Jesus for he will lead the way; how you speak when you show love, what do you feel in your heart for the son of God; do you want to live your life now washed and cleansed, to have purification in your mind, body and soul, to have Jesus in your life, the blood of our Lord will give you life, that you have never experienced before, as he asks you will you pick up the cross and follow me, your Lord.

7 The burning passion that I feel deep down inside, I listen my Lord and follow what you say, I try and do; what is right, not like before, for I am a different person now, transformed by God, now in a different light, not in this world, but living in the light; to stay away from; the pits of hell, to be a creation of God, taken by the hand; I cannot live without my Lord God; the word and truth of God, that saved my life, he cast away my sins; he died to give me life, the cross I now hold, I am a disciple, a follower of the messiah; Jesus Christ.

105
The only answer;
the Lamb of God, Amen

1 Oh God my soul it thirsts for you, my flesh it longs to be with you, as righteousness it shall flourish; like the palm tree full of life; glistening in the stars of the night, as you look up with love in the heavens above, the only answer is the lamb of God.

2 Do not be at war with the carnal mind, for your mind will then be at war with God; believe in God then search your heart, educate yourself and cleanse your mind, take up the cross of Jesus Christ, the Bible morality and the 10 Commandments of God; your character renewed and your ego now gone, the only answer, the Lamb of God.

3 I say unto you about your carnal mind is it your option, or the option of God; who has more power, the last answer in the end, you will stand before him regarding your sins; so who's option are you seeking, God's or man's; flesh or spirit, for I say unto you, beware of the world; for if the world hated me it most certainly will hate you; be a conqueror in Christ, if the world hates you then rejoice; for you will be a winner in the eyes of your Lord Jesus Christ, the only answer, the Lamb of God.

4 Greater is he that is in you, than he that is in the world, for there is nothing impossible for those who believe; for the word of God teaches us all; walk away from the created problems of the world, gaining your crown from heaven above; listen to the angels as they rejoice, another sinner saved from the world; so be still and know that I am your God; be on your guard and stand firm in your faith, draw courage and strength from what God gives to the saved, the only answer the Lamb of God.

5 My heart overflows from your tender love; as my lips recite the composition, a great theme from God, with my Lords chosen words, a tender heart that overflows; the words of God given with joy, hope and grace given to embrace, the words of Jesus made manifest; to all my children listen and learn, the only answer, the Lamb of God.

6 The Kingdom of God does not consist in talk, but in power, power that's been given to us all, faith in everything we've needed, it's through the Godly life and knowledge in him; who has called us by his own glory, and the goodness and love that's within; according to the riches of your loving kindness God; that you have granted me the power and the strength, my Holy Spirit alive within me, filled with joy and peace, the only answer, the Lamb of God, as I pray in worship amen and amen.

7 Lets come before you oh Holy one as we raise our hands to you high, we summons your power and your strength; as our flesh is weak most of the time, our understanding so limited in knowledge; as we believe what our world has to tell, for man has no understanding about our great king in heaven; oh come to me child of wisdom, for the truth will come to you, and I will give you all the answers, a calling from me to you.

8 Verily, verily I say unto you, that I came as a witness to testify, so that all might believe through me; are these not written in scripture my child, that Jesus is my name, I am the son of God, I am the beginning and the end, I came in flesh to be sacrificed; to save all that I can from your sins; so listen all my children I want all to have eternal life with me, I say unto you, love me, with all of your heart and believe in me, the answer the Lamb of God, to have eternal life through me.

9 Through love and faith I believe my Lord, for eternal life is what I do seek, I am totally devoted to you Jesus, a deep calling, that you did give, as I sleep and wake you are there; you are never far from my side, I turn to you for answers, and Lord you have never let me down, It took me awhile to realize that all I asked for you did give, my eyes are opened spiritually, my eyes they now do see; you are a miracle worker, a practitioner that's ready to heal, we need to rely more on our Lord Jesus, than what this world can give.

10 So let us pray and lift our hands up high to our creator and our King; with so much love in our eyes with tears streaming down our face, for all the good works he has done, with words and the creations done with his hands, with so much beauty we forget to look at, all that's living so great and small, everything has a beginning and it also has an end, but if you take up the cross and follow him, then eternity he will give, I am the first, and the last, I am the beginning and the end, I am the alpha and the omega, I am the answer, the Lamb of God, let's give thanks. *AMEN*

106
Church Rapture

1 Oh Holy God from most high, King of Kings and Lord of Lords, a Judgement seat where your church goes, to meet and see our Lord; for all that we have done, while here on Earth; oh how we can be glorified to be in Heaven at last, and it's all because of our deep love, for our Messiah Jesus Christ; Church rapture, the priesthood of Christ.

2 In a twinkling of an eye; taken by God, being alive while on earth; we are his church; believer's with faith, deep love for our Lord; but the ones that are first, were the dead in the graves, the dead in Christ, to rise in the clouds; we come together all in the clouds, we will all see our Lord, face to face, the church rapture, with our beloved Lord, and his grace.

3 The world in which we live is not a joyous ride; for many do not believe in our Lord Jesus Christ; that's why our Lord comes to take his church home, glory to God in whom we so love, the world it will now crumble and fall, please now repent and ask to be saved, God he has mercy, for the antichrist he will come, and he will try to destroy whatever he can; however God he is watching and he has a mighty plan, the Church rapture will be watching from heaven above.

4 Nations against nation, kings against kings, the antichrist is getting God's people; to take the mark of the beast; the believers who refuse will suffer the blade, they saw the evil beasts, true plan, people cried and prayed; right to the end, while 4 horses of doom, the power of Satan's work on the Earth, Jesus is getting ready to take his revenge, with war and bloodshed, famine and death, a physical change on Earth as thousands are dead, but the safety in heaven the rapture of the church, watching in silence; what is taking place on Earth.

5 The 7 trumpets of God, and his angels ready to take charge, and the 1st of these trumpets was fire, hail and blood; followed by the plague of the insects much larger than man, insects we could have once held in our hands, their sting it's so painful, which lasts 3 months, many cannot stand the pain and wrath.

6 The Angels with bowls who through blood to the Earth, to contaminate our waters, no more quenching for our thirst; heat and darkness, will cover all of our Earth; the terror and horror thousands will endure, unbelievers in Jesus no repentance at all, many will still fall, for no love for our Lord; you could be saved, but you have no faith; there are still Angels to come to deliver your fate; his lights still turned off, with hail as large as your garbage bins, with nowhere to run no escape for your sins; you chose darkness over me, live in darkness on Earth.

7 It's Armageddon time, the fight between good, and bad; get ready Satan to be cast in the lake of fire; you are no match for our God our King; for you and your army, for what you have done, evil will never win, against the son of God; and with God's heavenly children; the church; safely wrapped in his arms, a thousand years of peace, finally hear last; to live with peace and joy, where Jesus will reign.

8 Our crowns that we were given; we placed at God's feet, our glorious and majestic king of kings; to bow down in honour for giving us life, we look at you our Lord with such love in our eyes, your guidance and Grace bought us into your arms, you saved us all Lord when you took all our sins on the cross; but it's our deep love for you, and all that we have come to know, the truth the love, the faith and the trust, and all this is our Lord Jesus Christ.

9 The blood and the cross of our Lord Jesus Christ and the full understanding in the words of God; however the truth really lies in the blood of Jesus Christ; our gracious Heavenly Father who gave us his son, is truly to be blessed and worshipped in heaven above, to be home one day to be in our heavenly church, to have all knowledge that God will reveal, which cannot be given to us in our flesh; the full revelation which heaven does best.

10 As the thousand and seven years pass, with the renovation of Earth, the wicked and wicked dead in the graves, will face God; in the great white throne, judgement in Heaven; to face all their sins, where there will be wailing and gnashing of teeth, when they will finally understand that Jesus is real; and the sinners doom is over, cast into the lake of fire; no more pain, for the believers in God, no more wickedness to hurt , and the lovers of God; with no more lies, no more tears, I am so honoured to love and know my beloved God.

11 Now look up into Heaven Church, and what do you see, the kingdom of Jesus; the New Jerusalem is coming, in the clouds' for all to see, and look at our teacher, on his white throne, look and feel his love all around; our Earth so radiant, no more darkness to be felt or seen, Eternity at last, in the kingdom of our Lord Jesus Christ.

107
Spiritual blessings by Gods Holy Church above

1 Oh praise the Lord, and our Holy righteous Father in Heaven; as Angels have rejoiced, as my name has been written, in the Lambs book of life, to bow to your knees, to cry out to your Lord, I need you God, take me in your arms, I turn to you, I can't do this on my own, I have failed so much, I need you my Lord God, as spiritual blessings granted by God, spiritual blessings by Gods; Holy Church above.

2 Galactic Planets never seen before, the structure so massive; one billion light years across, a light year can travel at 100, thousand miles per second, but in a twinkling of an eye we are bought up into Heaven, we cannot comprehend something so grand, as our Earth will look like a floating speck of sand, so how great is our God, our Father in Heaven, the creator of all, truly spiritual blessings, given by God, Spiritual Blessings by God's Holy Church above.

3 When we open the word of God, and realize how powerful he is, you can understand, why angels bow down to him, day and night they sing by worshiping his name, singing Holy, Holy, Holy, is his name;

oh praise our Lord as grace abounds; spiritual blessings that you can feel all around, spiritual blessings given by Gods holy church above.

4 The God that we serve holds the seven seas, in the palms of his hands; stand look and listen at the vastness as the waves they break; but God holds what we are looking at like a drip from a tap; God through the planets out into the vastness, like we throw a ball that we catch; he through stars like glistening diamonds and he knows each one by name, all that's in the heavens, can you even comprehend that; he picked up dust from our world, he breathed on it to create man; took a rib from that creation, then woman was made; as they become one parents to us all; what an awesome creator is our wonderful God; spiritual blessings by Gods holy church above.

5 Our God made a covenant to all man, that he said he would keep for all time, for eternity to God is nothing at all, and his loving kindness endures forever more; so magnificent in all his glory, we will serve him every day and night; his promise is that he will never leave us, pick up the cross of his beloved son, and pray for all to follow, and love and heal the sick, for God he gives you the power; if only you would believe; the holy spirit dwells in you, can you feel the love within, believe and trust in Jesus, and don't forget to forgive, remember all have sinned, and do not cast any stones, do not expect to remove a speck from anyone, but remember the beam in your own eye; spiritual blessing are given for all to see; open your eyes for they are a vast as the seas; spiritual blessings by God, his wonderful holy church above.

6 You are a joy God; my joy and my peace, peace you will give us each time we pray, we can call and you will listen, much more; than we can comprehend, we can pray and you will be present, with your angels by your side, now as a child of the king, and our only way to heaven, we must understand the importance of our mistakes, and repentance, we can become a real family united as one in the kingdom of heaven where our Messiah reigns; as you watch over us, with love and hope;

to turn to you, with complete love and faith; you are a patient God, you will never leave us, that's our spiritual blessings by Gods Holy Church above.

7 Spiritual authority we have been given, it is power on Earth from God; but how we do waste it; this gift that came to be; we must live in obedience in every way; Jesus is our Lord and our Saviour and we must preach the word of God to all; for Jesus he came to preach the truth to all; rebuke all wickedness, for it is not from God at all; just live to be like God, full of pure love for all; if you want life it is the only way, to believe in the son of God; spiritual blessings by Gods holy Church above.

8 I say unto you, receive me for I am your Lord; I will grant you all that you ask, pray and call upon me in your times of trouble and I will give you my peace; make God your power, and darkness will back down, for light is in and all around; receive me and darkness will have to leave, in Jesus' name, our church our God, Jesus Christ and power; fight for the word, the power within, given by God, for all believing Christians; spiritual Blessings by Gods Holy Church above; Spiritual blessings God's spirit within.

9 The inspiring word of God, its truth in which we live, receive me oh Lord, as I give myself unto thee; my love ever so deep, I am caught up in your church, Oh rapture me oh Lord, when the time does come; don't leave me behind, your beloved child of faith; I have confessed all of my sins, which was done between you and me, a covenant that's been done that no one else can break, your mercy is like none other, you're as loving as can be, repentance is so easy, for they are between me and my king; we have an understanding, that he gives with so much love; when you turn to him in forgiveness; for all your past mistakes, he takes you by the hand; then wipes away all tears, he sends you in the comforter, then he resides within; you are no longer lost, you understand what's done, you have finally found Lord Jesus; you have picked up the cross.

10 Oh my Lord and saviour, you are in control; in control of all, including myself, you are in control of what is going to happen on Earth, no time for peace, darkness it rules; it will not be pleasant, not nice to see; but you do come back in all your glory; on your white horse for all to see, people afraid who didn't believe; come take away Jesus the evil of this world, an awesome God, who has done so much for all; it breaks my heart how people's eyes are so blind, they are so heart hardened, so arrogant by the world, if they could only see before it's too late, to repent and accept Jesus as the son of God; the love I have in my heart for Jesus my Lord, these prayers your reading are from the word, the word is Jesus made manifest, to give you life and to give you peace; Gods merciful love for all his children, spiritual blessings from Jesus Christ.

11 Crush the thief that comes to steal at night, as Jesus he did under his feet, you have the blessings when you have God, don't let a thief take your peace, given by God, you have the power his name is Jesus Christ, fight the enemies that control your life, you have an awesome God by your side, he loves you, and he won't cause you harm, he is light all around, he can take darkness away, the enemy hides in all dark places, it has no right to come near you, call Jesus in, and it will have to flee; have faith, love and trust, and feel the light around, that is the light of God, showing you the way.

12 How beautiful you are; your radiance it shines, it touches the church, and it touches my heart; tears flow so fast, rolling down my cheeks, my Holy Spirit alive, my Jesus within; the joy the faith the love that you bring, the children of God, the church in which we pray; to our God within, your face it blinds; and binds your church in faith, the Lord God who is the stronghold of my life.

13 Heaven and Earth must die, to save the children of God; to take evil away from your beloved church; Oh praise our God; Jesus our King, for the New Jerusalem is coming a new Earth in which we will live, no more tears will be shed, no more sicknesses, we will be healed, our king Jesus on his white throne as he will watch over us, there will be no more fear, no more darkness will enter in; pure love all around, oh praise our dear God, for giving us his only beloved son; to have come and fought darkness, with his army of angels by his side, to win with strength and so much power, my Lord my God, Satan never had a chance; so let's all praise and sing, in your Holy and righteous name, for the prince of darkness will be gone at last; Praise our God and our beloved church; with spiritual strength, spiritual blessings by Gods holy church above, my king Jesus is seated at the right hand of father God; Holy, Holy, Holy as we pray amen.

108

For my beloved God Almighty

1 My exalted God how I come before you with so much love and grace, I wake thinking about everything that you have done, all my wishes and prayers that you have made come true, many in which I never realized that you had answered until you reminded me, such fools we are to think that we have done this from our own actions our own hands, do we not yet understand that without you we are nothing.

2 Oh God most high, I find myself seeking from you all truth so to live my life fitting for you; we need knowledge and wisdom to live in peace and harmony; without corruption and sin, many believe their thoughts are their own; good and bad, and that their bodies and all thoughts are theirs, we are ignorant to acknowledge or comprehend the truth, we need saving and acceptance, my beloved God almighty, I long for goodness, sincerity, acceptance, biblical truth from the word of God, the word can set us free.

3 We can fight for biblical truth so more and more people do not become detached from the word of God, Jesus he came to minister the truth, not to be ministered to, we can be saved from the world and deceit; if we do not program ourselves to the lies, there is only one God, one truth; which one do you want to live by; the higher

power of God almighty or the power of what this world gives,
I found great love like never before, this love can only be delivered
to you by God.

4 The Earth needs satisfying with fruits from your word, for you alone
are the creator, the creator of all; you alone can make your thoughts
known to people, the children all from God; you alone can transform
our Holy Spirit, the Holy Spirit given by God; you alone my Lord Jesus
are the true vine; the gardener is the father in Heaven; you alone can
set us all free, you alone are my Love within.

5 I say unto you abide in me and I will abide in you; and hear my words
about this vine, for it is I that am the vine and you my children are the
branches; live in me and I will live in you, for a branch cannot bear
fruit of itself unless it abides in the vine; My Lord I cannot live without
you, all by dead fruit you have trimmed of, so that I can live in you and
the good fruits can produce; I abide in you as your words abide in me.

6 Bless us oh Lord, so that we shall not walk in the counsel of the
wicked, nor stand on the paths of sinners, neither sit on the same seat
as the scoffers; we only seek to study in the word of God, to follow
the right path of righteousness and meditate on it day and night; for
only then can we prosper and succeed in all we do; oh God almighty
we praise and glorify your Holy name, my beloved God almighty.

7 My Lord most high fix all your laws so they are placed on my heart,
all words and truths; so our hearts will overflow like a water fountain,
filled with emotions and love, that only our loving God can give; light
up our pathway so that we do not lose our way and stray; you are our
only way to salvation, our Lord Jesus Christ, he will wash us whiter
than snow, and give us peace and tranquillity, for we seek to live in the
kingdom and become like our messiah, our king, our saviour.

8 On your white throne of glory, as you look down upon your children
and the transformations as they seek you, their hands held high as

they look up to you with such love in their eyes as they pray, the angels rejoicing for every child who finds the grace and wonder of their saviour Jesus Christ; crying and seeking, for mercy; love and salvation, the repentance of sins, as they become new Christians in faith and believing; your miracles we need, when we fall to our knees; for our sins are so bad; we know that its only you Jesus who can set us free, you sacrificed your life, to set us free from sin, life is in your blood; it was our only fighting chance.

9 To live a life in God, that we never had before, the life that we once lived, was a sentence of only death, what we thought was right, was just a life of sin, it just wasn't right, in the eyes of our sinless Lord; who died to set us all free, and the only way to this life, it was the living blood; of our Lord Jesus Christ.

109
3¹⁄₂ years

1 I am the word and I came to be, I was born in Bethlehem with a star above me, a king is born, the king of the Jews, told by the prophets, the ones that knew, But Herod he was king and he heard about this news, he was the king, no new born boy; I am the king he replied I am the king of the Jews; then he put in an order, that all newborn baby boys must die.

2 As innocent blood was spilt, that displeased God; he heard all of these mothers and children's cries, he felt their pain in Heaven above; but God he knew what had to take place, he came to Joseph and said; take the mother and the child Jesus away, for if you do not, the child will surely die; for King Herods men, in the morning they will arrive; this new born king he must be saved, he is the king to spread the gospel around, the word, the truth, sent from Father God above; I gave up my son Jesus; so he can save this world, a saviour of sins, to have eternal life.

3 I was named Emmanuel; Jesus, before I was born and my mother was Mary, chosen by God, Her husband was Joseph, they are both of a descendent line; they are descendents of King David, which is my royal bloodline; a perfect plan by our almighty God, for I was Gods only son, to learn your ways, to became flesh, to live with you and teach each day, to write it down for future use.

4 I lived my life; my parents hid me well, but King Herod he thought I was, disposed off; Herod he died, the murderous fool, for he died thinking he was the true king of the Jews; this murderous fool who shed innocent blood, a fool with no love; in his heart; he killed his own son for getting in his way; a foolish king in every way; but King Jesus had plans in years to come, to change history until the new Jerusalem comes; now he will walk with the disciples; the ones that he will choose, spreading the gospel, the good news; 3 · years listening to his awe filled words, filled with love and truth all around.

5 I had many visions during all of my years, speaking to my father who filled me in, these visions that I had they did come at night, they were of my father, our Father God; a father who taught me very well, to listen and to learn to heal the sick, miracles that I done to have witnesses, I was born in flesh to take away sins, to give all God's children some fighting chance, to believe who I am, the son of God.

6 I obeyed my parents, here on Earth, a request from the commandments of Father God; I done my chores that I was expected to do, my father was a carpenter, by trade; but many skills I learned with the family I had, but the word of God, was where my true heart laid.

7 My Father in Heaven I must obey, I am the son of God and no blemish I have, I do not have much time, I have so much to do, I must preach the word, for 3 · years of ministering; is all I can do, I was tested by Satan, when he offered me so much; He even asked me to jump, if I was the son of God; look out over there, look how high we are, I can give it all to thee, if you walk with me; Satan is a deceiver, and I cast him away; he cannot be trusted, he is full of sin in his heart; I rebuked Satan and you must too, I will cast out Demons from the words of my mouth.

8 I have left the family home, to travel and to preach, with so much love in my heart, I have many people I must meet; but I had brothers and sisters who did understand, but my beloved mother Mary had tears rolling down her face; with so much love in her eyes for her miracle son; but she knew in her heart that this day must come; two of my brothers followed me to preach the word of God, one he opened up a church, he believed in God; he understood who I was, the son of God.

9 3 · years and it's all about God; for 3 · years to heal and raise the dead; the truth and the word, must be spread around, the people are amazed at what I did tell; but I had a heavenly father, who loved and taught me well; I knew what was ahead of me, for I felt all the pain, I felt all of the sins placed upon me; but Father he said, son, you must Go ahead; I felt love all too well, for the children of God, I did love these people, that I need to save.

10 I had twelve disciples that I searched and found; but I already knew who I was seeking to preach my works around; they were to be

my followers to spread the gospel of truth, to listen and to learn all I will tell; to have faith and trust to write all that's taught, to be a witness to, the son of God; to teach all nations when I am gone; but they struggled they loved, they even cried, but they needed to believe, and forget their flesh; but my miracles they witnessed, in awe they felt; but they did still struggle with what they saw; but my disciples where loyal and stood by me, even though one was taken by Satan the thief; he hung himself upon a tree; now the time had come and their hearts become sad, when they were told, I was to leave this world; their hearts became sorrowful, for the love of the son of God.

11 Their eyes were opened; when I rose again, I stood before them, telling them to preach, what I have told them, what they had seen; you are my witnesses, go and tell all; keep faith, love and trust, and spread that around; teach to all nations, all around the world; the truth must be told, to all who have ears, to open up their eyes so they can spiritually see; tell that God is love, you can be saved, for all of your sins, repenting for all that you have done; with sincerity in your heart, believe in God, believe in the truth, be saved by your sins, by the blood of our messiah, Jesus Christ; he died on the cross his body was shed; he gave up his life; so you could live, repentance a must, to be given life, in the heavenly realm, where your Father and Jesus reside.

12 I was crucified a threat, a crown of thorns on my head; this was done by people who had no faith; their hearts so hardened, spiritually blind; only believing the false teachings done by man; they are covered with sins, no trust or belief, in the son of God, who came to set them all free.

13 Many will be hated, who believe in me and Gods word, the truth of God though, it must be told; and you all must understand that for 3 · yrs I preached and I healed, and I never gave in, just to save you all; I planted a seed, so believe in God, and save as many as you can preaching the gospel of God; with the love of God, I can promise you this, the reaping and the blessings you will truly receive; and blessings from heaven as God is watching over thee.

14 I will open the eyes to all who love me, giving you all the blessings in your Holy Spirit from me, where I will reside deep within, do not grieve what I have given you; but keep joy in your hearts; with peace, faith and trust, as tears will be overwhelming in your eyes, that's how close I am, a heartbeat away; I am a blessing to you, as you are to me, as your eyes become opened, each time you pray, you will feel my love for you, when you become stronger in your faith; with sins cast away; in the repentance you gave; your trust and belief in the blood Jesus gave, it had to give new life to a beloved child of Jesus Christ.

15 My Lord in 3 · years you preached the word, in 3 · yrs you had given so much; in that 3 · yrs your truth and words spread so far, Lord the word of God has transformed many thousands of lives; my God so almighty, your deep love so grand, in 3 · yrs your miracles have amazed, Lord even since the beginning of time; you have proved your love time after time.

16 3 · yrs in ministry and your life was taken so short, you were 33 so young so strong; your precious blood was shed for all to see, humiliated and mocked, punished brutally; but all that they accomplished, was that your devoted believers, fell more deeply in love with thee; our faith and our believing become powerfully strong, to our king of kings, our saviour our Lord, and knowing the real truth, Jesus is the son of God, he rose again, to save all.

17 Your life was brilliantly planned from the beginning of time, to save our lives, taking sins, and casting them away; your 3 · yrs when you spread the word of God; the disciples, your followers, where to continue your work; to spread the good word, when you ascended to heaven, our disciples oh Lord said our beloved teacher, he had so much love to spread; for all of Gods children, young and old; he wanted to save he had compassion for the poor, the sick he healed, he brought the dead alive; we walked with Jesus; we loved; we cried, we miss our beautiful teacher, whose name is our messiah Jesus Christ.

18 We prayed, and yes we loved our 3 · yrs as he preached; he had incredible patience for all who searched for him, even when many didn't understand; his parables in the way he spoke; he is someone special, he is truly the son of God; we spread the Gospel, we wrote his words, the words of the mouth of Jesus Christ, Jesus is the word made manifest; many of us disciples we died, murdered for our fellowship with our Lord and our deep faith; but not before we hid the gospel all over the place; our words had to get through, to all who believe, to live and breathe, the word of God, the words of our teacher, the love of Christ, he touches our hearts, he does give life; he fills you with an everlasting love deep in your heart.

110

Do you choose, eternal life

1 Has God not suffered more than anyone, It does sometimes takes a deep hurt, to have a deepened for God; and it's that in which our Lord uses in such broken world, it's this world in which we live; your suffering which will lead you to God, so do you choose eternal life.

2 The gift of eternal life, what is heaven really like, Heaven I say unto you, is like being awestruck, not like this rushed world, for heaven its tranquillity, a calmness like a wonderful waterfall; calmly flowing over you, washing and cleansing you all at the same time; the overspray of water flowing over you as a baptisms of purification; heaven is like this only infinitely deeper, do you choose eternal life.

3 What the Bible describes about Heaven it's true; but far greater than we can ever imagine, my Lord we can visually be placed in our minds, and our dreams of what heaven is like, Lord explain the difference between Heaven and eternal life, for are they not the same, I say unto you; that eternal life it is not a place nor is it even a length of time; I am eternal life, just as God is the source of all physical life; he is the source of all spiritual life too; do you choose eternal life, in and through me.

4 I say unto you listen to my words, God he made your body, he knew you before you were born, does not your body need food, air and water, for if these things were to be taken away from you, would you not surely die; I say unto you, that the same holds true to your spirit; for God he created your spirit to be joined to him, and so without him, it will surely die; there will be no eternal life, do you choose eternal life.

5 Come to me and listen more, for I say to you this, when God offers you eternal life; God he is offering you himself; I live in the heavenly kingdom, I watch all you do; and people cannot go to heaven; until they no longer live in the fleshly bodies that they have; but listen unto me, you can have eternal life now; let those who have ears let them hear, understand what I now say; for eternal life doesn't begin when you die, eternal life begins now; the moment you put your love and your faith, in the messiah Jesus Christ; for it is then that I reside, in your Holy Spirit in which I gave; the moment you change your ways, your new life, I will give unto thee.

6 The trinity many do not understand, even though many say that they comprehend, for there is no greater intention, then to be joined together with the creator, of our Heaven and Earth; the first is to let God guide you every step of your faith, the word of God is life changing, if heaven is where you want to be based; to guide you out of the mess, that your life has been in, which is of sin.

7 We do need Gods strength; to guide us all the way; for nothing is impossible, if you believe; in what God, can do for you; power he gives you when you believe with all your heart; God is the almighty, its eternal life he gives unto you; the power in the Holy Spirit, the strength and the love to.

8 For those who choose to have separation from God, understand that hell does exist; for there is that existence, and is this an existence one wants to take; I say unto you this, God accepts what people do choose, for God offers forgiveness to everyone; so if you choose to go it alone, you have then become separated from God; do you want eternal life.

9 God cannot make everyone go to Heaven, for love cannot force a relationship on all; we were all created to have the ability; to choose freely as we please, to live in good or in bad; this is why humanity suffers so much grief, it's because of the separation from God; and If you are spiritually blind, you will not understand this; do you want eternal life; God doesn't choose anyone to suffer at all, it grieves him when his children fall away, they are heart hardened, ignoring their God; they have chosen not to accept him, because of their lack of faith; they rely on this world, trapped in lies and deceit; separation and unbelief; it is what they choose to believe, so I will tell you my beloved children, those who have ears let them hear.

10 Love worketh by faith alone; you walketh only by the path that you choose; I call on you to receive me, the love trust and the faith I will receive; so live in me and I will live in you; choose me over this world; I gave you the right to make mistakes, I give you the choice to receive me and repent; so will you love me as I love you, will you believe in me and trust me, put all your hope and faith in me; to live in me as I will live in you, then If you do, give yourself unto me, with all your heart and your soul, and I will set you free, feel and want everlasting eternal love and peace.

111

In the expression of the Holy Spirit, My Messiah Jesus Christ

1 I am so thankful my Lord that my heart has been moved, like a sacred heart, the flame of God, for I am a Holy believer and united in you as one; my Messiah as we bow down and pray unto you; I feel tenderness in my heart, devotion in faith with you; now with a powerfully changed heart, from bearing the good news, the gospel words of God; in the expression of the Holy Spirit, my Messiah Jesus Christ.

2 My living hope, Jesus Christ, our care giver of hope; I reach out to you with a pure heart and love, a new changed conscience, a conscience longing to be completely pure, I proclaim the word of God with all of my heart and soul; I rise to the occasion to write and spread the word, in the expression of the Holy Spirit, my Messiah Jesus Christ; the Holy Spirit is the breath of God, which empowers within, the believers in the truth and faith believing.

3 Lord Jesus, my faithfulness is strong in your sight, my prayer and words, in your presence I give unto you; let your light shine through us; my Holy one, as we are united together, together as one; flooded in your revelation, supernatural fruits that you give, the goodness, righteousness and the truth; I come to you my saviour, it's my passion to grow stronger in faith; I hunger for my Lord Jesus and praise him for the washing and cleansing of my sins.

4 Beloved Jesus Christ, our King; as you shall guide me with your counsel; receiving me to glory, for you light my lamp, my Lord you illuminate all my darkness away from me and my family; which you have filled us now with love and light, that shines before us; search me oh God, and know my heart well, oh try me God, know my anxieties; take away any wicked ways, pull me in the right way, make my ways straight; so to everlasting peace, I believe that you abound in me in hope, love and faith; in the power of the Holy Spirit, bringing justified faith; through our Lord Jesus Christ.

5 Lord I pray thee; that I overcome every form of darkness, as a strong soldier of our Lord Jesus Christ; who is our anointed one; I seek only to live life empowered by Gods free flowing grace, which is our true strength, given unto us, found in Jesus by union with him; we must stay free from the chains and the sufferings; given by us from evildoers of the world; we must abide in Jesus for the word of God it cannot be chained; I have suffered much heartache lord; but it does benefit your chosen people, to hear such words, to discover the overcoming life that is in Jesus, and experience such a wonderful journey that lasts forever, to be joined with him in his death, we are united with him in life, joined with him in his suffering, we will reign in his triumph and we have trust and faith in the words of God.

6 I will hear what our Lord will speak, as he speaks with such love and grace, to his people and his saints who bow down on their knees and give thanks; oh come to me all you who labour, and who are heavily laden and I will give you rest and peace, so take my yoke upon you, and learn all about God; and all the love that I teach; for I am meek and lowly in heart; and my peace I give unto you, my yoke is easy and my burden is light, do not taste fear for I am here by your side, I look deep within your soul, and I take away all your pain, in the expression of the Holy Spirit, my Messiah Jesus Christ.

7 Gods peace he will leave you, his peace he will give you, and not as the world gives does he give you; do not let your hearts be troubled neither let fear trouble you; for darkness cannot harm you, for you cast it away in the name of your Lord Jesus Christ, he will give his children peace, Jesus he will bless his people with healing, for he is the great practitioner.

8 These things which you have learnt, received, heard and saw in me do them; for the God of peace will then be with you, filling you with love and compassion, through our Lord Jesus Christs mercies, we are not consumed because of his compassions for they fail not; they will be new every morning, as you meditate on his words at night, for God he is great in his faithfulness, in the expression of the Holy Spirit, my Messiah Jesus Christ.

9 Think childlike, for I am God your source; for I say unto you, cast your cares unto me' do not let your mind be troubled, do not walk that road, that trail of thoughts your mind wants to take you on, it's the darkness, the enemy, who wants you to continue in your fears; and if you do not release it to God, it will continue to get darker; so cast it away for you have no future in the thinking about all your past and present troubles; and my peace I will give unto you.

10 Think on thinks that are truth (the word of God) being just for (God is a just God) Love for (God is Love) forgiveness of others (for God forgives you) and praise the Lord (for he is Good) the peace of God passes all understanding; for he will keep your heart and mind in perfect peace, trust in me and keep your mind stayed on me; pick up the cross and follow me, for I am not changed, I am the same yesterday and today; forever, I am stable; in the expression of the Holy Spirit, my Messiah Jesus Christ, our saviour and our King.

11 My voice oh Lord, all my cares I shall give unto you, you shall hear my voice in the morning, oh Lord in the morning I will direct it to you, as I look up with love in my eyes, with compassion, you will wipe away my tears, the comforter you will send me, and your words are in the expression of the Holy Spirit, my Messiah Jesus Christ.

12 My gracious Lord Jesus, will you show me the path of life; as the path of righteousness you walk me on, it will be in your presence, in fullness and in joy; for in your right hand there are pleasures forever more; you reached down from heaven and you rescued me, you took me by the hand and drew me out of the deep waters; you spoke to me in words of love, forgiveness, mercy and compassion; you washed and cleansed me whiter than snow; for the repentance of my shame; you took my sins and cast them into the deep depths of the sea, to be remembered no more.

13 Oh the Lord over all, your voice is upon the waters, the God of glory who thunders in his mighty power, we sing praises to you our king Jesus; who rides in the clouds above all; Lord Jesus your peace surpasses all understanding, it guards my heart and my mind, through the Holy Spirit given unto me; the Holy Spirit of perfection where you reside, the work of righteousness is peace; for this effort of righteousness is quietness and an assurance forever; in the expression of the Holy Spirit, my Messiah Jesus Christ, I give deep worship and thanks to thee.

14 No fear of darkness will come upon me, because of the love and protection of my Lord Jesus Christ, his blessings and words are power, the words made manifest in his Holy Name; you alone are all I can put my trust in; whom have I in heaven but you; neither is there anyone upon Earth that I desire, for it can be only you; you know my deepest desire, you know my deepest thoughts, you know what I long for, for you hear my deepest sighs, you catch my flowing tears, you hold my heart in your hands; you whisper in my ears; I am here my beloved child, you talk to me in my sleep, you show me dreams of love and peace, I meditate on heaven, for one day you will take me there; you truly are the son of God, you truly are our king, your passion and understanding, my Lord Jesus I truly love thee.

112

I am not ashamed of the Gospel of Jesus Christ

1 Oh Lord indeed you have made my days as handbreadths, as my age is nothing before you, for certainly everyone at his best state is but vapour; but my Holy one when with rebukes you correct us, for iniquity, you make ones beauty melt away like a moth; surely then is not everyone but vapour; my Lord Jesus I pray you with love in my heart, for I am not ashamed of the gospel of Jesus Christ.

2 The world it only blinds us; why; you do not even know what will happen tomorrow, what is your life, when you are just a mist that appears for a little while, and then just vanishes; but fear not; for I am with thee, I will bring thy seed from the east and gather thee from the west, thus says the Lord your God; who will make a path for thee.

3 My Holy one, I am not ashamed of the Gospel of Jesus Christ, for you are faithful and just to forgive, you died on the cross and took all of our sins, and you suffered for all, you forgave us cleansing us of all unrighteousness; for all have sinned and fallen short of the glory of god the father of all; I will without hesitation pick up the cross of my Lord and my saviour, I follow you with all my heart and soul, with praise, worship I honour you; I bless your Holy and righteous name, your promise to all who follow you, is that everyone who calls on the name of Jesus Christ will be saved and have eternal life, given the Holy Spirit, where you reside.

4 I say unto you that even so there will be more joy in heaven over one sinner's repentance than over ninety- nine righteous people who need no repentance; Lord your kindness and lovingness and mercy is why I say unto you with love and joy and grace that I am not ashamed of the Gospel of Jesus Christ, I will speak the word of God to all that I can even in rejection, I will send mercy and blessings to all, I will hold my hands up high to my King of Kings and Lord of Lords.

5 I receive thee oh Lord Jesus, I walk in you, rooted and built up in you, and firmly established in the faith and the gospel, as I have been taught; abounding in it with thanksgiving; for I am not ashamed of the Gospel of Jesus Christ, for the more I follow in the footsteps of Jesus Christ; the more my Holy Spirit transforms me, and the more it transforms me the more I find that guilt takes over and rebukes what I have done wrong in the name of Jesus Christ; I am more full of love and respect, hope, faith and trust; that the gospel will transform us each and every day filling us with the truth, healing and blessings and a life of eternal life in Jesus Christs Holy and righteous name.

6 How I wait on you Lord Jesus for all the strength that I need each day, I need that courage in my heart to face what the world and darkness has to throw my way, to try its best to keep me away from my Lord Jesus and to take away my peace, peace that has been lovingly given in the trust and faith of Jesus Christ; Oh yes Lord I wait with contentment for it is great gain in your name and in your eyes, it is the very reason that I am not ashamed of the Gospel of Jesus Christ, its closeness to a great healer and king, purity and deep loving kindness.

7 The wisdom that comes from Heaven is first of all pure, then peace loving, considerate, and submissive, full of mercy and of good fruits, to be impartial and sincere, oh how kind is our Lord, how good is he, I am not ashamed of the Gospel of Jesus Christ, for this God of ours is full of mercy, the blood of our Lord Jesus Christ is life, everlasting.

8 Oh blessed be our Lord Jesus Christ who daily hears our prayers, and bears all our burdens, for its God who is our salvation, who will not fail nor forsake you, we can draw from the gospel of truth, and fear not, nor be afraid.

9 The eternal God is our salvation and underneath is his everlasting arms; he will drive out all our enemies before us, Jesus is always near us, draw on his strength and never be discouraged for he is our God; Jesus will strengthen and help, hold and love us into everlasting victory, with his right hand he will never let go his children whom call upon him for salvation and truth, no I am not ashamed of the gospel of Jesus Christ, and I will forever praise pray and worship in his Holy and righteous name, amen

10 I give thee thanks to you God who gives victory through our Lord Jesus Christ, my rock and my salvation, my high tower; I shall not be greatly moved, but steadfast in his deep love, he has healed me when my heart was broken; he bind up my wounds, bringing me peace and harmony, sending me the comforter, Oh my great practitioner; in the presence of our God almighty we must always pray to him giving thanks for all he has done; our Lord in one body, one hope, one love, one gospel, the gospel of truth, our Lord our king Jesus Christ.

11 The chastisement for our peace was upon our Lord Jesus; for it was by his stripes we have been healed, by his blood that was spilt we have been saved, he was wounded for our transgressions, and bruised for our iniquities, our Lord he is gracious to us, and he blessed us and he will make his face to shine upon us, and he will give us our peace in hard times; Jesus is love and grace in abundance, his word is a lamp unto my feet and a light unto my path, I love you my Lord Jesus Christ, my king of kings, I praise and glorify your Holy name.

12 I put my trust in you oh Lord with all of my heart and soul, I try not to lean on my own understanding and the understanding of our deceitful world, in all your ways oh Lord I acknowledge you; for it is you who will direct my paths, I am not ashamed of the Gospel of Jesus Christ, it's the fear of God that is the beginning of knowledge, but the foolish despise wisdom and the instructions of the word and truth of God and the Gospel.

13 Lord Jesus I love and trust in you all the days of my life, to live in you is to live in peace and you have shown me that in so many ways; to feel and to be secure and to be at ease of all dread and evil, I do understand that I have your love and forgiveness; the peace of mind that Jesus gives is like none other; the healing that comes from the blood of Jesus is life, the light that he shines forth to you leads to life everlasting, for he alone is the light of this world; the counsellor, the Holy Spirit, whom Father God sent in his name, he is our teacher of all things, and I speak of our Savour; and Jesus Christ is his name.

14 I am not ashamed of the Gospel of Jesus Christ, for it is God who works in you to "will" and act in order to fulfil his good purpose, I say unto you to commit thy way unto me Jehovah your God; oh trust in him, and God he will bring it to pass, he will walk you in the path of all righteousness, in faith, hope and trust; you will walk by faith and not by sight; Oh how great are your works God for thy thought are so deep, I will give you Lord repeated thanks and praising you in the depths of my heart for all to hear and listen I will speak your Holy name; I will shout with joy and love for you Lord God almighty who has ransomed me.

15 Blessed is the God of Israel, for he visits all people who call out to him, sing I am not ashamed of the Gospel of our Lord Jesus Christ, for our God he is wonderful, oh how his words are filled with love, shout to heaven singing praises as your eyes reach to his filled with tears and love; for its his mercies that are poured out to all who pray and receive him, as there Lord and saviour; Holy, Holy, Holy to our Lord God almighty, worthy are you to be praised.

16 Lord from the source of your righteousness is my justification and from your marvellous mysteries is the light of my heart, oh how my eyes are gazed on you, do you see Lord how my eyes fill with tears as I pour out my prayers of devotion, do you read my heart for all the love that I feel towards you, I can't see the depth but I know it's there, I cannot comprehend this deep feeling, but I know you do, for you alone gave it to me; Lord know that when my eyes are gazed upon you it is of that which is eternal, on wisdom that is concealed from people, on knowledge and wise design, hidden from people on a fountain of righteousness, I am not ashamed of the Gospel of Jesus Christ, before you Lord I will bless your Holy Name as I move my hands and bow my knees in worship, for you thy great goodness, the good news, the king of all I pray Amen.

113
Blessed are you; Lord our God

1 Blessed are you; Lord our God, Our Messiah our King, and glory to our God most high, for words cannot express how your greatness has transformed our lives; and the children of God have placed you on their hearts, we believe and trust and have the deepest of faith in you; oh God most high; we pick up thy cross and follow you, we have repented our Lord, for you who died to save all; "My beloved Lord" I tell you in my heart you didn't die for nothing at all; our hearts do ache for our deepest love, for our beloved Lord, our saviour king Jesus, the son of God.

2 We walk with you every single day, we read the Gospel, the good news from you; "our journey Lord" that we are more than willing to embrace; stay with me Jesus to the very end, you are my saviour my loving grace; when I close my eyes I walk with you in dream state; you hold my hands and we lovingly pray, a dream that fulfils me each of my waking days, I guess what I am really saying Lord is to never leave my sight, for blessed are you my Lord Jesus Christ.

3 Thanking you Lord Jesus, It's so easy to do, when you live every day, with the one who truly loves you; united together as one body in Christ; our journey together, one true Christian life; the blessings from God, from heaven above, the life giving answer, the blood of Christ, the bread of life; transforming lives, believe and trust in your Lord Jesus Christ; for the Lord he says love me with all of your heart and soul, I will never leave you, you will never be alone, oh you touch me heart Lord in such a loving way, I feel the love inside, I take your loving hand, and as I look to you, another hand touches me back, I know that it is you; it's the hand of our Lord Jesus Christ, blessed are truly you.

4 Blessed are you our Lord God; the one who is never far away; and blessed am I, who feels you by my side, for blessed are we for our Lord and our God, who gives us the time of day; the one who answers our prayers, who watches our every steps, who talks to us, who lights up our paths, the path that leads us to Heavens Holy Gates.

5 Oh blessed are you, Lord our God; the master of the universe the great creator of all; who has sanctified us, and with his commandments to wrap ourselves in the fringes of Gods words, the Jewish prayer shawl that Jesus wore.

6 Oh God how we all marvel at the love that you give, your loving kindness is felt by the children you have saved; and no one can save us but our Lord Jesus Christ, so we need to pick up the cross and truly follow him, to express in our words, that he is our Messiah and our true King; our Messiah in Heaven who we will gaze upon one day, this day that we will keep placed deeply in our hearts, the day we will meet our Lord Jesus Christ.

7 My heart so overwhelmed with the deepest of love, and how amazing and true that Gods words are, the word of God and it's amazing power; and how it can just turn your life around, these powers are the words of Jesus Christ, the breath and the power of the holy Spirit given; the power of creation and the power to heal, to even make the lame, walk again; Lord but my words are so numb, not because I don't know what to say, I am numb because of the love and affection that I have for you inside; to many words at one time, to express to my Lord, Jesus Christ, Oh blesses are you, Lord our God.

8 Oh blessed are you, oh Lord our God; if you read my heart Lord, you will find where my love is formed, the Holy Spirit you have given me so deep inside, the transformation of our lives it's here where this power lies; the God within; the love and the truth, the words of God, righteousness he gives, and the pathway to joy.

9 Our precious Lord, our royal king; your words are written on my heart for all to read and hear; you're a poet my Lord, so beautifully expressed, but then you are the word made manifest; so it's not hard to comprehend, our Holy and righteous King, tell me over and over again, and I will write them all down, the words from Heaven, the angels they will sing, so keep speaking to me Lord, for blessed are thee.

10 Blessed are you Lord our God, forever keep us deep in your heart, read us deeply as you forget all our sins; place us in protection under the righteousness of your angel wings; hide us deeply from all our regrets; as we live and breathe our lord and saviour everyday; we were called together; united as one; as we find our way; to live eternally with the son of God, I feel you Lord, you're getting closer day by day, to save all your children to whisk them away; blessed and Amazing is our teacher; our Messiah our reigning Heavenly King, our Lord Jesus Christ, and Holy is your name, as we pray all together. Amen and amen.

114
Oh how bad do you want; God's Mercy and Grace

1 Only for you; for your Glory Lord God; for your presence I await; My God, my amazing grace; let it come your loving kindness, let it flow, let it pour upon us; as we search and seek your Holy embrace; oh how bad do you want; God's mercy and grace.

2 Why is it Lord; that destiny takes more than a moment, and why is it, that we realise our dreams and visions take such hard work effort and endurance; and periods of times that are so tough that sometimes even to keep going is such a struggle; Oh how bad do you want, God's mercy and love.

3 Oh look at the man called Moses a man of great destiny, a great hero for many of the Old Testament, a great man who had saved many thousands from Egypt, who took on the Pharaohs with God's strength love and mercy for his people; a calling from God to save his entire nation, after 430yrs of slavery; Moses suffered many emotions and struggles but he never gave up entirely, he tries, however even Moses gets rejected by God, but 40yrs later God calls Moses to his Holy mountain, and comes to Moses as a flaming bush, this flaming bush of God's loving kindness; forever changes Moses life; Oh how bad do you want God's mercy and grace.

4 How bad do you want to be free; how bad do you want to be different, how bad do you want the purpose of God in your life, how bad do you want God's love, his peace and joy and to put on a smile upon your face; how bad do you want to be well; how bad do you want your family home to be lit by God's illuminating love; and to hear your children always saying, I love you mum and dad; so how bad do you want God's mercy and grace.

5 How bad do you want God to make a difference in your life? And are you willing to change your direction to Jesus Christ; to open your eyes to his kingdom in Heaven, and to close your eyes to the world in which you live in; can you think about why you need this change, what has this world really done for you? Where do you really belong? How bad do you want God's mercy and grace?

6 How bad have you been mistreated or how bad have you mistreated others? Are you living by God's grace and faith, and do you feel you even deserve God's love and grace; how bad is your calling, what is your true destiny, do you want to get to know God's love and faithfulness, love and faithfulness that you will not get from this world; the kingdom of God's is compassion and mercy, love spread out for all; Jesus Christ is our saviour; our king and our Lord, how bad do you want God's mercy and grace.

7 Do you find yourself at the mercy of unkindness, darkness trying to devour you around every corner, are you afraid to face every day; are you longing for God to shine his light; and to be saved; are you longing for God to shine your way, to fulfil every moment of your day; to feel the freshness and breeze surrounding your every step; then look up and reach for Jesus, the word; he will take you by the hand and show you real love; he will lead you away from the darkness that you face, now how bad do you want God's mercy and grace.

8 How bad do you want God's mercy and Grace, its small steps to God is all it will take, understanding that Jesus only wants you by his side; your repentance in heaven, where angels will rejoice, another sinner saves by God's mercy and love; and gladness that you have accepted "Jesus Christ" as your Lord; Join the family in Heaven where true love is all around, Jesus will read your heart to see your devoted love, and if you are loyal, he will reside there as well.

9 A change of direction, giving up the world that is full of sin; for it is a better choice to do so in the end; the word of God, the love, trust and faith; a true family in Heaven, waiting for us to embrace, A heavenly father, our loving Jesus Christ; no sickness no pain no deception, no sin; Just grace, and mercy is all they give; accept our Lord and saviour for he is the only way, so pick up the cross of our Lord Jesus Christ today; he is loving and caring and he wants you to repent, and if you do his promise is he will see you in the end; Oh how bad do you want, God's mercy and grace.

115
As I live and breathe to know your ways

1 Let us come before his Holy presence, with love and joy and thanks giving; let us shout for joy to our Lord as we pray before him; as you walk among us and be our God, as we your people, we will live and breathe and learn your ways.

2 I can never escape from your spirit; I can never get away from your Holy presence as I live and breathe to learn your ways, my heart rejoices with my new found life with my Lord and saviour Jesus Christ.

3 For your promise to us is that where two or three are gathered together, you will be with us as we pray; your promise is if we remain in you, that you will remain in us as well; oh glory be to God for he will never leave our sight; for no branch can bear fruit by itself, it must always remain with the vine; and neither can we bear any fruit, unless we remain in you; as we live and breathe to learn your ways, Lord Jesus Christ my saviour and My King.

4 For those who say they live in God they should live their lives as Jesus did; Lord as I live and breathe to learn your ways, do not cast me away from your presence, do not take your Holy Spirit from me, I love you with all of my heart, and I will repent for my ungodly deeds, for your promise is to your children; is that you will be with them always.

5 Holy, Holy, Holy Jehovah of hosts most high; the whole Earth is full of your Glory, Oh worthy are you to be praise, as I live and breathe to learn your ways; my Lord, my God and my Holy one, you deserve the glory the honour and the praise; Lord you alone created all with your hands, your Holy word and breathe created all things, the word made manifest is power beyond our belief; and it's because of your desire that we exist; created in your image my Lord, in all my heart I give thanks to know, my Lord Jesus Christ.

6 My beloved Lord and Saviour, whom I praise and worship alone; you have changed my very essence; and done many miracles in my life, as I live and breathe to learn your ways for I have such a long way to go; I turn to my Lord Jesus to teach me what I need to know; and with your patience and understanding I put my faith and love in you; and I know my saviour I will get there, for its your promise that you will help me, and that you will never leave my sight; so I will achieve my goal and be more like you; to have my place in Heaven, and to see my king upon his white throne.

7 I say unto you; as it comes to pass in the last days, I will pour out my spirit on all flesh, now the Lord is the Spirit and where the Spirit of the Lord is; there is liberty, for the son Jesus Christ shall therefore make you free, you shall be free indeed.

8 My beloved gracious Lord, if only we would all live a life filled with your law and your love, following in your Holy example, you loved us enough to offer yourself as a sacrifice; which was a pleasing aroma to God; and as we are a pleasing fragrance of Jesus Christ to God; among those who are being saved and among those who are to perish; it will be that whoever will accept and call on our saviour Jesus Christ will be saved; we pray in your Holy name that many more will pick up the cross of our Lord and repent and live in Christ, to have everlasting life.

9 Lord my God, I exalt you in the Heavenly realm, and how every knee shall bow in reverence; I give thanks to you forever as I live and breathe your ways, for it is great peace have those who love and want to learn your laws; for nothing can make them stumble; and happy will be those whom you discipline, oh my Lord and saviour, for the ones you teach they will receive rest from the days of adversity; I have astounding tender affection for my Lord Jesus Christ, in your Holy name I pray to thee.

10 I say unto you all my children, to be joyful and grow in maturity and you will receive wisdom beyond your years; encourage one another, living in peace and harmony, do not allow self promotion to hide your heart, and abandon every selfishness and you will receive revelation of spiritual insight, I am God of mercy, and my peace I give unto you, love me as I love you, for I have called you to live a life of freedom in the Holy Spirit; however do not view this wonderful freedom as an opportunity to set up a base in this world, for this freedom in which I speak off it means not to indulge yourself and to become completely free as to serve one another, expressing love in all that you do, do not agitate the Lord your God, as to be brought under judgement.

116

Adorned with blessings

1 Oh Holy one blessed be he, as my Lord he put his hands on me; for I was adorned with all blessings 5360 I became to be; I was raised up and I grew to be the length and width of the world; and the Holy one gave me 72 wings which grew on me; 36 on each side, and each one covered the entire world,

2 The Holy one gave me 365 eyes and each eye was as the great luminary moon, which shines light on all; I was called Metatron; you would know me as my Earth name "Enoch" I was adorned with blessings from the Holy Jesus Christ; the 365 eyes I was given are 1 for each day of the year; 72 wings for the 72 nations of the world, my wings cover the world, Oh Holy one blessed be he for Metatron I am but my God he calls me "youth" for I was taken from Earth and in Heaven I am the youngest of them all.

3 I your Holy one Jesus Christ came on the morning of the 6th day being Friday; I commanded my wisdom to create man from seven consistent applications; **1** being mans flesh from the Earth; **2** his blood from the dew; **3** his eyes from the sun; **4** his bones from the stone; **5** his intelligence are from the swiftness of the Angels and the clouds;

6 his veins and his hair are from the grass of the Earth; **7** his soul is from my breath and from the wind; adorned with blessings; from the Holy anointed one, blessed be he,

4 And **7** being the perfect number for I gave **7** natures to the flesh- hearing; the eyes for sight; to the soul – smell; the veins – touch; the blood- taste; the bones for endurance; to the intelligence- enjoyment and peace; I am your Lord God the creator of all, adorned with blessings that I have given unto all.

5 I created speech a saying from all knowing; I created man from the spiritual and the physical nature; and from both come man's death, life and appearance; so adorned with blessings and with love, for I your Lord Jesus give a testing of man the free will to either love or hate me.

6 I say unto you for a day in your courts is better than a thousand outside, I would rather stand at the threshold of the house of my God, than to ever consider to dwell in the house of wickedness; I would rather be adorned in blessings from my beloved Lord Jesus, my God; for my heart and my soul overflow with abundant joy and peace, my soul is filled with deep gratitude in the presence of his love; this love for my saviour is beyond our understanding.

7 My heart and my flesh cry out for my living God; as my soul it yearns for the courts of the Lord God; Lord you have made known to me the ways of life; you have filled me with gladness with your presence everyday; you are generous to a fault, you have lavished your favour upon my business, my home and my beloved family, adorned with blessings for the love of our Lord.

8 Oh Lord how great you are to me ; as you are robed with honour, adorned with blessings in all your royalty and majesty; and to all who love you deeply; you are an honour to love and to be in fellowship with, for your beloved church; in worship Lord you will cover us like a curtain with peace, love and faith and in trust and hope you will bring us abundant joy; giving us the revelation of spiritual insight, all these blessings from our beloved teacher Jesus Christ our Messiah.

9 My Lord Jesus; my greatest passion, my anointed one; what a wonderful teacher you have been; I understand in my heart that I still long for more knowledge and understanding; a long spiritual journey have I still yet to go; oh I pray thee Lord; to lift me up; for all my prayers are with you, Oh Lord God in an acceptable time and in the multitude of you mercy; hear me; in the full truth of your salvation.

10 Lord I know in my heart your loving kindness is abundantly great beyond anyone's comprehension; turn to me my Holy one in accordance of your mercies, for how I deeply hunger for the knowledge, truths and wisdom of the words of God, for you alone are the word made manifest; I lift up my eyes of love and compassion to worship you in your Holy kingdom; and Lord all the strength and the love that you have poured upon us, we do feel adorned with blessings from our saviour Jesus Christ.

11 You are power and Glory; the doors and the widows of the heavens; the wheels and all the halls, you are the greatest of them all, adorned with blessings is our Lord Jesus Christ; who gives us his all; Oh Lord place your laws upon our hearts; and be our Lord and father till we meet face to face, I give myself to you with all my heart and soul, I am ready to come before you to face my wrongs hear on the Earth; and my deepest devotions are to my wonderful Lord Jesus Christ; AMEN

117
You rose again to save the lost

1 Jesus Christ you died upon the cross and you rose again to save the lost; forgive me now of all of my sins; come and be my saviour, my Lord and my friend; change my life to make it new; and to help me my King to live for only you.

2 Another special day about my Lord, as our hearts still deeply break for what you went through; your body punished as you received all our sins, do many of us not understand; that we crucified our saviour our King, that we sent you to the cross; but you rose again to save the lost.

3 How you must love us all, to suffer such pain, for you were stripped naked and mocked, as they nailed you to the cross; our beloved Lord how humiliated they made you feel; as you cried out to Father, father forgive them for they know not what they do; them not knowing at all, that they nailed our true king, but you rose again to save the lost.

4 Your believers Lord; suffer because of our sins; when we celebrate your birth and your death here on Earth; it's not enough for what we have done; you are our special Lord our beloved King, oh hear our prayers and forgive our sins; our deep love for you will never go away, we married our saviour when we gave ourselves to him; feel our deep love as you reside in us; as you rose again to save the lost.

5 Do we really understand or even comprehend, what love really is, that you suffered at the hands; it's you our King Jesus that understands real love, we can only pray and ask our Lord to show us the way; to be our teacher our father and our true friend; you are the only way to heaven, our true home above; and it's you our Lord Jesus, you rose again to save the lost.

6 Compassion and mercy that you have for us all; and it's this deep love that we hunger for; you pick us up when we fall; you pick us up when we call out for you; you planted the seed to help us to grow; to move us closer to the kingdom above; this kingdom we seek is our heaven called home; to a God a father who loves us all; who rose again to save the lost.

7 Our Lord Jesus Christ, he loves us all; he died on the cross, and he suffered for all; remember our King, it isn't hard to do, your children Jesus we pray deeply, because we really love you; our Lord our saviour we pick up the cross, we are followers in faith, truth and love, as you rose again to save the lost; **Amen my Lord from your saints in love.**

118

Lord I am the one to blame and I've caused all your pain

1 The Messiah to all, a king of kings; the city was Jerusalem, time two thousand years ago, the people called him Jesus and his crime; was for all the love that he showed; but you gave yourself, the day you wore that crown; I am the one to blame and I caused all your pain.

2 You've taught me love that only you could give; you died for me and took away all of my sins; you have shattered my heart, filling my eyes with love felt tears; oh thankyou Lord for showing me a better way to live; you have stolen my heart in such a loving way; all of me I give to my Lord, my King; Lord I am to blame and I caused all your pain.

3 My Lord Jesus you could have told Father; father take me away; I am not guilty, I am not the one to blame, I am sinless; Father I am not going to pay the price; but your Love for us Jesus was so deep; Lord I am the one to blame and I caused all your pain, you Lord died for my sins; you knew my beloved Lord what you had to do to save us all; from our bodily abuse, that causes our sin.

4 My Lord Jesus as you walked right through the city gates; you looked up onto the hill that hill of fate; three crosses you saw, two crosses that had two criminals; one on each side of yours; the pain you where enduring as you carried your cross, your body stripped from the beatings you took; you fell to your knees because of the weight, this was also because of the sins that you took; all of our shame that you felt that day was almost too much for you to take; Lord I am the one to blame and I've caused all your pain.

5 His disciples were to watch over him; one hour was all Jesus asked from them; as he walked to pray to father God; for supported was all that he did need; he looked up to Father will tears rolling down his face; he cried out to father; father let this cup pass from me; Father he cried; not by my will but yours; Lord I am the one to blame; and I have caused all your pain.

6 You struggled with abuse and punishment; when all you wanted to do, was to show us how much love you have for us all; our great teacher our prophet our Lord; but it ended up being what they thought was your fate; our Messiah our King the saviour of all; you showed them in the end; that you were the son of God.

7 The love and the miracles that you showed for all; wasn't enough to show people who you were; they mocked they cursed you, for what you had done, but you were there to teach, to bring the church to life; to preach the Gospel, the word of God; to all generations, to save the world; but many were blind, because of their sins, they only wanted to condemn the son of God; but the Christians they accepted the son of God, our Messiah our Lord our true King Jesus Christ.

8 My Lord, my saviour, I am the one to blame I caused all your pain; you died for me; you saved my Life; and if it wasn't for you, I would not be where I am today; you were sentenced on the cross at Calvary,

died in agony; which you went through for me; when you took me by
the hand and said father it is finished; this child is mine and is saved.

9 Oh how my love for you is so deep inside; with our entire faults and
complaining, you still love us all; the compassion and mercy, the peace
that you give, the path of righteousness that you have lead me in;
just feels so right; knowing you are near me; for I need your strength
I need your touch, for your Holiness you take my breath away; a father
a son so full of love, that only wants love in every ones heart.

10 Lord I am the one to blame and I've caused all your pain; we need
to repent to be saved by God; so we can wipe away all the tears
from his eyes, he died for us, to give us life, but we are throwing it
away for the sins of the world; let him not have died for nothing at all;
repent for your sins, give yourself to our Lord; every sinner saved, all
the angels will rejoice, and heaven above will write your name; in the
Lambs book of life, and all your sins will be remembered no more; for
by grace you have been saved by the Lord.

119
The word of "God"
so loving so true

1 Lord; our Saviour, my reigning king; the peace and joy that is in my life; that you have brought to me and my family; what does one say, to how we all feel, the word of God has transformation beyond our wildest dreams; our lives so different, we are all at peace, we even walk around with a smile on our face; we think before we speak, watching what comes out of our mouths; these things we would not have done before, before we found "God" for the words of God are loving and true.

2 You teach me these words almost every day, which is bringing us all so much joy when we bow down and pray; as you speak to me the word of God, I'll listen and learn. And I'll put pen to paper and write; the words of God so loving and true.

3 I say unto you my people on Earth, you know not what you do, for many turn away from me; any chance that you can, however the truth of the matter is do you want to find the time; to seek me out, to listen and to learn the word of God and the truth; for the word of God is loving and true.

4 Come to me my people I say unto you; but you hear not my words; I say unto you seek me child; but you go with your day; I say unto you; do not be troubled child; for I am here by your side; but you push me away; letting anger build up in your heart always; but the word of God is loving and true.

5 Let go off this world and turn to me; let go of this world it's all I want from thee; it causes to much anger, deception, pain, lies and sin; If you get to caught up in it, then I cannot get in; for you build up walls that I can't get through, eyes and mind so troubled; that you cannot break free; so call on me and I will hear your prayers, turn to me and give me a chance, I am your God loving and true, I am compassionate and loving and I am your only chance, do you want to be saved; for the word of god is loving and true.

6 Compassion and love is what I can give; I will wait for you; when you are ready for me; mercy and kindness is waiting my child, turn to me and know I am your God; can you hear the angels rejoicing above, it's the heavenly kingdom for another saved child; the words of God; loving and true.

7 Believing and faith is needed with deep love; it will open your heart; and it's there that I can reside; I will work on you every single day, scraping away all your sins; that you have; repentance will come easy for it will be something you will want to do; and It will be no option, once you turn to me; I will know your heart, and every essence of you; that's why I come to you for your heart is now true; and the words of God are loving and true.

8 A new life child is what I gave thee, for you have searched me; and made me your saviour and king; your love for me; it's true in your heart; live in me and I live in you; believing in me is all I want from you, I saw your suffering; I saw your pain, and for all that has happened; it has not been in vain; you are a different child because of your love, your trust and your faith in the word of God; the word of God; loving and true.

120
Compelled by God's Love

1 Do you feel draw to our Lord Jesus, do you think about his day and night; does he make you smile, does he fill deeply the depths of your heart; does he overwelm you with tears rolling down your face; do you understand your compelled by God's love and grace.

2 You have been drawn to God and there is a reason why; it could be as simple as that he has a job for you in this world; or a more serious reason, to save your life; so whatever the reason, whatever the call, you are driven by a force; compelled by Gods love.

3 Jesus is love who suffered for all; and he has always been with us, just waiting for our call; now give yourself in prayer to the one who loves us the most, he is seated at the right hand of the father God; he will answer your prayers, he is our saviour Jesus Christ.

4 Compelled by Gods love; our Lord Jesus Christ; your love shines in our eyes; our faces glow, knowing you are by our side; in our hearts where you reside, a rushing force which is driven by love; our Lord Jesus Christ, our walk with you, it gives us life; to face the day anew, we are born again in Christ, we are compelled by God's love, that only Jesus can do for you.

5 Jesus has changed people's lives all over the world, and his power is becoming stronger, and there is a good reason why; Jesus is coming back soon, in a little while, however remember my children, 1 day is a thousand years in the Heavenly realm; my children need to spread the word of God; and more people are needed to be saved, for the love for my children is important to me, so be compelled by God's love and your Messiah Jesus Christ.

6 There are many of my children all over the world; they are suffering at the perils of selfish wicked times; many are abused, not feeling loved at all; wondering why they were even, born at all; do you feel their pain; search deep within, where Jesus resides; for he is our saviour and our King; he feels their pain and their suffering and if you are feeling it to, it's the compassion from him; so open your hearts help where you can, be compelled by Gods love, feel it deep within.

7 Save as many as you can, by drawing on God's love; and do you really believe that you have done enough; people cold; nowhere to live, when you are snuggled up cosy and warm in bed; they are crying with hunger, children are dying, every second of the day; with no food or water for many days; and people are watching as their loved ones are dying in their arms; and when you think about what we are throwing away each day; its unimaginable how many lives we could save.

8 Would you feed a family and save a life, are you being compelled by God's love, a driven force by Jesus the son of God; for your brothers and sisters are dying all over the world, are you shedding tears for all who have died; the unknown the unloved, the forgotten, that have suffered in our cruel, and selfish world; are you compelled by God's love to try and do more.

9 Thrown away and left to die, does it not break ones heart; but it also does break Jesus' heart as well; feel his love and pain deep inside, but they are also his tears rolling down your face; so if your heart is breaking for the underprivileged suffering in the world, rest assured that Jesus is feeling it deeply as well; he resides in you; you have become one, your compelled by God's love, the Holy spirit within, to save as many of Gods children as you can.

10 Do not give up, or think you have done all you can; do not even think that you can wipe your hands; many have died, another lost soul, another loved one crying out for help; when many have thrown away food they disliked; It is that easy for many in this world, many don't even know what it is like to starve, to go without or have nowhere to sleep, no water; to even have a sip; no clothes to wear in the freezing cold; we have the government to help us eat, but in their countries they do not care whether they live or die.

11 I have given you life; I say unto you, very few dollars is all you need; have you done enough to save the lost; compassion and mercy, is what I do teach, are you driven by love, that I supplied you with; you're touched by God's grace if your heart feels compelled; you cannot stop the strength of the Holy Spirit given, for you will feel the pain all over the world; your love will be deep, compelled and driven to save all; it's the God within; your Lord Jesus Christ; who has healed the suffering with the word and the touch of his hands; be compelled by Gods love and save as many as you can; your driven by the spirit, given by love, this is God in heaven and you are his beloved child; one saved person is your saving grace by God.

121

Lord you are the beginning; And the end

1 we have found love that never runs dry; Lord we know it comes from the depths of the sky; and how our love in our eyes are fixed on the one, the one who has no end; the one who stands strong and for all time; and for all your believers; that this faith has no end; for Lord you are the beginning; and the end.

2 Your love goes on forever oh Lord; your love goes on bringing so much joy; and its forever that our hearts will seek our Lord Jesus Christ; in everything that we believe from the skies to the oceans depths; in the beauty that it holds made from our Lord Jesus hands; it's this love that goes on to the end; for Lord you are the beginning; and the end.

3 Through every rise and fall, Jesus remember in our hearts you called us to be yours; and one thing I do know for sure; I am a child of the kings; I am writing this for you all, I was called to write these beautiful words a gift from God to share his words, a poet is the Lord his words made manifest; that is how he created the world in which we do live.

4 From dawn break and into the night our Lord Jesus is with us guiding us each day; know that he is with us, walking by our side; in righteousness we will walk for the pathway he will light; you are our saviour and our sweet rejoice, in an upside down world, thank you for calling us into yours.

5 Your arms forever opened wide; you took me in and you saved my life; your loving promise to keep me safe, to hold me tightly, with a strong embrace; and to never let me go; oh my Lord you are the beginning; and the end, your love is forever eternal; it will never have no end; you have a plan for your children, and that's to save as many as you can; to never suffer no more deception, to be never again lead astray; to suffer no more pain, and all tears are wiped away; I love you my Lord Jesus, you are the son of God in every way.

6 Lord Jesus your love is unfailing to all, and your love is never shaken; your hope given to all it awakens your love deep within us; and how can we not recall all that you have given; how can we not pray in thanksgiving, to our Lord Jesus Christ our King; for you are the beginning; and the end.

7 Holy, Holy, Holy Lord God almighty; no measure knows your worth; face down is where you found me; on my knees is where I cried out to thee; for if you had sort perfection, I would have died, trying to reach it; But my gracious and Holy righteous Lord, in your forgiveness and merciful heart; it's my broken heart that you wanted; my repentance, my Lord you truly got it, my deep affection you have, for we are united as one.

8 A heaven rejoicing for it has my broken hearts sound; for it now sings in heaven Holy, Holy, Holy is your name, for you are the beginning and the end; you own the sound of every broken heart; in heaven; in Jesus name, one in unity for all time; as you burn in me all your desires. Living once wrong, now a new child in Christ; a passion burning, for worthy is your name, and into your greatness, we will walk your way.

9 Forever now Jesus I will call on you; and every moment of my day Jesus I will think of you; and you will hear my soul crying out for you; forever connected, to never let each other go; darkness may enter, but it will be rebuked; before it takes hold; in Jesus name it has no hold; we are now one my Holy Spirit where you reside, it's a great feeling Lord that you are so close by; never alone, always at peace, completely change because of you my beloved King.

10 In my heart now I have just one word; it's **L.O.V.E** which comes straight from you; you are pure love, our sinless king; your love radiated through to all that you reach, you are the answer to everything; people when you feel god's love reach out to you; it's our Lord Jesus Christ reaching out for you; so follow our Lord and never let him go.

11 Jesus he will change your lives; and give you back much more; little by little each day he will work, and before you will know it; he will be totally yours; he wants you, and loves you; he is patient; and kind; his mercy will endure for the longest of time, repent immediately for what you have done; he wants you right back on the path which you fell; he will take you in his loving arms; he will scrape of the bad that he does not want; we must always pray in worship to our Lord Jesus Christ, and remember to always thank him for saving your life.

122 The Lord's Prayer

1 Our Father which art in Heaven,
I am the Alpha and the Omega, the first and the Last,
the beginning and the end;
Hallowed be thy name,
Holy, Holy, Holy Lord God of hosts most High,
Thy kingdom come;
New Jerusalem for all saved;
Thine will be done;
Sacrificial Lamb, Gods command to save all from sins;
On Earth as it is in Heaven;
Heaven and Earth will pass away;
a new Heaven and earth will be united as one;
Give us this day our daily bread;
Repentance and forgiveness of sins and iniquities;
and forgive us our trespasses;
I forgave you for your sins;
As we forgive those who trespass against us
and lead us not into temptation;
Love one another as I love you;
and deliver us from all evil;
Lord God's final Judgement of Satan, to the pit of fire;
no more suffering for his children;

For thine is the Kingdom;

Love and receive Jesus as your Lord and saviour;

For the power and the Glory;

Jesus reigns forever- King of Kings, Lord of Lords;

Forever and ever;

Eternal life in the New Jerusalem; with Jesus Christ;
and all of God's children pray.

AMEN

123

The Holy Communion (Prayer)
Bread

Maintain thy place with all care: both of flesh and Spirit; make it thy endeavour to preserve Unity for which nothing is better bearing with all people, even as the Lord did with thee supporting all in love, having thy Spirit always awake.

Guard for yourselves and for thy whole family or congregation, over which the Holy Spirit has appointed you as overseers; to shepherd and to tend; to feed and guide the church of God; which I your Lord Jesus Christ, brought with my own blood.

The blood of Jesus has opened the grave; the blood of Jesus it has opened Heaven; the blood of Jesus it keeps Heaven opened for all sinners, with repentance true to their hearts; for God being the judge of all and Jesus Christ the mediator; so let us all together in one Unity and with child like persevering, and expectant faith; let us open our souls to an everlasting experience of this wonderful amazing power of our Lord Jesus Christ.

As we gather here today in the Holy Communion with the body of our Lord Jesus Christ; the life giving bread and the Holy cup; for life is in the blood; faith in the blood of Jesus Christ it produces great power and results.

There are three that bear witness on Earth; the Spirit and the water; and the blood of Jesus, and these three agree in one; **1**- Water- baptism unto repentance the laying aside of your sins; **2**- The blood of Jesus- Redemption in Jesus Christ; **3**- The Spirit- is he who supplies power to the water and the blood; so also the spirit and the life giving blood; possessing living power in Heaven; the heart of people in man.

Christians are unleavened; there is no leaven- no evil; for we have been perfected in Jesus Christ; washed and cleansed out of the old Leaven, for we have been made unleavened in our Lord Jesus Christ our Passover Lamb, a sacrifice for all.

My beloved Lord and Saviour Jesus Christ; I feel totally blessed to be in your presence; to partake in the last supper, and we do this with love, honour and respect; I lift up my hands to you; for you have shown me what a great sacrifice that you have made for us, giving us this Holy gift to partake with, as we hold this bread in our hands, not only do we feel blessed and privileged, but we are taking you Jesus as the living bread.

My Lord I can do without many things, but now that we have found you, we cannot live without you; I have grown so much stronger in my faith, trust and believing, and more love for my brothers and sisters; Lord you are my spiritual teacher, my spiritual strength and so much more; you make me feel so loved, a loving feeling in my Holy Spirit like none other, it's a transformation given by you; I lift my hands up to my King, in honour; I humble my heart to you in a childlike faith, with a childlike heart.

I lift up this Holy bread, the Holy sacrament; for the greatest gift and sacrifice; that no one can ever out do, you are Lord over all; Lord you have saved washed and cleansed many thousands of your children of all sins; sins that you took for us upon thy cross; as you suffered and bore all sins; sicknesses and diseases; you have given and changed all believers, turning all our lives around; through the blessings of the Holy word of God.

I believe through your body and shed blood, that my body is healed from the crown of my head to the very souls of my feet; that every cell and every organ and every function of my body has been restored and renewed in our Lord Jesus Holy name including my mind, my body and my soul; I lift my hands to you oh Lord giving thanks for I believe in you, I have total faith and trust in you; I praise and I glorify your Holy name, I thank father in heaven for his precious and royal son, I believe Father that you sent your son to save us of all of our sins; and that he did rise again, I believe in the word and the truth in the Holy scriptures, and the truth of God the father, My Lord Jesus Christ you are the living bread; and all of Gods children they pray **AMEN.**

Now partake in the life given bread of Jesus Christ.

124
The Holy Communion (Prayer)
The Cup

Lord Jesus the Lamb of God, fill your blessings upon this Holy cup which I hold in my hands the cup which contains your royal and Holy blood; make this Holy blood effective in us; for we give ourselves unto you, to bring us to faith and to keep us faithful, for the heart of the spirit is in the blood of Jesus Christ; who through the eternal spirit offered himself without blemish to God; Lord Jesus purify our conscious from dead works; so we serve our living God.

The answer is in the blood of Jesus Christ; the living bond between the spirit and the blood that cannot be broken; but our conscious rises up and condemns us, where do we turn; we turn to our Lord and our saviour; we turn to the suffering and the death of Christ; for it is the blood of our saviour that is the only cleansing agent that can give our conscience relief in our life and our peace in death.

We must place ourselves under the teachings of the Holy Spirit; for our God so loved the world that he gave his only begotten son; that whoever believes in him; shall not perish but have eternal life; for God has prepared for those who love Jesus; and for those who trust in our Lord, the best is yet to come; we will see the all satisfying glory in God; and this is eternal life; to rescue us from final judgement.

For Jesus Christ having being offered once to bear the sins of many; he will appear a second time; but it will not be to deal with sins, but to those who are eagerly waiting for the arrival of our saviour and king; for by grace you have been saved, through faith; the Spirit of God that dwells in us as a seed of life, this is the powerful effect of the life giving blood of our Lord Jesus Christ, which is leading us.

Our Holiness we will always walk by faith and hope, you have given us a holy spirit which teaches us about your deep love for us; and that in your eyes you love us perfectly; our new found faith and walk as devout Christians is your leading and calling; to be united as one; our understanding of the great sacrifice you made for us; a gift you gave freely through your precious holy-royal blood, we thank you Holy one; for excepting all our shameful sins; we poured from our hearts, through our words, and our heartfelt tears; a repentance we all shared deeply to our Lord; we couldn't hide nothing from you; and we greatly will acknowledge reminders of our sins; a covenant done only between me and my Lord, that no one can break.

I put on my Holy Prayer shawl; out of love, devotion and respect for your beloved Holy Land of Israel in which we pray in honour; Lord you make us feel completely content, satisfied; blessed, as our spiritual teacher, divinely working in us; so we can become more and more like our Lord, a pure child, innocent and sin free.

I will obey you Lord, for I know it is not my will; I humble myself to you, thanking you for the path of righteousness you lead us to, and I do understand that you will lead me back, when I fall and become troubled; as your power it is my promise; I am fearfully and wonderfully made; as my body is stretched over the cross of my

Messiah, and the new covenant is Infallible, secured by your precious blood; remembering my sins no more, and forgiving my inequities; for the spirit it gives life, and the fear of God is upon my heart; I persevere as your power it is my promise, your commandments oh Lord place them upon my heart; for I seek them.

Holy and righteous Heavenly father, open our eyes spiritually as we pray, giving us the noblest visions and the highest aspirations; and the deepest convictions of our Christian fellowship; in this we pray in truth and sincerity as devout Christians; for it's in our high moments of worship; as we will forever renew our vows of loyalty to our father and our Lord Jesus Christ in thy Heavenly kingdom, the Holy kingdom in which we seek.

Lord strengthen us in our noble purposes, helping us as we take of the fruit of the vine which symbolizes the life blood of your precious son, as we are also deeply reminded of our Lords suffering at Calvary of our master upon the cross; we serve you Lord for it is our desire; forever and consistently in our heart and our soul.

As we are about to consume your precious blood, the heart of the spirit, the blood of the new covenant; a special covenant; for this covenant it will not fail; as we give thee thanks for all who have accepted our Lord Jesus Christ as saviour, who did shed his precious blood and gave commandments to his Loyal disciples to teach all nations and baptising in the name of the father and of the son and the Holy Spirit.

As we come before you today our Lord Jesus; we hold this cup up High, saying this cup is the new covenant in my blood, do this as often as you drink of it; in remembrance of me; for you are proclaiming my death until I return.

Is the cup of blessings in which we have just blessed at the Lords supper not sharing in the blood of Jesus, for indeed it is,

Is not the bread in which we have just partaken in not a sharing in the body of Christ; for indeed it is, since there is one bread which is the Lords believers; who are many united into one body, we are partakers of the one bread; which represents the body of Christ; and the Holy cup which represents the blood of Christ.

Drink from the Holy Cup

Repeat

In this we pray in the name of our Lord Jesus Christ who is our King of Kings our Lord of Lord's, he is our saviour and our Messiah, for life is in your precious blood; and all of Gods children pray, **AMEN**

We as believers in our saviour must always stay strong in our faith and our believing in the Holy Spirit, for faith and love in the flesh and blood in his passion and resurrection being both fleshly and spiritually; and in total unity of God with you, for in our Lord Jesus we are all sons and daughters of God, through faith.

Our holy and eternal God, maker of heaven and Earth and our father of our souls; who was called to us to be in fellowship with thee; for he has given us all good works to do; to take our lives and to let us be consecrated in the work of the church, Lord to thee; in the spirit of our Lord; he came not to be ministered to but to minister and to give his life for many; in the name of Our Lord Jesus, **Amen.**

125
Devotionals; Words of wisdom, to strengthen your faith

1 I say unto you my child; pay close attention, to your father's words, for insight will bring you great success.

2 God's words should be lived by; they will provide you with empowerment and spiritual insight.

3 The key to unlocking the kingdom of God is truth and knowledge; this comes with clinging to the word of God; it is God's treasure, this will be given to all who receive the word of God.

4 Discernment comes from wisdom and understanding; to learn to become wise; to teach the immature to become wiser in doing so this will also give you greater skills in leadership; and in all that you do.

5 Live in the obedience and devotion to God; paying close attention to the insight revealed to you in the words of god; to bring you success which will bring you peace, grace and calmness in all your thoughts; to guide you in all your decisions in the company of people that you will come in contact with.

6 Always stay faithful to God; saying "no" to all temptations in your youth, "peer pressures" saying "no" to things that will take you away from God; Robbing someone or doing a robbery; stealing of any form; lying; causing harm to another person, shedding blood; crime is no way to live, if you want to live in God; life is in the blood, life is only in your saviour Jesus Christ, "Repent" and ask for forgiveness, your God is a loving and forgiving Father, if your heart is genuinely sorrowful he will forgive you of your sins.

7 This is the same as above for the older generation; do not Lust over anything, sexual desires or other pleasures of the body, do not get intoxicated, do not blaspheme, or curse anyone; do not have a lying tongue; do not cover up crime for others; do not commit adultery, do not look at anyone with lust in your heart for this is still adultery.

8 Neither should anyone become such a fool as to cover up your own deceptions for do you think that your Lord your God would be a fool as to not know your true hearts desires, your deception, rebuke all darkness and come back to a pure heart, do not mock your lord your God, who knows all truth.

9 Come to me and pray for I will not turn you away; and those who have ears let them hear; do not continue in your stubbornness, and laugh at what I teach in the word; of the true Gospel.

10 In your times of darkness and stress, depression and heartache, do not let your heart be troubled; for I will send in the comforter, I am the Lord your God; remember the world hated me long before it hated you; I will never leave you nor will I forsake you, do not allow fear of any kind consume you.

11 Do not turn your back on me; pick up the cross and follow me, accept me as your Lord your God, do not have any other God before for, and I will give you my peace.

12 Treasure all that I have given you, in all strength and wisdom and your burdens will become light, and train your heart to live and walk in my footsteps; and in how I would have applied a task; train your heart in the words of God; and meditate on these words; listen to when I speak and accept my advice.

13 Call out to me in your prayers, ask and I will give unto you; then open your heart to full comprehension of what you have received from me; train your children and future grandchildren in the word of the Gospel; teaching them of love, joy, peace and harmony; insight and in strength to love and to believe in me with all of their heart and soul.

14 Above all teach them to fear thy Lord God; in wisdom and in knowledge, I am a loving and a compassionate God, the fear is to keep all; on the right path of 'all" righteousness, to abide in me, for me to be able to abide in you; do not stray from me, repent for all your sins, live in me and I your Lord God, will live in you.

15 I say unto you to keep yourself away from lies and manmade rules and regulations in religion; for the word of God is the truth; Jesus Christ he died to set you free from manmade religious untruths; your poor choices and the deceit you choose to listen to corrupts your judgement; If it doesn't sound right; it isn't right so walk away, and do not let it enter into your thoughts to take over; believe only in the word of the Gospel and its teachings; and the truth will set you free.

16 Always trust in your Lord God completely, do not always rely on your own opinions and the opinions of unbelievers who mock the word of God; believers of God should only rely on the gift given to you by God "the Holy Spirit" this is your true heart of love and kindness, faithfulness, and your trust in Jesus Christ; God almighty will help you in every decision, so never let your mind stray nor second guess for that is darkness trying to lead you away from God.

17 Your beloved Lord God he loves his children, he will never lead you away from him, he only wants the best for his children; he will never deceive you or lead you on the path of destruction or harm, that is the work of the darkness and lied, deception of this world, not the kingdom of God; if you have been lead by a still small voice trying to keep you away from making a wrong decision, then listen and obey, never try to correct God; when things end up going wrong how many times in the past have you said I knew I should not have done that, I should have listened to my first decision; God he is love and compassion and he is patient; he will never put you in harm's way; for he loves you unconditionally.

18 Embrace all truths given to you, these decisions are life changing pointing you to follow your Lord God; to a brighter life of happiness and joy, beauty and grace to you and your whole family; so follow in the right path of righteousness; the word and the truth of Gospel; for eternal life in the kingdom of God.

19 Love me with all of your heart and soul; cherish all the words of your Lord Jesus Christ the son of God; he will protect, love and guide, praise and honour you; and in fellowship he will never depart from you; for you are united as one in fellowship in Gods heavenly church; the heavenly realm where Jesus is seated at the right hand of Father God.

20 Repent all your sins and I will cast them into the deepest oceans depths and never shall I remember them no more; do not dwell on the past; for I forgive your inequities; for if you are truly sorrowful in your heart, your sins are forgiven.

21 Jesus Christ is the anointed Messiah who suffered on the cross, a sacrifice for all our sins, he has taken us out of the evil world of sin and deception and given us a free life, setting us free; through our salvation, for this was Gods desire; he gave us his precious son; for us to have life to turn and change our lives around and to turn to him and the word of God.

22 Make God your passion and become a true trustworthy and loyal servant; follow the gospel of God for it is the true and only Gospel of God; receive Jesus as Lord and saviour; do not allow persecution from anyone, neither let anyone harass you because of your fellowship and love of the anointed messiah; he is your only way to salvation, let no unrighteous one; lead you astray; walk only in love and peace, faith and in truth and righteousness; and the truth will set you free.

23 Confess before God in all truth for you have been saved by grace and faithfulness; not by religious laws; remember always God accepts you; by the gift of grace and the gift of his son; Jesus he lives in you, by accepting him as the son of God your Messiah, and by loving him above yourself; worship no one accept Jesus Christ the son of God, and worship no other God, but God the Father; you have become one, nailed with him in crucifixion; for by grace you have been saved; he is the manifestation of wisdom; your new found life in Jesus Christ is the gift of the Holy Spirit, it is your reward, your new birth, bringing you to maturity in Jesus Christ the anointed Messiah.

24 God made a covenant which is his son Jesus our Messiah; this has fulfilled our new life in Jesus; it is a solid contract, we are under the power and grace of our Messiah, saved by faith and entering into a life with him, cleansed and washed of all unrighteousness.

25 Always give praise and thanks in prayers to God; and do so with great Joy; for your union with God is to be cherished above everything in fellowship in Christ; pray with confidence for God has a permanent place in your heart; only God knows how much you dearly love him.

26 Pray to God for your love to grow even stronger; increasing beyond measure to bring you into richness and the revelation of spiritual insight in every area of your life; including your family life; your work, your scriptural readings, and your bible studies, and your prayers; then wait and you will have your request answered; you will be filled completely with the fruits of righteousness that is only found in Jesus Christ; the anointed one.

27 Put all your hope no matter what in Jesus; clinging to him passionately; and he will openly reveal all to you before everyone's eyes; let Jesus' love magnify you in all you do; let Jesus work on you on all areas of your life, transforming you into a new person being worthy to serve him; and in all your heart and your soul.

28 keep all love in your heart for it will give you confidence; Jesus relies on this to further you in maturity, faith and strength; your walk with Jesus will keep you loyal and faithful in righteousness; his trust in you will be to spread his word and his love for all; to save sinners and to bring them into repentance.

29 Never be shaken up by an unrighteous unbeliever in Jesus Christ; when you speak his name stand strong in your faith; and pray for the unbelievers in secret; asking for them to be saved and to turn to Jesus for salvation and truth, for Jesus is the only way.

30 People will always rise up against you it has been this way for over 2000yrs, actually since the murder of Adam and Eve's son Abel; their son Cain, he murdered his only brother out of the jealousy; for God had respect for Abel; because of his righteousness; so Gods encouragement for you is that he will prove that he will return again; and show all unbelievers the truth; God has already shown you his love and privilege, not only to believe in him but that he died for you, now that's love "right".

31 Spread the wonderful word of God to whoever will listen; you can powerfully change hearts in all; "it has changed you already" every believer of the Gospel already bears good fruits of eternal life; do you not already experience the reality of God's grace.

32 Our God he is the creator of all; for through the son everything was created in the Heavenly kingdom and on Earth; all that is seen and unseen, all things great and small; he is the beginning and the end; he also existed before anything was made, and everything has found completion in him, he is Jesus the son of God, he is the head of the body; which is the church.

33 If you have or had always been distant from God, living in darkness, with evil thoughts and actions, or ashamed of all your sins, and actions; Jesus is divine power he has brought you back to him "restored" and in faith, he has released his supernatural power onto you; he also sacrificed his own body as a sin offering; you have been brought with a price; so that you can dwell within him, in his presence you are now Holy and flawless, restored and renewed in Jesus Christs Holy name, Amen.

34 Now walk with God, walk in the wisdom of God, and do so especially before unbelievers; make it your duty to make Jesus known, by letting every word that you speak pour from your mouth only of love, peace, joy and grace; Jesus is your Lord; listen for all the rejoicing and give respect, and you will receive respectful answers from all those who are asking you about your new faith in Jesus, for they are seeing the new change within you, "Jesus".

35 I say unto you give careful attention to your spiritual journey and cherish all that you have been taught in the word of God; live what you preach and release even more in abundance to what is inside of you to all who will listen to you.

36 Live your life now in God; be fully empowered by Gods flowing grace, feel it flowing over you like a beautiful waterfall; for this is your true strength; it is found in Jesus the anointed one; it is your union as one together; a washing and cleansing.

37 Trust in the word, of your God; for the word of your God will never change; God never changes, neither does he waver in his faithfulness to us; God's is firm foundation; and this firm foundation of God has been written in two inscriptions, your Lord God recognizes those who are truly his; and everyone who worships and glorifies his Holy name must always forsake, wickedness.

38 My children stay away from all foolish people who want to argue or be verbally aggressive and foul mouthed; for they are immature; they will only generate more conflict by staying around them, you are entertaining their behaviour; you are a child of God; a true servant of Jesus Christ will avoid being argumentative, and would only be peace loving; humble, lowly at heart and gentle; you should help and seek to find the truth, being patient towards the immature.

39 Find wisdom, be aware that the cultures of our society are changing dramatically, sinking to its lowest, a degradation that will be very difficult for all God's children; people of today are becoming more ignorant of the word of God; they are not teaching the new generation of our future children; the word of God hardly exists in our schools; Easter and Christmas are hardly discussed about the meaning of these two important history times; the birth and Death of our Messiah, it is no longer a topic to be discussed, it is disgusting, what our society has become, this is the work of darkness that people cannot see, and parents are allowing it to happen, they are not speaking up; so our future children who will eventually and completely not know who God the father is or Jesus Christ; they have no hope, and their hearts will become hardened; Christians are already being targeted for their faith and beliefs in Jesus, the son of God.

40 Our world is becoming self centred and lovers of themselves; they are becoming more and more obsessed with more money, better cars, larger houses, holidays, dining out, partying, and putting themselves before their children; their lifestyles are more important than their children, many are not even having children; people boast about their greatness and high lifestyles, strutting around in their arrogant pride, mocking what is of right standing as they are still continuing to ignore their families; these are ungrateful; ungodly, spiritually blind; not seeing the world falling apart around them while they are living it up in the world, their delight is the world more than the pleasures of our loving caring God, who can save the sinner who will repent and be saved by changing their lifestyle; so child of God stay away from the corruption of the world and such people, who will pull you into the darkness and sin of the world, instead pray for them into repentance.

41 The followers of God will always come under attack and persecution and difficulties; however live passionately and faithfully as a worshiper of Jesus Christ our king, the anointed one, remember he was persecuted but he hungered to get his message across; this is the same hunger he gives to his children who follow him; by preaching this good news; by sharing these prayers; Jesus preached this good news of the Gospel; he taught the true meaning of love; so never listen to a arrogant heart; but advance yourself in strength and put on the Armour of God, stay steadfast in truth and in faith in your Lord Jesus Christ for he will never forsake you.

42 Every word of God in the Holy Scripture has been lovingly written by the Holy Spirit of Jesus Christ; the breath of God; the word spoken over creation, the word made manifest, this same power has been given unto you, giving you the strength to take the right path; to live a cleaner life from this day forth; to repent immediately when you have sinned and give it to God, this is taking the right path of righteousness; god he leads you into a deeper pathway of godliness; you are a servant of God, mature and prepared to walk in righteousness; fulfilling all Gods desires that are placed by him unto you, your Holy spirit to do Gods work. **AMEN**

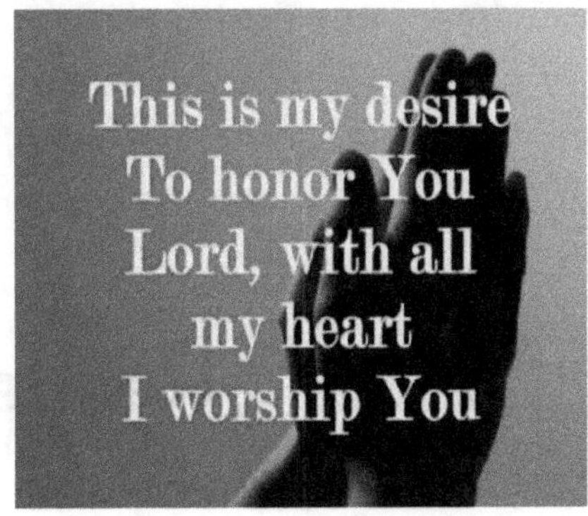
This is my desire
To honor You
Lord, with all
my heart
I worship You

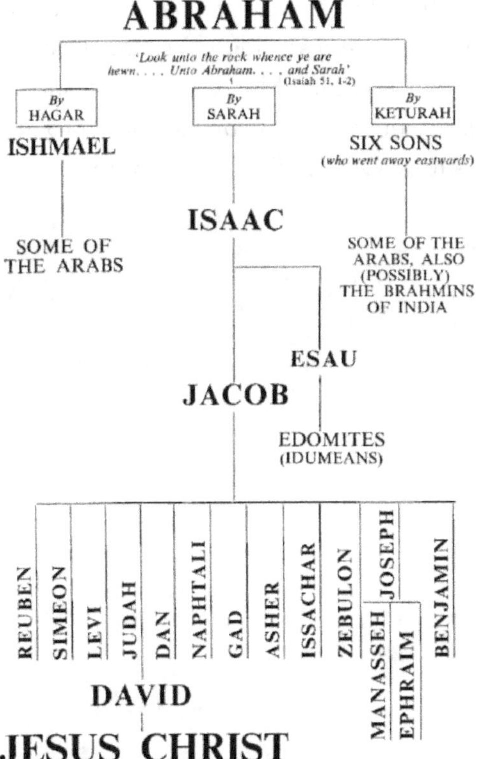
ABRAHAM
'Look unto the rock whence ye are
hewn. . . . Unto Abraham. . . . and Sarah'
(Isaiah 51, 1-2)
By HAGAR
By SARAH
By KETURAH
ISHMAEL
SIX SONS
(who went away eastwards)
ISAAC
SOME OF
THE ARABS
SOME OF THE
ARABS, ALSO
(POSSIBLY)
THE BRAHMINS
OF INDIA
ESAU
JACOB
EDOMITES
(IDUMEANS)
REUBEN
SIMEON
LEVI
JUDAH
DAN
NAPHTALI
GAD
ASHER
ISSACHAR
ZEBULON
MANASSEH
EPHRAIM
JOSEPH
BENJAMIN
DAVID
JESUS CHRIST

My Beloved Readers

I send you all my love and deep prayers thanking you for purchasing this book, I hope it gives you as much blessings as it has done for me; Our Lord Jesus Christ has change my life in such an amazing way; the changes that he will give you as well; lets share always in these wonderful prayer words that Jesus has blessed us all will and spread the words to all who will listen, let us vote the bible in our Lord Jesus Christs Holy and righteous name. GOD BLESSES YOU ALL.

Minister Lynda